Deadly Deals

Books by Fern Michaels

Return to Sender
Mr. and Miss Anonymous
Up Close and Personal
Fool Me Once
Picture Perfect
About Face
The Future Scrolls
Kentucky Sunrise
Kentucky Heat
Kentucky Rich
Plain Jane
Charming Lily
What You Wish For
The Guest List
Listen to Your Heart
Celebration
Yesterday
Finders Keepers
Annie's Rainbow
Sara's Song
Vegas Sunrise
Vegas Heat
Vegas Rich
Whitefire
Wish List
Dear Emily

The Godmothers Series:

The Scoop

The Sisterhood Novels:

Deadly Deals
Vanishing Act
Razor Sharp
Under the Radar
Final Justice
Collateral Damage
Fast Track
Hokus Pokus
Hide and Seek
Free Fall
Sweet Revenge
Lethal Justice
The Jury
Vendetta
Payback
Weekend Warriors

Anthologies:

Snow Angels
Silver Bells
Comfort and Joy
Sugar and Spice
Let It Snow
A Gift of Joy
Five Golden Rings
Deck the Halls
Jingle All the Way

Published by Kensington Publishing Corporation

DEADLY DEALS

FERN MICHAELS

ZEBRA BOOKS
KENSINGTON PUBLISHING CORP.
http://www.kensingtonbooks.com

ZEBRA BOOKS are published by

Kensington Publishing Corp.
119 West 40th Street
New York, NY 10018

All Kensington titles, imprints, and distributed lines are available at special quantity discounts for bulk purchases for sales promotion, premiums, fund-raising, educational, or institutional use.

Special book excerpts or customized printings can also be created to fit specific needs. For details, write or phone the office of the Kensington Special Sales Manager: Attn.: Special Sales Department. Kensington Publishing Corp., 119 West 40th Street, New York, NY 10018. Phone: 1-800-221-2647.

Zebra and the Z logo Reg. U.S. Pat. & TM Off.

ISBN-13: 978-1-4201-0686-2
ISBN-10: 1-4201-0686-4

First Kensington Books Hardcover Printing: December 2009
First Zebra Books Mass-Market Paperback Printing: April 2010

10 9 8 7 6 5 4 3 2 1

Printed in the United States of America

I'd like to dedicate this book to
two wonderful friends,
Miss Jill and Miss Patsy,
the awesome ladies
of Dorchester Jewelers
here in Summerville, South Carolina.
You rock, ladies.

Prologue

It looked like a cozy building, and it was . . . in the spring and summer. Ivy covered the brick walls, and flower beds abounded, all tended by the new manager of the Quinn law firm, a twelve-member, all-female firm, as everyone was quick to point out. In whispered tones, of course. Previously owned by Nikki Quinn, one of the infamous vigilantes.

In the fall and winter, the three-story brick building in Georgetown took on another appearance. Usually smoke could be seen wafting up through the chimney from the fireplace in the spacious lobby. A wreath of colorful leaves adorned the stark white door.

The Monday after Thanksgiving, the building took on another transformation. A fragrant evergreen wreath with a red satin bow almost as wide as the door arrived from a grateful client in Oregon. Inside, the fire blazed; the birch logs from another grateful client somewhere in the state of

Washington had arrived like clockwork the day before Thanksgiving.

It was a low-key firm; all the lawyers were friends, each of them helping the other. There was no shortage of clients, but that hadn't always been the case. At one point the firm had struggled to keep its head above water, but that had all changed when the vigilantes were captured, then escaped. The media had had a field day as they splashed the news that the Quinn law firm's owner was one of the infamous women. Within twenty-four hours, there had been long lines of women, some men, too, queuing outside to be represented by the now prestigious-cum-outrageous, famous law firm.

Nancy Barnes, the firm's office manager, was fairly new to the firm. She'd replaced her aunt Maddy, who had retired to stop and smell the roses a year after the vigilantes had gone on the run. She knew the firm inside and out, having worked there summers and holidays for as long as she could remember. She herself was a paralegal but had found out that management was more to her liking. She had a wonderful rapport with the lawyers and clients. At Christmastime alone she had to have a friend come by with a pickup truck to take all her presents home, gifts from the lawyers, gifts from all the grateful clients.

Nancy Barnes loved her job.

On the first day of October, Nancy was huffing and puffing as she struggled with an oversize pumpkin that she had somehow managed to get into the lobby after opening the door and turning off the alarm without dropping the enormous squash. She knew by the end of the week there would be about twenty more pumpkins around her scarecrow-and-hay arrangement, brought in by the lawyers themselves, as well as the paralegals and secretaries.

Cozy. A feel-good place to come to when in trouble.

Nancy looked up to see a young woman coming through the door. Her first thought was that she looked like a deer caught in the headlights. Fragile. Scared. But there was a spark of something she couldn't quite define. Yet.

Nancy Barnes was a chunky young woman who wore sensible shoes. She had curly hair, *unruly* curly hair, and a bridge of freckles that danced across her nose and rosy cheeks. She wore granny glasses and always had two or three pencils stuck behind her ears or in her hair. It was her smile that put new clients at ease, or maybe it was her first words of greeting; no one was ever quite sure.

"Good morning. What can I do to help you?"

"I'm Rachel Dawson, and I need to talk to a lawyer as soon as possible. I don't have an appointment. I'm sorry. I just . . . what I did was . . . My husband doesn't know I'm here. I can't afford to be here." The woman flapped her arms, then said, "But here I am."

"I'll tell you what. Walk around here to where I am. I'll get us both some coffee, and you and I can talk. What that means is after you tell me your problem, I'll decide who would work best with you. We have doughnuts, too."

Rachel Dawson tried her best to smile but couldn't bring it off. Nancy could see she was fighting back tears.

Settled at her desk, with coffee Rachel Dawson wasn't going to drink, Nancy asked gently, "Tell me what you're comfortable telling me so all of us here can help you. I want you to think of this firm as your extended family. Everyone here works for the client, and it doesn't matter which attorney is assigned to you. Do you understand that?"

"I can't afford to be here. My husband is going to be upset when he finds out I . . ."

"Let's not talk about payment right now. But for the record, we do quite a bit of pro bono work. I'm usually the one who makes that particular decision, so we aren't going to worry about whether you qualify or not right now. Tell me how we can help you."

Rachel Dawson fooled Nancy. Before she spoke, she gulped at her coffee and drained the cup. "I can't have children. It's me, not my husband. I've had every test in the book. I'm thirty-seven. My husband is thirty-eight. We both have very good jobs, but right now I'm on a leave of absence. We were desperate to have a child, but the wait was so long, and going outside the country didn't work for us. A friend of a friend told us about a lawyer who arranged adoptions. We went to see him a year or so ago, and in the end what we did . . . what my husband did was donate his sperm to a surrogate. It was all legal. We paid the lawyer a hundred thousand dollars. I don't know how much of that went to the surrogate. We paid all her medical expenses. I even drove her to the doctor's when she had to go. She was a student at George Washington University. We bought her clothes, food, and paid her rent.

"She gave birth to twins, a boy and a girl. We were overjoyed. I can't tell you how giddy we were. We went into panic mode the day we found out. We had to redo the house—you know, make room for two babies instead of one. I guess I should tell you we had to borrow forty thousand dollars from our parents. Call us foolish, but we'd been saving for a college fund even though we had no children. We hoped that we would eventually be blessed. We're savers, Miss Barnes."

Nancy watched Rachel peer into her cup. She seemed surprised that it was empty. So Nancy reached for the cup and went to the kitchen for a refill.

"We were so happy. It was like suddenly our life was now complete. We didn't sleep. We sat up and watched the twins sleep. I guess all new parents do that. My husband took leave, too, for a month, so I could get things working. We couldn't afford a nanny, and our parents helped out. We literally thought we'd died and gone to heaven."

Rachel reached for the coffee and again drained the full cup. She set it down precisely where it had been. Nancy waited, knowing the worst was about to be revealed. She wasn't wrong.

"Then our world turned upside down. A letter came in the mail from a lawyer saying his client, the surrogate mother, wanted the twins back. We thought about fighting back, but we had seen cases like this played out in the media, and the birth mother always got the children. Our parents offered to mortgage their houses. We were going to cash in our retirement funds and the college fund but were advised not to do that. My husband talked to several lawyers, and they basically told us to move on and put it behind us. I went to the lawyer we used to arrange the adoption. I called and called, and he didn't call back. I went to his office, and they wouldn't let me see him. I thought about going to the newspaper, but the truth was, I wasn't strong enough mentally or physically for that kind of onslaught. You'll find out sooner or later that I had a mini-breakdown. That's what they called it, anyway."

Nancy looked down at the small recording machine, which she'd decided to use at the last minute. As usual, she'd forgotten to mention it to this frail woman sitting in front of her. "Mrs. Dawson, I'm recording this conversation. I hope that's okay. I should have told you that before I turned the machine on."

"That's okay. Is there anything you can do for me and Tom?"

Nancy's mind raced. Was there? "I'm going to

turn this off for a few moments. Then I'm going to get you some more coffee. I have to make a few phone calls. Will that be okay? I think I know just the person to help you."

"Truly! You do! Oh, my God, I'll do anything. Anything at all if you help me."

"Which lawyer did you go to, to arrange the adoption?"

"Baron Bell."

"Baron Bell?" The name shot out of Nancy's mouth like a bullet. "Baron Bell refused to see and talk to you after . . . after . . . ?"

"Yes, Baron Bell. He seemed like such a nice man. He's always in the papers, and he's an advocate of everything. Everyone Tom talked to backed away when he told them it was Mr. Bell who had arranged the adoption."

"Who is the surrogate mother?"

"Her name is Donna Davis."

Nancy ran to the kitchen, refilled Rachel's coffee cup, and took the filled cup back to Rachel, then walked down the hall to an empty office and called her aunt Maddy. Midway into the conversation, she said, "I don't know what to do with her, Maddy. Nothing like this has ever come up before. I'll be honest. I don't think any of our lawyers here at the firm will agree to go up against someone like Baron Bell in what could become a high-profile case like this one. Talk to me, Maddy."

Nancy listened. She reached for a pad and pencil and scribbled furiously. "Maddy, are you going to do what I think you're going to do?"

"Can you think of anyone better?"

Nancy smiled. "Actually, I can't. Wouldn't it be wonderful if . . . Rachel could get her babies back for Christmas?"

"It's the time for miracles. I'll do what I can. Keep me in the loop, honey."

"Will do, Maddy."

Back in her office, Nancy sat down and reached for a small pad. As she wrote down Lizzie Fox's name, address, and phone number on a slip of paper, Rachel Dawson kept on talking. "I think this is some kind of baby ring. Tom says I'm out of my mind, but on my really bad days I would go to the park and just sit. I talked to a lot of nannies and young mothers. One of the mothers looked at me when I told her what had happened, and told me about someone else the same thing had happened to. I have her name right here in my purse. I even went to talk to the adoptive parents, and they're in the same position Tom and I are in. They used Baron Bell, too. Their surrogate is a student at Georgetown. Is there any way, any way at all, we can get our babies back for Christmas? We had such plans. Our first family Christmas." Rachel burst into tears.

"Rachel, I can't answer that, but the person I want you to go see is just the right lawyer for you. Trust me when I tell you she could take on Baron Bell with her hands tied behind her back and blindfolded. If anyone can help you, it's Lizzie Fox."

Rachel Dawson bolted upright. Her tears

stopped in midflow. "She's the lawyer that . . . She was . . . the vigilantes' attorney."

Nancy stared across the table, her gaze steady and direct. "Yes," she said softly.

"Oh! Oh! When should I go to see her?"

Nancy's phone rang. She picked it up and listened. All she said was, "Thanks, Maddy." She turned to Rachel. "Right now. You can walk to Lizzie's office from here." Nancy was out of her chair and around the desk. She put her arms around the woman's thin shoulders. "Just tell Lizzie everything you told me. Be sure to give her the other surrogate's name. By the way, is your surrogate still living wherever she was living before the birth of the twins?"

"She is. I . . . I would park down the street, hoping to get a glimpse of the twins. They never seem to leave the apartment. I guess she has a babysitter while she goes to class. I was so obsessed. I don't know how to thank you. Will Ms. Fox work out a payment plan for us? Do you know?"

"You'll work something out. I wouldn't worry about that right now. Just go and talk to her, and I wish you all the luck in the world."

Nancy waited until Rachel Dawson was through the door and out of sight before she walked back to her office. She called her aunt, and they talked for ten long minutes. Nancy was smiling when she hung up the phone. Then she laughed out loud. "Rachel, honey, you are in such good hands," she murmured under her breath.

Chapter 1

The most famous address in the world—
1600 Pennsylvania Avenue

Trailing behind the Secret Service agent escorting her to President Connor's private quarters in the East Wing, Lizzie tried her best not to gawk at the magnificent Christmas decorations. She was not, she had to remind herself, a starstruck tourist. She was there for lunch and so much more.

The president herself opened the door and literally dragged Lizzie inside with a whispered, "I'll take it from here, Agent Goodwin." She smiled warmly at her friend. "God, Lizzie, I am so glad to see you! I mean I'm *really* glad!"

"Me too, Madam President." And she *was* glad. She and President Connor had a history. Then they wrapped their arms around each other in a bone-crushing hug, strange for two such elegant women.

President Connor laughed. "Stop with that 'Madam President' stuff. In here we're Lizzie and Marti. I *need* you to call me by my name, Lizzie. I don't want to forget who I really am. Can we do that?" She sounded so anxious, Lizzie nodded.

Lizzie looked around. "Pretty fancy digs, Marti. This is my first time in the White House. I'm impressed. The Christmas decorations are beautiful."

"If you have the time, I'll give you the tour after lunch. Right now I want you all to myself. I can't thank you enough for accepting my invitation. You look so happy, Lizzie."

Lizzie smiled as she was shown to a deep off-white chair that would have held both her and Cosmo. She watched as the president sat down across from her and kicked off her shoes. Lizzic did the same thing, and they giggled like two schoolgirls.

"There are no words to tell you how happy I am, Marti. I wish I could say the same for you. You look like you have the weight of the world on your shoulders."

Martine Connor forced a smile she was far from feeling. "I *do* have the weight of the world on my shoulders. See how bowed they are. And before you can ask, the world slowed down for some reason this week to allow me time for this luncheon."

"You want to talk about it, or is it all NTK? Your approval ratings are in the seventy percent range, so you must be doing something right."

Martine shrugged. "I had a hard time getting used to having every second of my time budgeted. Sometimes bathroom breaks are a luxury. There's always a crisis that has to be dealt with brewing somewhere. You know me. I'm cool under fire. It's when I get up here that I lose it."

Lizzie blinked. "This was what you wanted, Marti."

Martine brushed at the soft bangs falling over her forehead. "Yes, and if it weren't for you . . . and . . . your friends, I wouldn't be here. I know that, Lizzie. It's with me every second of every day. That's why you're here, isn't it? That's why you accepted my job offer, right? You're here to spell it out to me. Again."

Lizzie stared at her old friend. She gave a slight nod. "Six months. Pro bono. I walk away unless the job proves to be something beyond my expectations. I have to admit, I was surprised you agreed to my terms."

Martine burst out laughing. "Oh, Lizzie, I wish you could have seen the expressions on all *their* faces when I listed your demands. I thought the lot of them would choke to death. Nine to five! Every weekend off. Pro bono. I realize one hundred sixty-eight thousand dollars is a lot of money, and yet it isn't much to live on here in the District, what with rent, travel back to one's home state, taxes, everyday expenses, and maintaining two residences. It's hard to raise a family and keep up two residences, all for the sake of doing one's duty. When I told them you weren't interested in adding the White House to your résumé, because yours was impressive enough without it, several of them had to be resuscitated. It's safe to say your fame has preceded you. Actually, Lizzie, you're a legend in your own time, and I, for one, am honored to be called your friend. How does your new husband feel about your taking on the job?"

Lizzie leaned forward. "You know what, Marti? My husband is that rare breed of man who only wants to see me happy. If all it takes is his approval, he's all for it. We take turns traveling on the weekends. You need to give him a huge slice of credit for helping get you to where you're sitting right now." Lizzie looked around and lowered her voice. "Is this place bugged? Are you recording me?"

"Lizzie!"

Martine's outrage was so total, Lizzie relaxed. "What I was going to say was, my husband numbers among his friends some of the most powerful, some of the most respected, some of the richest people in the world, and those he doesn't know personally, he has access to via those same friends in his Rolodex. You should see his Rolodex, Marti. I think it's safe to say your own cannot compare."

"What are you trying to tell me, Lizzie?" There was an edge to Martine's voice that did not go unnoticed by Lizzie.

"Nothing, Marti. I was simply commenting on your question about my husband."

"Point taken."

There was a knock at the door, and a white-coated waiter indicated that lunch was ready in the little breakfast nook, as requested by the president.

"Our lunch is ready. It's one of the perks here.

I hope you enjoy it," Martine said as she rose and led Lizzie down the hall. When they reached their destination, she nodded to the waiter to show that he could leave. "I know you don't like to eat heavily at lunch, and most days I don't have time for lunch. We're having sesame-crusted salmon, grilled asparagus, and a garden salad."

It looked delicious, but Lizzie wasn't hungry. She lifted the glass of iced tea set by her plate and clinked it against Martine's. "Here's to a thankful Thanksgiving and a Merry Christmas, Madam President."

"And the same to you, Lizzie."

The bite was still in Martine's voice, Lizzie noticed. Well, she hadn't invited herself here. She was the invitee. She smiled as she mashed the salmon on her plate. Martine was cutting her asparagus into tiny pieces. Lizzie couldn't help but wonder if she was going to eat it or if she was just playing with her food, too.

"Does my office have a window, Marti?"

Martine offered up a genuine smile this time. "It was one of your requirements, so yes, your office has a window. You did say you would be willing to negotiate the second half of the year. Is that still on the table?"

Lizzie mashed the salmon some more. "Yes, but no promises. So, tell me now, who do I have to watch out for?"

"Everyone would be my guess. You've been Googled so much since we made the announcement, I'm surprised the site didn't shut down. You're the next thing to Public Enemy Number

One at Sixteen Hundred Pennsylvania Avenue. My chief of staff understands that you are to have direct access to me twenty-four-seven. Of course, he went ballistic, but we're on the same page now. Everyone is replaceable. He understands that, too."

"Guess you aren't going to eat that asparagus. You must have a hundred little pieces on your plate."

"You always were perceptive, Lizzie. I'm listening when you're ready to talk."

"My friends are very unhappy, Marti. I thought you would have gotten the message when your Secret Service agents were thrown into a Dumpster and their weapons and badges were sent back to you."

Martine started to mash her salmon the way Lizzie had. "We're going to have to put all this food in the disposal so the kitchen doesn't get their knickers in a knot. I did get the message. I wasn't amused. We had to do some fancy dancing to explain all that."

"I bet you did. My friends weren't amused either. You have six months to keep your promise."

"I can't believe you're giving the president of this country an ultimatum! And if for some reason I can't deliver on the promise in the allotted time, then what?" Martine asked in the same frosty tone.

Lizzie smiled. "Marti, I might be many things, but I'm not clairvoyant."

"What? Are you seriously warning me that the

vigilantes can penetrate the White House? Is that what you're telling me? Are you telling me they're smart enough to outwit the best of the best? It's simply not possible. What are they going to do, hold a gun to my head and make me sign a pardon and then we're all going to disappear in a puff of smoke?"

Lizzie was pleased at the look of pure horror on the president's face. She continued to smile. "I said no such thing. That's your interpretation. Although the ladies did take on your Secret Service and come out on top. And if I remember correctly, that little neighborhood White House luncheon you sponsored didn't go over so well either. Your guests were more impressed with their ride home, compliments of the vigilantes, than they were with your luncheon, the photo op, and their souvenirs."

Martine Connor got up and carried the two luncheon plates to the sink in the main part of the kitchen. She scraped the plates and turned on the garbage disposal. Lizzie listened to the loud clunking noise followed by a shrieking, grinding sound.

"The plumbing leaves a lot to be desired," Martine said.

"You could call a plumber," Lizzie volunteered.

"It doesn't work that way here. In the real world, yes. I can't even describe to you what it's like living here. I can't step out and go to the drugstore to get shampoo. If I want to do that, I have to notify the Service a month in advance.

Then they have to empty out the store so I can shop. I can't go to a bookstore. I can't drive a car. I can't use my credit cards or carry money. If they ever find out I have that phone, they'll probably pack me off to Outer Mongolia.

"You know what I miss, Lizzie? I miss going out to the mailbox for my mail. I miss all those catalogs I used to get by the pound. I always looked forward to Sunday afternoon, when I'd browse through them and order something. You know what else? I made potato pancakes one day. They came up here on the run and said I was stinking up the White House and not to do it again. They fucking told me I can't make potato pancakes! It was the onion I put in them. I'm not excusing my language either."

For all of a minute, Lizzie almost felt sorry for her old friend. Almost. Then she burst out laughing. "Remember that old saying, 'Be careful what you wish for, because you just might get it.' You wished for this, we made it happen for you at the eleventh hour, and now you have to live with it. And you have to honor your debt. That's the bottom line."

"God, Lizzie, how cold you sound. That's the real reason you agreed to sign on, isn't it? You're here to protect your friends, and if it means taking me down, you'll help them do it, right?"

Lizzie just smiled.

"Goddamnit, Lizzie, say something."

"Where I come from, Marti, and where you've been, a person is only as good as her word. I really should be going. I've taken up enough of your time today."

Martine Connor turned to stop her furious pacing. Lizzie thought she looked great in a honey-colored suit, with a copper-colored blouse underneath her suit jacket, which was open. Her haircut was stylish, and the feathery bangs falling over her forehead were new, too, since the last time Lizzie had seen Martine. She looked presidential.

"But we haven't had dessert, and I was going to give you the tour. Lizzie, I'm sorry. I'll find a way. I promise you. Please, I need you to believe me."

"It's not me you have to convince, Marti. I'll pass on your message. Six months. Not one day, not one hour, not one second longer. I'll report in on January second. I hope you have a wonderful holiday. Are you staying here or going somewhere?"

"Camp David. I plan to sleep through the holidays. Do you want to hear something really sad? I don't have a single soul I can invite to spend the holidays with me. Well, that's not quite true. I had several people I was going to invite, but the Service said when they vetted them, they were unsuitable. *Unsuitable!* That's what they said. I'm whining, and I didn't want to do that. I apologize."

Lizzie stepped forward and wrapped her arms around the president. She squeezed hard. "Six months, Marti," she whispered. "Now, how do I get out of here? Is that guy with the 'football' still outside the door? Oh, one last thing. Watch out for Baron Bell."

Martine grimaced. "You mean the marine with the nuclear codes? Yes, he's out there. You just walk past him. It's that simple. One of my agents will take you home."

Lizzie stared at the president. She could feel her eyes start to burn at what she was seeing on her old friend's face. She lowered her voice to a bare whisper and said, "I wouldn't want to be you for all the gold in Fort Knox."

The moment the door opened, Martine Connor shed her personal persona and, in the blink of an eye, was once again the president of the United States. "Thank you for that observation, and thank you for coming, Lizzie. I enjoyed our luncheon. I hope we can do it again soon. Happy holidays to you and *yours*."

"Don't eat too much turkey, Madam President." Lizzie flinched at the sound of the door closing behind her. She straightened her shoulders and walked alongside the agent escorting her to a black limousine, where another agent waited to drive her back to her home.

Lizzie kept her eyes closed all the way home, her mind racing as she sifted, collated, and made mental notes.

The moment she was inside her cozy little home, she shed her lavender suit and donned a pair of jeans and a warm, fleecy shirt. She had the crazy urge all of a sudden to make potato pancakes. But first she had to check things at her office, call her husband, then call the mountain. Maybe she should call the mountain first. Or maybe she should wait, think about her visit some more, and make the potato pancakes first. Multitasking, so to speak.

Before she did anything, though, she was going to make herself a pot of strong black coffee to get her adrenaline levels up. While the coffee was dripping, Lizzie fiddled with her CD player, then slipped in one of Cosmo's favorite CDs. Frank Sinatra's mellow voice filled her kitchen. She immediately felt the tenseness leave her shoulders. Then she made herself a sandwich, the kind of sandwich Cosmo raised his eyebrows over but later admitted was tasty. Swiss cheese, lettuce, fire-roasted peppers, and one slice of salami. That mess she'd mangled back at the White House couldn't come close to the sandwich she was devouring. There wasn't a crumb to be seen when she finished.

Then Lizzie moved at lightning speed. She called the mountain, then she called Jack Emery, then her office. She had two calls left to make when she poured her coffee. The first call was to Nikki's old law office, where she asked more questions than she answered. She had one call to go before she could call her husband. With business taken care of, she could talk for hours if he had the time. At the crack of dawn, she'd be winging her way to Vegas to spend

Thanksgiving and the rest of the holidays with Cosmo. A radiant smile lit her features.

Lizzie was huffing and puffing when she opened the doors of the fireplace, placed the logs just so, and threw in a pile of birch kindling. The fire blazed instantly. She then moved a pile of silky red cushions near the hearth so she could curl up and be comfortable.

One more trip to the kitchen to replenish her coffee. She was walking through the dining room when retired judge Nellie Easter picked up the phone. "Lizzie, Judge. Several things. I want to wish you and Elias a wonderful Thanksgiving and a Merry Christmas. I'm leaving in the morning for Las Vegas." They made small talk for a few minutes, with Lizzie asking about Elias's new grandbaby and his other children before she got down to the real reason for her phone call.

"Nellie, tell me everything you know about Baron Bell. And ask Elias if he knows anything. Better yet, use the speakerphone, if he's agreeable."

"Baron was always a gentleman in court. He fights to win for his clients. He and I belong to five or six of the same organizations. He's been Man of the Year for so many years, I've lost count. He used to do a lot of pro bono work. Lovely wife, kind of timid, stays in his shadow. Two grown children. One is a doctor at Georgetown, and one is a public defender in Georgia. Several grandchildren, who he dotes on. No matter the cause, you can count on him for a donation, and he gives his time willingly to any worthy cause. He plays Santa every year for some children's group, and it always makes the paper. He always arrives in a sleigh with his helpers, either on wheels or with horses pulling the sleigh, and he does it at his own expense. It's usually quite an event. As far as I know, I never heard a hint of any kind of scandal. He's quite wealthy, and as you know, there are always a few who will take a swipe at you for that. Elias said there's a file on him at the Bureau, but nothing bad is in it. There are those among the recipients of his generosity who think he's the Messiah. Why are you asking, Lizzie?"

"No one is *that* perfect, Nellie. What's his flaw?"

"If you believe his court record, his PR, then he is *that* perfect. Why? What happened to make you ask these questions? Did I also mention he has a pass to the White House? That means he's invited to *everything*. So he's on your radar, eh?"

"A little under it, but he's there. Do me a favor, Nellie. Ask around. See if there's anything of interest there. Then call the mountain and share it with them. Are you going to spend Christmas on the mountain or just Thanksgiving?"

"We are. We're coming back Sunday night but will return the following weekend. Elias said his family is heading for a warmer climate. We both like the cold, and both of us are looking forward to spending the holidays with old friends. I'm sorry you won't be joining us."

Lizzie laughed. "Thanks, Nellie, and one more time, happy holidays!" She sighed happily. Now she could curl up and talk till she fell asleep. Business was taken care of.

She had packed before she left for the White House and would be ready to go as soon as she rolled out of bed in the morning. Damn, she'd forgotten to call Maggie at the *Post.* A minute later she had Maggie on the phone. She spoke quick and fast as she explained about her meeting with Rachel Dawson. "There's something there, Maggie. I could feel it. It isn't good either. I'll be working on her case while I'm in Vegas." Her final words were, "The window of time is going to be short, Maggie. Make it work if you can. See you when I see you."

Life is good, Lizzie thought as she settled into her nest of colorful cushions.

Across town Maggie flipped open her Rolodex, then looked at the clock. Four o'clock. She punched in the numbers and waited for Abner Tookus to pick up. He did on the fourth ring.

"I thought you said you were taking my name out of your Rolodex," was all the computer hacker said by way of a greeting.

"I lied. Just the way you lied to me about working for Big Blue, and even then you lied some more, saying you were going on a honeymoon. You snookered me, Abby. I want my pound of flesh."

"Call someone who's fat and can afford to lose a pound or two. I don't have any to spare. I'm working. That means I have no time to do anything for you."

"You better find the time, and this one is for free. F-r-e-e! That job you have, the one that is paying you in eight figures? That's all compliments of me. I can take it away just like . . . that," Maggie said, snapping her fingers.

"Go ahead, take it away," Tookus blustered. "I hate nine to five. I hate wearing a suit and tie. You want to fall back and regroup and call me again like in twenty years?"

"Nah! I'm going to come over to those plushy digs where you work and rip the skin right off your face. What I can't decide is, should I do it before or after I sic the vigilantes on you? Now, if you're really nice to me, I'm going to forget you challenged me. Truce?"

"Truce. What do you want?"

Maggie's voice turned syrupy sweet. "Not all that much. I want everything there is to get on one Baron Bell. I want it from the moment he came into being in his mother's womb until this very minute, and after that I want hourly updates."

"You gotta be kidding me, Maggie. Mr. Squeaky Clean himself! Mr. Man of the Year! Mr. Personal Buddy of every power broker in Washington! That guy is the Easter Bunny, the Tooth Fairy, and Santa Claus all rolled into one. He is beloved and cherished beyond belief. What'd the son of a bitch do to put him on your radar screen?"

"Just never you mind, Abner. At the moment, Baron Bell is *under* my radar but rising to the top. That's all you need to know. I want this by nine o'clock tomorrow morning. I do not care if you sleep or eat. Is that clear? If you're one minute late, you will find yourself skinless. Nice talking to you, sweetie."

Maggie let loose with a deep sigh. She had no doubts at all that Abner would come through for her. But whether he would have anything worthwhile that her friends on the mountain could use was another matter entirely. Well, she was the master of spin, if she did say so herself.

Time to get ready to close up shop and head for the mountain with the others. She could hardly wait to sit down to a Thanksgiving dinner with all the trimmings prepared by Charles. She smacked her lips in anticipation.

At least she wouldn't be going empty-handed. Abby's file would be her gift to the host. She laughed as she envisioned Charles's expression when she handed it over.

Chapter 2

It was Thanksgiving eve, and the compound on Big Pine Mountain was quiet. The reason for the silence was the late hour and the fact that snow had been falling for the past nine hours. A giant white blanket covered the mountaintop, making it picture-postcard perfect.

Charles Martin prowled the confines of his command center, his thoughts all over the map as he stared down at the paperwork Maggie Spritzer had brought with her earlier in the day. With the investigation his own people had done, he felt like he had a solid basis to move forward when the guests left on Sunday and the Sisters got down to the mission at hand. He now walked out of the command center, slipped on a heavy mackinaw, and opened the front door. A blast of early-winter air rushed through the room. He smiled at the high drifts of snow on the porch. He stood under the overhang and fired up his pipe. The smoke from the cherry tobacco in his pipe and the heady scent from the evergreens were an intoxicating mixture. He loved it. Loved seeing the steady snowfall, knowing all his chicks inside were safe and sound. For now.

Tomorrow they would all sit down to a huge dinner he would begin preparing in just a few short hours. They would all pray and give thanks for so many things. He hoped his voice didn't falter when he offered up his own thanks. As he puffed on his pipe he thought about the son he'd never gotten a chance to know. He knew that if he let the tears flow, they'd freeze on his lashes. He shook his head to clear his thoughts. It wasn't that he was banishing all thoughts of Geoffrey, but that it was unbearable to think about his son, the traitor.

Charles listened to the silence around him. He wondered what it would be like to live in a world as silent as the one he was standing in. Never to hear the sounds of laughter, never to hear the wind rustling in the trees, never to hear the birds chirping early in the morning. *That* was an unbearable thought. He shifted his mental gears to the work at hand. Not that dinner was work. He could prepare a Thanksgiving feast with his eyes closed. What he couldn't do with his eyes closed was figure out what was going on with Baron Bell. Or with his eyes open, for that matter.

He whirled around when he sensed a presence. "Myra! What are you doing up at this hour?"

"I'm up because the bed got cold. Why are you standing out here, Charles?"

"The world looks so clean and pure right now. It's so perfect, I just want it to be like this forever, but that's a foolish wish on my part."

Myra reached out and nestled her hand within his. "It is beautiful. The snow came early this year. I'm ready to get married now, Charles. I thought maybe on New Year's Day. I'd like Nellie to marry us. Say something *now,* Charles, because I don't think I will get the nerve again to make this commitment."

"But you didn't ask me. You made an announcement. I'm supposed to get down on my knee and *ask you.*"

"Well, what are you waiting for?" Myra asked.

Charles dropped to one knee and reached for Myra's hand. "Myra, will you marry me on New Year's Day? If you say yes, I promise to love and honor you into eternity."

"My answer is yes, Charles. Will you make the announcement at dinner?"

"If that's what you want, then, yes, it will give me great pleasure to announce our betrothal. You just made me the happiest man in the world." Charles moved his arm and wrapped it around his beloved's shoulders. "What made you pick this moment in time, if you don't mind my asking?"

"Well, Charles, we aren't getting any younger. In fact, we're getting older by the day. If that isn't enough of an answer, I realized I don't like cold beds. And you're right. This moment, right now, this instant, is so perfect, it just seemed like the right time. I'm going to have Annie stand up for me. Whom will you choose, Charles, to be your best man?"

"Elias. You don't think the boys will be upset, do you?"

"No more than the girls will be upset with my choosing Annie."

"I don't have a ring for you, Myra."

Myra laughed. "The ring isn't important. Just ask Elias for one of his cigar bands. That will do nicely."

Charles reached for his bride-to-be. "My life is now complete, Myra. I think we should go inside before we both freeze to death out here, and then there won't be a wedding at all."

"I think you might be right. Come along, my darling. I'll help you get started with your Thanksgiving dinner."

Charles pretended horror. "My dear, you are worthless in the kitchen. But you can watch me. Let's have an early breakfast. You can brown the buns and make the coffee and squeeze the juice. We received a box of Baby Bell oranges with our food order yesterday. Wait till you see them. Each one is more perfect than the other. And to think you can get them only at this particular time of year. Amazing."

Myra linked her arm with Charles's. "I'm going to learn to cook, Charles. I've been watching the Food Network."

Charles laughed all the way across the compound as he half dragged Myra through the deep snow.

Thanksgiving dinner was everything everyone had hoped it would be. Good friends breaking bread and giving thanks together. Chef Charles accepted the accolades heaped on him with a gracious smile. The conversation was light, at times bantering, but always in good taste. Even Murphy and Grady whooped their thanks at the heaping plates Charles set out for them, but instead of turkey, they had roast chicken.

Jack passed on the pumpkin pie, saying he was allergic, and went with the pecan pie. The others hooted with laughter at the remembrance of the truckload of pumpkins back in Utah. One and all agreed that it seemed like a lifetime ago.

Coffee and brandy were served in the living room, in front of a blazing fire, which Elias and Bert maintained. Outside, the snow continued to fall. Relaxing music, golden oldies that no one objected to, played softly.

Even though there were football games on the big-screen via satellite, no one opted to watch them. All were content to sit and revel in the peaceful atmosphere with good friends.

When Charles walked into the living room carrying a huge silver tray with two bottles of champagne, they all knew something interesting was about to happen. Myra, at his side, held an identical silver tray with exquisite cut-glass wine flutes.

Nikki looked over at Jack and winked. The heirloom crystal flutes had appeared months ago, brought from Myra's farmhouse to the mountain by Nellie. This, whatever this was, must really be important. Feeling a nudge to her shoulder, Nikki turned and wasn't surprised when she heard a whisper in her ear.

"This is Mummie's big day, Nik. She's finally going to do it."

"About time," Nikki said under her breath. She risked a glance around the room, but no one seemed to be paying attention to the fact that Barbara's spirit was in attendance.

Charles uncorked the first bottle of champagne. They all watched the cork sail upward, then spiral down to land at Myra's feet. The second cork went upward, spiraled down, and settled at Charles's feet. The little group clapped their hands.

"Nice going, Barb," Nikki mumbled.

"You should see what I can do when I put my mind to it." The spirit giggled. *"Shhh, here it comes."*

Charles cleared his throat. "I have an announcement to make. I've asked Myra to marry me, and she finally said yes. I asked her on bended knee in the snow at four thirty this morning on the front porch. I hope you're all as happy for us as we are for ourselves. So, let's drink a toast to this happy couple."

Nikki wasn't sure, but she thought she saw her spirit sister settle herself between her mother and father. Then again, maybe it was the smoke that suddenly billowed out of the fireplace before it was sucked back in and then straight up the chimney. "Nice going, Barb."

"Thanks, Nik. Give them both an earthly hug for me, okay?"

"You got it!" Nikki untangled herself and got to her feet to accept her flute of champagne. To Charles and Myra, she whispered, "I have orders to give you both an *earthly* hug. One earthly hug coming up," she said, wrapping her arms around Charles and Myra without spilling a drop of champagne.

"She was here, wasn't she?" Myra whispered.

"Oh, yeah, she was here." Nikki smiled. "She approves."

"I felt her right beside me," Charles murmured.

"She was between us, wasn't she, Nikki?" Myra asked.

Nikki nodded. "Smack-dab in the middle. I am so happy for you both."

The little group started to sing "For He's a Jolly Good Fellow" and then they switched up to "For She's a Jolly Good Lady." All off-key, but no one cared.

Cushions and blankets appeared out of nowhere as the happy guests sprawled wherever there was room. No one noticed until later that Annie and Isabelle had left the living room and returned to the building where they lived.

"I saw how unhappy you were, Isabelle. I know how you feel. I pretty much felt like a third wheel myself. Suddenly everyone became a couple. Don't get me wrong. That's a good thing. I don't think anyone will miss us, at least not for a little while, and even then they'll think we ate too much and are taking a nap. Everyone has a partner but you and I. I think we should do something about that, and I think we should do it *right now!*"

"And that would be . . . what?" Isabelle asked tentatively.

What indeed? "Well, you did tell me and the others on one or more occasion that you thought that guy in the Vegas casino was pretty hot. There for a while after we got back to the mountain, I thought you were pining for him. You said you looked right into his eyes and liked what you saw. You know the guy I'm talking about, the one you socked in the eye! You even remembered his name. Stu Franklin. He said if you ever take a vacation, you'd be able to find him on the beach in the Caymans. You said if we were ever pardoned, that was the first place you were going. You even asked Charles to have his people run a profile on him, and if I'm not mistaken, you have it in your possession."

Isabelle sighed. "All true, but that was then and this is now. How do you suppose one would go about finding someone on the beach in the Caymans, someone who is hiding out from the law?"

Annie could feel herself getting into it. "*I know people,* Isabelle," she said vaguely as her mind raced. "Listen, you're an architect. Draw me a picture of him from memory. Do it *now*."

Isabelle ran to her room and returned with a sketch pad. Her drawing pencil moved swiftly, with sure, deft strokes. Ten minutes later she held up Stu Franklin's likeness.

Annie stared at the picture. "Damn, girl, the man looks *hot!*"

"He was so hot, Annie, I felt like my eyebrows were on fire. How else do you think I was able to draw such a likeness? I wonder if he remembers me or his invitation. He probably has hundreds of beach bunnies running after him."

"Trust me, honey, he remembers you. He singled you out." Annie wondered if what she was saying was true. "You're beautiful, and he was helping *you*. He didn't have to do what he did that day. I think it's safe to say, he meant every word he said."

Isabelle threw her hands in the air. "What good is this going to do me except make me more sad that I'm alone?"

"Not for long. Come on. Put your jacket and boots on, and let's go to the command center. I told you I know people."

Outside, the snow was still falling.

"Do you think it will ever stop, Annie?"

"Oh, who cares? You need to be thinking of crashing waves, white sand, sultry breezes, and that . . . that guy on the beach. I wonder if anyone told him he's safe from prosecution. See, that's your . . . your reason for calling when we finally locate him. Even a lame reason is better than no reason, because he probably already knows, but there's no way for you to know that he knows. Did that make sense?"

"Well, yes, in a cockamamie way."

They were in the command center, and Annie was standing at Charles's workstation. She took a deep breath, picked up one of Charles's special encrypted phones. She dialed a number from memory and waited. Isabelle watched her and knew in her gut that whatever Annie was up to, she was going to pull it off. She walked off, sensing that Annie didn't want her eavesdropping on her secret private conversation.

"So, do you know who this is?" Annie said to the person who answered the phone.

"Ah, Miss No Name. Just for the record, I'm wearing my magic decoder ring. That means our conversation is safe. Are you calling to wish me a happy Thanksgiving?"

"Among other things. Are you keeping your eyes on my half of our business, *partner*?"

"Twenty-four-seven. Did you have your dinner yet?"

"I did, and it was wonderful. I need a favor and I need it *now*."

The voice on the other end of the line grumbled. "What is it with you women? You always want everything *now*. Since I'm three hours behind you, that means I have not had my dinner yet, and my 'now' is not the same as your 'now' with the time difference."

"Don't worry about it," Annie snapped. "You'll be eating turkey for a week anyway. I want you to find someone for me right away.

You did say you were . . . well, what you said was you . . ."

"The term you're looking for is . . . 'connected.' Which I am. All right, all right. What am I going to get out of this deal? *If* I decide your request is worthy of my expertise."

Annie swallowed hard. What would the girls say? What would Myra say? "Well, Mr. Fish, partner, you get *me.*"

Oh, God, did she really say that? Obviously she did, because Fish was sputtering on the other end of the phone. Annie listened.

"Oh, get over yourself, Mr. Fish. Admit it, you don't have a clue as to what to do with me. Not to worry. I'll show you."

Oh, God, did she say that, too? She blinked when she heard laughter on the other end. Annie listened again.

"What do you mean when? It's not like I'm free to come and go as I please. When you least expect it, I'll be there." Annie groaned inwardly. She rather thought there was a song with lyrics like that. She felt her face flame. "So, give me your fax number, and I'm going to send you a picture of the man I want you to find. Think in terms of *rewards* for a job well done. The kind you never dreamed of, that's what kind." Annie squeezed her eyes shut, knowing she was going to have to powwow with the girls to come up with *rewards.* Her whole body felt so hot, she wanted to run out naked in the snow. Fish was still sputtering on the other end of the line.

Annie slid the drawing into the fax machine

and punched in the number Fish had managed to give her during his sputtering.

"How long is this going to take?" Annie asked. "Did I also mention that I . . . we need the man's cell phone number and we want a guarantee that he will answer it when we call? You can do that, can't you, Fish?"

More garbled words.

"What? What? Are you saying you lied to me? You said you worked for some secret branch of the government no one has ever heard of. You said you were a terrorist and a mercenary. I believed you. Otherwise I wouldn't have called you. Oh, I cannot believe I tumbled to your silver tongue. You can just forget those rewards."

She listened, her eyebrows shooting upward.

"Well, that's more like it. The rewards are back on the table. Of course I'll wait for your call. Where do you think I'm going to go? No, I'm not sending you a list of the rewards. Well, maybe I could send the first three." Annie made kissing sounds into the phone before she broke the connection.

"Isabelleeeeeee!" Annie screeched at the top of her lungs.

"Oh, no, your source said he couldn't help. It's all right, Annie. You tried, and I appreciate it. I guess it just isn't meant to be."

"Shut up, Isabelle. It's in the bag. In a few hours you will be talking to Mr. Franklin. It's what I promised to get the information for you."

"Oh, Annie, what did you promise? Are you saying you can't deliver on your promise?"

Annie told her. Isabelle blinked. Then she blinked again before she doubled over laughing. When she finally stopped laughing, she managed to gasp. "I think we can come up with a suitable list of rewards. We might even be able to come up with *instructions.* You do realize what the problem is, right?"

"Oh, God, what could be worse?" Annie groaned.

Isabelle started to giggle and couldn't stop. "Following through," she finally managed to gasp.

Annie sat down with a thump. "What should I wear?"

"You aren't getting it, Annie. Zip."

"But . . ."

"A promise is a promise, Annie."

Annie rose to the occasion. "My dear, if you can make contact with Mr. Franklin, I can certainly honor my promise." *YIPPEEEEE!*

Four hours later eastern standard time, Annie's cell phone rang. She bolted upright from where she'd been dozing on the sofa. She gave Isabelle a shout to wake up where she, too, was dozing by the fire. "My phone is ringing. I think this call might be for you, honey."

Isabelle reached for the phone and said, "Hello, this is Isabelle."

"Well, Isabelle, this is Stu Franklin. There's this guy standing here with a gun to my head, and he's telling me to talk pretty to you. Not that anyone needs to tell me something like that. I'd appreciate it if you'd tell him he can leave me now so we can have a private conversation. I'm going to put him on the phone right now, before he blows my head off."

Isabelle managed to squeak out, "Thank you for your help, sir. I appreciate your doing this for me on Thanksgiving. I hope I didn't take you away from your dinner."

The voice on the other end of the phone mumbled something that sounded like he was glad he didn't have to kill anyone on Thanksgiving. Isabelle was so light-headed, she had to sit down.

Stu Franklin's voice was soft, cultured, intimate sounding. "Somehow or other, Isabelle, I thought you would have gotten in touch with me in a more conventional way. But, I admire your aggressiveness. I'm glad you called. Are you having a nice Thanksgiving?"

"I did . . . I am . . . I was until . . . oh, never mind. I didn't spoil yours, did I?"

"No. I just had a hot dog with all the trimmings on the beach. Did you have the whole enchilada, meaning a turkey with all the trimmings?"

"I did. I love hot dogs with all the trimmings, too."

"I saw that picture you did of me. Pretty good. Are you an artist?"

"No, I'm an architect. I feel . . . I feel kind of foolish and pushy right now. Maybe someday I can explain what made me . . . what I mean is . . ."

"Just for the record, I would have gotten in

touch, but I didn't know how. I was hoping you might take me up on my offer one of these days."

"That's kind of hard, but I'm working on it. We have two feet of snow where I am right now."

"It's sunny and eighty degrees where I am. There's not a ripple in the ocean, and it's sapphire blue. There aren't many people here right now, which is unusual. I guess the economy is as bad as they say it is."

"Has anyone told you that you're free from prosecution? If not, you can come and go as you please. We . . . we took care of that for you."

The silence on the other end of the phone lasted so long, Isabelle had to say, "Are you still there?"

"I'm still here. No, I didn't know that. Well, this is a wonderful Thanksgiving, after all. But, how do I know it's true?"

"Because I tracked you down to tell you. I don't lie. I think we might, I say might, be going to Washington soon."

"Is that an invitation? If it is, I accept."

"It is. If you give me your phone number, I can call you if it happens. You can call me anytime but not at this number." She rattled off a number, which Stu Franklin said he memorized.

"Let's talk, Isabelle. I want to know what happened that day at the casino. I want to know all about you."

And so Isabelle told him while Annie pretended to snore lightly on the sofa.

Chapter 3

While their faces were rosy pink with the frigid temperatures, they were also glum. Except for Annie and Isabelle, who for some reason spent the whole holiday weekend smiling.

The snow had finally stopped late Saturday afternoon. Sunday was spent clearing it away with snowblowers. Now they had single-file paths that led to the different buildings. It had taken them hours, but they had managed to clear out a wide path to the cable car. All that remained to be done was to deice the gears, oil the machinery, and hope it didn't start to snow again before the assembled guests were due to depart.

"I don't think I've ever been so tired in my whole life," Jack said as he trudged back to the main building. He looked over at Nikki, who looked just as tired.

Inside the main building, Charles was waiting with rum cake, hot coffee, and a pot of hot chocolate loaded with marshmallows. Food to go had been packaged for those who wanted to eat turkey during the coming week. Only Maggie and Jack had said they wanted food.

The Sisters were moaning and groaning about being frozen to their bones. Myra looked around, an indulgent smile on her face. She knew the girls would curl up in front of the fire that she and Annie would tend after their guests went down the mountain.

"They're so tired, Myra. We need to tell Charles that morning will be time enough to get down to business. Do you agree?" Annie asked.

"I do agree. What I'm thinking is you, Charles, and I can work and get things set up, laid out. And then we just present it to the girls tomorrow morning."

"What about that mysterious guest Charles said is coming to the mountain at dawn tomorrow?"

"I guess we deal with it tomorrow morning. The girls are adaptable, you know that. Look at them. They can barely keep their eyes open. I think that once our guests are gone, they're all going to go to sleep and sleep through the night. Even the dogs are exhausted," Myra said, pointing to Murphy and Grady, who were stretched out in their dog beds near the hearth.

Myra and Annie were always sad, even gloomy, when it was time for their guests to leave. That day was no different.

Two hours later they watched as everyone pulled on boots and heavy jackets.

Charles appeared with a carton that held

thermos bottles full of hot chocolate. "You'll need it when you get to the bottom of the mountain. More snow is predicted after midnight, so it's a good thing you're getting a head start. Please, all of you, drive carefully, and check in when you're home safe and sound."

Everyone promised to do so.

Nellie and Elias were the last to leave. Myra hugged her old friend and whispered in her ear. "I know you won't forget, Nellie, but if you can't find it, call me. I want to get married in my daughter's wedding dress. I think . . . I think she might like to know I'm getting married in her dress. At least I hope so. It was so beautiful, Nellie. All those seed pearls that were hand-sewn."

"Don't worry, Myra. When I come up next weekend, I will have it with me."

"Nellie, if I'm not here, just hang it in your room. We might be . . . Well, we *might* be off the mountain, *working*. I don't want Charles to know. It's a surprise."

"Understood. Thanks for a wonderful weekend. Elias and I will treasure the memory. Stay warm, my friend."

"You too."

A last round of hugs and kisses followed. The two dogs slept through the departure. By the time the door closed behind their guests, the girls were making a mad scramble to the living room, where they snatched at pillows and comforters to make nests for themselves.

The moment the table was cleared of the

cake plates and cups, the girls were sound asleep.

"The fire will last a good three hours, so I suggest we adjourn to the command center, where I can brief you on our agenda. If we're to accomplish our goal, we'll need to stay on a very tight schedule," Charles told Myra and Annie.

The trio bundled up, then checked on the girls one last time before they left the building. The first thing Charles did was rebuild the dying fire in the main room of the command center.

"Myra, I don't know if I should feel special right now or if I should feel dismayed that you and I are the only two at this orientation," Annie grumbled. "So much can be lost when we translate for the girls."

"Not to worry, Annie. I think the two of us are articulate enough to make it happen where the girls are concerned. If not, oh, well," Myra said, throwing her hands in the air in a devil-may-care gesture. "And, may I say you are looking particularly . . . sparkly this evening, Annie. Did something happen I don't know about?"

"Whatever in the world are you talking about, Myra Rutledge? What could have happened up here on this damn mountain that you wouldn't know about?"

Annie's face was so pink, and she was so flustered, Myra knew she was onto something. "You have a point, dear, but you do look . . . uh . . . guilty."

"I do, do I?"

"Yes, dear, you do." Myra did her best not to laugh at her friend's discomfort.

Annie was saved from having to make whatever comment she could have come up with when Charles took a seat at the round table. Three stacks of folders had mysteriously appeared while Annie and Myra were talking.

"So, Charles, who is the mysterious guest who is to arrive in the morning? What happens if the cable car is frozen? Then what do we do?" Myra asked.

"We'll deice it and spray some hydraulic oil. Our guest is Tobias Tyson, also known as Tee or, as his . . . uh . . . colleagues like to call him, MF. For Magic Fingers. Mr. Tyson is a . . . safecracker. Top of his field. Two stretches in the federal pen for his expertise. He very graciously agreed to my invitation to join us here and to teach one of you the tricks of his trade."

"Which one of us? Whose safe are we going to crack?" the two women asked at the same time.

"That's up to Mr. Tyson. But to answer your question, it will be Baron Bell's safe that you are going to crack. My intel tells me the safe is like the man himself, or the self he portrays to the public—benevolent and old-fashioned. I have here many articles and pictures of the man, and the safe is always prominently displayed for some reason. It is an antique and weighs several tons. Impossible to steal, but not impossible to crack."

"Tell us what you've learned from your people and the files Maggie brought to the mountain," Myra said.

"On the surface, Mr. Bell is what he appears to be. He has a thriving legal practice, mostly corporate. He's a fine lawyer. Being benevolent, he doesn't advertise that he brokers baby deals. It's not something he does on a regular basis. From what we can gather, he does it several times a year. Once the deal is done, all the legalities are worked out, and everyone signs off on it, he's finished. An example is Rachel and Tom Dawson. Mr. Bell brokered their deal. I hate using that particular term, but that's what it was, a deal. As subsequent events made clear, the babies the surrogates bring to term are nothing more than commodities as far as Mr. Bell is concerned.

"Mr. Bell put the Dawsons in touch with a surrogate, who would conceive a child using Thomas Dawson's sperm. The Dawsons paid Mr. Bell one hundred thousand dollars. The surrogate had her own attorney, but we can go into that later. Right now we're just concerned with Mr. Bell. Mr. Bell's role in the matter was to end the minute the surrogate gave birth and the papers were signed.

"But when the surrogate gave birth to twins, which was not expected, as the second baby hadn't shown up on the ultrasound, things changed. The surrogate demanded more money for the second child, and the Dawsons didn't have it. They said they would try to come up with the money. Here is where Mr. Bell entered the picture again, presumably because more money from the Dawsons was involved. The Dawsons took the twins home. They managed to come up with a few thousand extra, but nowhere near what Bell and the surrogate wanted.

"Then the surrogate filed a suit with her own lawyer, saying she'd changed her mind and wanted to keep the twins. Bell bowed out and refused to talk or meet with the Dawsons. Not only couldn't the Dawsons defend a lawsuit—they were bankrupt—but since they couldn't come up with the rest of the money, they had to surrender the twins to the birth mother.

"Mrs. Dawson went through what she described to Lizzie as a mini-breakdown. Mr. Dawson wanted to kill someone. The couple's marriage is suffering because of all this. Then Mrs. Dawson got angry. She pulled up her socks and started to check on things on the Internet. She also spent a lot of time in the park, talking to nannies and young mothers, and came up with another case similar to her own. That's when she went to Nikki's firm, and the office manager sent her to Lizzie."

"Were the Dawsons given back their money by Bell?" Annie asked.

Charles shook his head. "No. Nor did the surrogate give back the monies they paid for her care during her pregnancy. The Dawsons could sue for the money, but they have no funds to work with."

"Why didn't the Dawsons go to the newspaper or the media? If Mr. Dawson's sperm was used, he is the biological father. That has to count," Myra said.

"They didn't want the public uproar they knew would occur. Mr. Dawson was afraid his employer would terminate his position if it came to light that he was embroiled in a family media circus. Mrs. Dawson more or less felt the same way as her husband. They did *talk* to several lawyers. When they told the lawyers about the demands for more money because a second child was produced, they were told that for the surrogate to make such a demand, and for Mr. Bell to be involved with the attempt to extort the money the surrogate demanded for the second child, was a crime. It is illegal to *sell* babies, so the one hundred thousand dollars and associated expenses paid the surrogate could not be part of a commercial transaction in which the baby was bought. The minute the surrogate demanded more money simply because she gave birth to a second child, she was breaking the law by trying to sell the second child.

"But when the lawyers were told that the only evidence that such a demand had been made was the Dawsons' testimony, they could tell the Dawsons only that they couldn't win, that as long as the birth mother testified that she had simply changed her mind and could not bear to be parted from her children, she would always get the kids. They were also told that Mr. Dawson risked having to contribute child support if he pursued the matter."

"But you said Mr. Dawson was the sperm

donor. Doesn't that count for something?" Myra demanded again, outrage ringing in her voice.

"It takes money to pursue any kind of action they might want to bring. And any suit they brought would undoubtedly be met with a countersuit. Right now, Myra, that young couple is licking their wounds, and they don't know what to do. Lizzie is going to represent them pro bono. As a matter of fact, she's scheduled an appointment with Baron Bell for Wednesday. She's going to fly in, attend the meeting, and return to Vegas on the red-eye. She didn't explain the purpose of the meeting to Bell's secretary. Because of her reputation, they wouldn't dream of asking or putting her on the spot. The truth of the matter is they were probably flattered that she wanted to meet with Mr. Bell."

"Are we thinking Baron Bell and the surrogate's lawyer are . . . in this together?" Annie asked. "Who's her lawyer? Anyone we know?"

"From what I'm told by Maggie, she's a Lizzie Fox wannabe," Charles replied. "Maggie said she is full of herself and isn't even a good lawyer. Her name is Adel Newsom. From what I can gather, she tries to emulate Lizzie in everything. Her colleagues aren't kind about it when they discuss her."

Myra fingered the pearls at her neck. She looked toward the windows, but all she could see in the shiny blackness was her own reflection. "Do we know if they're just business associates, or are they . . . something else?"

"Oh, Myra, for heaven's sake, say what you

mean. What she wants to know, Charles, is, are the two of them shacked up?" Annie said.

"It appears to be so, but at the moment there is no proof. Maggie has her people digging *deep.*"

"What about the babies? Are they safe? What about the other case? What happened to that child?"

Charles closed his eyes. It looked to Myra and Annie like he was in pain. Somehow he managed to speak through his clenched teeth. "Bought and sold after the surrogate reclaimed the child. The same thing will probably happen with the Dawson twins."

"This is all about money," Myra said, her eyes brimming with tears. "How can people do that to innocent children?"

"People like that have no conscience, Myra. They go by the green stuff in hand. Well, I, for one, am going to relish going after them if Lizzie can prove they're the scum we think they are. And I, for one, will show no mercy where they're concerned. What else, Charles?" Annie demanded.

"We think there's a good chance the twins are about to be sold off to a new couple. That's why we have to do something quickly," Charles said.

"Maggie!" both women said in unison.

"Front-page picture of the Dawsons and their problem, along with pictures of the twins," Annie said.

"What if the Dawsons won't cooperate?" Myra fretted.

"If they think they can get the twins, I think

they might ignore the media circus. We can help them out financially. The downside is we're going to have to watch the surrogate, as well as the two lawyers," Charles said. "Everyone is under surveillance as we speak."

Annie reached for a yellow legal pad. She scribbled furiously for several minutes. "Give us the name of the second surrogate and the adoptive parents."

"The second surrogate is Joan Olsen. She's also a student. The parents are Beth and John Evans. She's a nurse, he's a doctor. Intern, actually. Like the Dawsons, they didn't want their employer, the hospital, to know what was going on. Newsom represented Olsen, Baron Bell represented the Evanses. They had essentially the same experience the Dawsons did, absent the attempted extortion. When things went sour, they tried contacting Bell, but he wouldn't return their calls. John Evans said at their initial meeting Bell spelled it all out for them. Once they took possession of the baby, and all the papers were signed, his part was done. Any future legal problems would have to be dealt with by another lawyer. Bell said he simply did not have the time to do a follow-through for the next eighteen years. Evans said he made a joke of it, and they signed off on it. So Bell didn't commit any obvious crime in that case. Morally, that's another story."

"What do we do and when do we leave?" Annie asked. "By the way, does Mr. Bell's safe have some kind of special significance?"

Charles smiled. "Think about it, ladies. Seeing a safe like that, an old-timey affair, complete with the engraved elk on the door, tells me Bell wants people to think he has a lot of things in there. It also tells people it's impenetrable. What it tells *me* is this . . . There's another safe in his offices. Snowden managed to secure and forward to me a complete blueprint of the entire office building. Mr. Bell's second safe is built into the floor under his desk. I'm sure he has one of those hard plastic sheets on top of it so that his chair can roll and move about with ease. Undetectable to the naked eye."

"So which safe do we want to crack?" Myra asked.

"Both," replied Charles. "If I'm right, the one in the floor will be a modern safe, digital, a snap for someone like Mr. Tyson to open. The old-timey Browning safe is going to be more difficult. You have to have a good ear so you can hear the tumblers. Not to mention a light touch."

Annie looked over at Myra. "This is exciting, don't you think, Myra?"

Myra thought the whole thing was frightening. Here she was, soon to finally marry the love of her life, but before she could do that, she had to take a hiatus so she could do a little breaking and entering and possibly pay a visit to the local jail.

"Absolutely, it's exciting," she snapped.

"Is that why you have such a death grip on those pearls around your neck?" Annie asked.

"No!" Myra snapped again. "I suggest you get rid of those chains around your neck if we're going to be breaking and entering. I can hear you clanking when I'm a mile away."

"You're such a poop," Annie sniffed. "What else, Charles?"

"There's not much that's going to happen through the night. Our surveillance is ongoing. I have a conference call scheduled with Lizzie and Maggie in the morning. Ted is going to see the Dawsons and the Evanses first thing in the morning to prepare them for whatever plan Maggie and Lizzie decide to run with. We don't want to tip our hand this early in the game."

"What about Adel Newsom? Who's checking her out?" Myra asked.

"I have it all right here," Charles said, tapping a dark blue folder. "She's a one-lawyer office with two paralegals and two secretaries. She does *not* do pro bono work. Never has. She drives a high-end car, wears only designer clothing, has a luxurious apartment complete with terrace. She likes fine wine and gourmet food. She also has a summer house at Rehoboth Beach. She spends many weekends there. Mr. Snowden's people visited her office here and her apartment and found nothing in either place to help us. I would like her to realize her security has been penetrated at the same time Baron Bell realizes it. That's when the rats start to scurry. Then Maggie follows up with her headline, whatever it turns out to be. At that point, it's all in your hands, ladies."

"Do we know who has the Evanses' baby?" Annie asked.

"Not at this moment in time, but we should know sometime within the next few days. We know where the twins are at the moment. By the way, the twins' names are Robert and Rita. The Evanses named their baby Benjamin. They called him Benjy. If it looks like the Dawsons' surrogate is going to flee, Mr. Snowden will deter her in some manner."

"I suggest we adjourn for the evening," Annie said as she offered up an elaborate yawn. Myra looked at her suspiciously, but Annie was oblivious to her friend's stare. "'Night, you two. I'm so happy for both of you. I can hardly wait for the wedding."

"Will you help me, Annie?" Myra whispered. "I want it all to be perfect."

"Absolutely," Annie said as she pulled on her boots. "We're all so happy for you. The girls were worrying about what color you want them to wear."

"Ice blue," Myra answered. "What color do you want to wear, Annie?"

"Well, I love purple, but that might clash with the girls. Whatever works for you, dear. I'll see you in the morning."

Myra followed her friend to the door. "You might as well tell me right now what it is that has you in such a tizzy. You know I'll find out sooner or later, and if it turns out to be later, then I just might get pissy. And we don't want that, do we?"

"Fish is going to be calling me soon. I . . . uh

. . . I called him and we had a very nice dialogue and we're going to do it again."

"Ahhh."

"Never mind ahhh. Try ooh la la," Annie called over her shoulder before she started to slog through the snow. It occurred to her when she was halfway to her building that she could have walked on the shoveled path instead of wading through the midthigh snow.

"Awawk," she mumbled as she brought herself out of her daydreams.

Chapter 4

It was barely light out when Charles set the last breakfast dish on the sideboard. The girls lined up and filled their plates. Out of the corner of their eyes, they watched Charles don his stout boots and fur-lined parka.

"I heard Charles's cell chirp, so that must mean our guest is at the foot of the mountain. That means he has to send the cable car down manually. Around four o'clock I saw him going out with the oil can," Kathryn whispered to Nikki.

"Why are you whispering?" Nikki asked.

Kathryn laughed. "I don't know." She loaded her plate with bacon and waffles.

"Do you think Mr. Tyson and Charles will confer before he springs him on us? It worries me that more and more people know our current address," Isabelle grumbled. Today she was eating sparingly and thinking about how she would look in her old bikini should she find herself on a beach in the Cayman Islands. Maybe she should order a new one and get some sun so that she didn't look like a snowbird when she hit the beach. She chided herself for such thinking, but she couldn't help but smile.

"You might as well tell us," Alexis said. "We've all been trying to figure out why you and Annie have been wearing these secret smiles. Share!"

Isabelle grinned, then looked at Annie, who nodded. She shared.

The girls clapped their hands in approval.

"Annie? It's your turn," Myra said.

Annie shared, her face flushed. "I talked a good game but . . . it's been like forever since I . . . you know." She was so flustered the girls forgot their breakfast as they jumped in with both feet to tease her. Annie's face turned a deeper shade of pink at their risqué suggestions. The suggestions ran from the sublime to the ridiculous.

"It's like riding a bike. It will come back to you."

"Just look mysterious and blasé at the same time."

"Be sure to use the word *performance* as often as you can."

"Candles, dim light, fragrant sheets are where it's at."

"Brush up on your athletic capabilities."

"You can find a tutorial on the Internet about hundreds of ways to use your tongue. They even have one for hand and toe usage."

Myra had to slap Annie's back when she started to choke. She was still sputtering, the others giggling, when the door opened. Charles led his guest into the dining room.

He was tall; his hair, snow-white. He was handsome and tanned. He was built like an athlete and moved with the stealth of a cat. He looked capable and hungry. He appeared to be of an age with Myra and Annie. It was his twinkling eyes that put the girls at ease.

"Ladies, your attention please. I'd like to introduce Tobias Tyson." It was obvious Charles wasn't going to introduce them by name, and it also looked like the tall stranger standing in front of them understood.

Tyson shed his white poplin down jacket and took his place at the sideboard. He filled his plate with fruit and muffins. Instead of coffee, he opted for hot tea.

Conversation consisted of the weather below the mountain, the coming holidays, and the Christmas trees that were going up in New York and Washington.

Later, all agreed they liked Tyson. He was well spoken on just about any subject. They all liked the fact that he looked whomever he was talking to in the eye. And, Yoko said, he smelled good. She wanted to know what cologne or shaving lotion he used so she could get some for Harry.

The minute the table and sideboard were cleared and the dishwasher was humming in the background, Charles left them to return to his command center.

Tyson unzipped the heavy bag at his feet. It took all his strength to lift a heavy door model onto the table. "This," he said, "is a replica—a scaled-down version—of the safe you will be dealing with." He pointed to a smaller unit. "This is a replica of a digital safe." He pulled a small square box out of the bag, powered it up, and said, "This will run through thousands of numeric codes in seconds and will give you the code you need within fifty-seven seconds." In a businesslike voice, he said, "Put your hands on the table so I can see them. When I tell you to raise your hands, do it and flex your fingers." He demonstrated how they should do it. "What's needed here is flexibility and a light touch."

The women frowned, openly showing their disapproval as Tyson touched their hands, shaking his head.

"Too short. Stubby isn't going to work. Knuckles too big. Those nails have to go, and so does the polish. It might chip, and it will be a clue for the authorities to follow. Too much jewelry. It has to go, too. Wrist's too thick. I'm looking for long, tapered fingers. Piano fingers. The pads of your fingers are too thick. Yours are too fleshy."

"Aren't we supposed to sandpaper our fingertips?" Nikki all but snarled.

"That's only in the movies. This is no movie," Tyson responded. "I was told that there is a security guard who makes his rounds of the building every twenty to thirty-five minutes. On the second go-round, the guard opens the office and checks the interior. Your window of time is small, so we have to make sure the person cracking the safe knows what she's doing and can do it with her eyes closed."

"I don't remember hearing anything about a security guard," Yoko grumbled.

Tyson looked over at the small, Asian American woman as though taking her measure. He didn't bother to respond. "Ahhh, perfect. Finger pad is just right. Good flexibility. No sign of arthritis. Nails trimmed just right. You'll do!" he said dramatically.

Annie was so befuddled, she didn't know what to do. When Tyson winked at her, she almost blacked out.

Isabelle leaned over and whispered in her ear, "I think you have a problem here, Annie. You went from no man to two men all of a sudden. I saw that wink. It was roguish. The others saw it, too. He's interested in you. I bet you could bring him to his knees if you tried."

Annie swallowed hard. *Feast or famine.* Tyson was waiting for a comment. *If* Isabelle was right, and the wink meant something, she did have a problem. Well, she knew how to wink. In the end, she made a kissing motion, then laughed. She smiled and kept smiling, to Tyson's discomfort. She leaned over and whispered, "You wouldn't know what to do with me. Trust me." She loved the man's startled expression so much, she decided to go a step further. She dropped her voice even more. "I know how to . . ."

Myra couldn't believe her ears. She gasped, and she gasped again as she whispered to Kathryn, who then passed Annie's comments down the line.

His ears red, Tyson made a production out of

searching for something in his bag. "You couldn't possibly . . . ," he muttered.

"Mr. Tyson, do I look like someone who makes idle boasts? I'm up for a sizable wager. Now, let's get this show on the road. Time is money. By the way, how much money are we paying you?"

Tyson told her.

"Really! I hope you can earn it. Shall we get started?" Annie wanted to be done with it all so she could go on the Net to visit the tutorial the girls were talking about.

Clearly flustered, Tyson asked Annie if she wore a hearing aid or if she thought she might need one to hear the tumblers turn over.

"My hearing is as perfect as the rest of me, Mr. Tyson."

The girls gawked, their eyes round as saucers. Annie never ceased to amaze them.

"Call me Tee."

Her heart beating like a trip-hammer, Annie did her best to pay attention and ignore the closeness of the man beside her. She liked the smell of the man and said so, her ear pressed to the makeshift safe door.

"Thank you. I don't think anyone ever told me she liked the way I smell before."

"Shhh, ah, this is the first one. Keep going. There's a first time for everything. What was it like doing two stretches in the federal pen? That's it. Number two. I thought you said this was hard."

"It is hard. It's the third one you're going to

miss. It wasn't a picnic, but once I made up my mind that I had to do the time, I did it and walked out a free man. Believe it or not, law enforcement calls on me from time to time to . . . help them. I do it gratis. How would you like to go dancing someday?"

"Dancing? You did that on purpose to throw me off so I'd miss it, didn't you?"

"I did. You have to focus, pay attention, and not allow yourself to get distracted. For instance, you could be going for the third tumbler, and the guard is a little early. You have to keep going and let the others worry about the guard. *Capisce?* The third tumbler is always the harder one. Once it took me nine times. Start from the beginning. We have all day. So, would you like to go dancing someday?"

Annie pressed her ear to the safe door. Suddenly she felt like crying and didn't know why. "Someday may never come, but if it does, I get to lead."

Tyson threw his head back and laughed. "You got it! Now concentrate."

"You may not know this about me, Mr. . . . uh . . . Tee, but I know how to multitask."

As Annie concentrated on the task in front of her, she found herself measuring the ex-con sitting next to her against Fish. The trouble was, neither one of them was coming up short.

Myra almost killed herself getting up from the table and running to the pantry off the kitchen, where the others were doubled over laughing. "She's a loose cannon. Someone has to rein her in," Myra said, her voice so garbled, the others could barely understand what she was saying. "This is *not* funny, girls. What if she . . . crashes and burns? Then what?"

"That is not going to happen. We're all going to take her under our wings and teach her a thing or two. That's not to say she needs teaching. It will be more like taking a refresher course." Nikki giggled. "You're getting married soon, Myra. You're welcome to sit in. You know what they say. You're never too old to learn new tricks."

Myra's hands flew to the pearls at her neck. "Oh, dear God!"

"Okay, fun's over. Time to get to work. Straight faces, everyone," Kathryn said. "Let's take the small safe and the digital gizmo, along with the instructions, into the living room and see which one of us is proficient at modern safecracking. I can't believe that schmuck said my fingers are too thick. I think I have nice fingers. Rings look nice on my fingers."

"Give it up already," Nikki snapped. "Do you hear me complaining that he said my fingers were stubby? I think we should push him off the mountain after he teaches us all he knows."

As they sat in the kitchen at the *Post,* Maggie scarfed down pancakes and sausages as she rattled off orders to Ted and Espinosa, who were trying to eat and take notes at the same time. "You can take Carmody with you if you feel you need more manpower. It's your job to convince the Dawsons and Evanses to go public. I want family pictures, not the ones you had earlier. All new parents take pictures all day long. I want a regular gallery. I want sweet, I want sad, I want devastated. Now, listen to me carefully." Maggie stopped eating long enough to show how serious she was about what she was about to say. "Only as a last resort are you to mention the vigilantes and their willingness to step in to help. You can mention that there will be financial aid to both families if they agree to go public and their employers terminate them because of the publicity. Take your food in a to-go bag and get on it. I want all this by noon, so get going."

"How am I going to eat waffles with syrup in a to-go bag?" Ted grumbled.

"Get some toast and a banana," Maggie said as she went back to her hearty breakfast. "Do a good job, and I'll treat you to dinner at Martin's in Georgetown. I'll even call ahead to see if we can get John Kennedy's favorite booth, the one where he proposed to Jackie. Booth three, or maybe booth one, where he would go to read the Sunday paper after Mass."

"Yeah, yeah, yeah," Ted said as he galloped out of the kitchen, Espinosa on his trail.

Forty minutes later, Maggie was back in her office. She took care of a few housekeeping details and settled down to wait for Lizzie Fox's call. She took the three-hour time difference as a personal affront to her own busy schedule as she watched the latest happenings coming in over the wires. Her eyes narrowed to a squint as she stared at her computer.

> Santa Claus, aka Baron Bell, and his elves will arrive in his personal antique sleigh, complete with sleigh bells and his eight worthy steeds, on the South Lawn of the White House for the annual children's Christmas party at the White House, hosted by President Connor and Baron Bell. The date is three days away.

Maggie's gaze raced through the news flash. Tree lighting. Tons of gaily wrapped gifts, snowballs.

The ultimate in photo ops. No mention who would set the sleigh down in the snow on the South Lawn or how they would accomplish this feat. Or how the horses in their Christmas attire would get there. Probably by horse trailer. Security would be worthy of a summit meeting.

Maggie pressed SEND. Five seconds later the article was on the way to the mountain.

Maggie reached for her BlackBerry. She sucked in her breath, then let it out in a loud swoosh as she alerted Ted to what she'd just read. Headlines of every size and shape ripped through her mind. It looked to her like it was going to be one hell of a busy week. Gut instinct told her she might get two special editions out of the forthcoming events. "Yesss!"

Promptly at nine o'clock East Coast time,

Lizzie Fox called. They updated each other, made small talk, then got down to business. Maggie read to Lizzie the article that she'd just e-mailed to the mountain. Lizzie burst out laughing, knowing exactly what Maggie was thinking.

"Maggie, before I keep my appointment with Baron Bell tomorrow, I am going to need written confirmation that the Evanses want me to represent them. I don't want to give Baron Bell one inch of wiggle room. I also cannot solicit the Evans family. They have to come to me. Rachel Dawson said she would do her best to convince Beth Evans, who in turn would have to convince her husband."

"Okay. Ted is probably at the Dawsons' right now. I'll text him and tell him what he has to do. The Evanses live in Old Town in Alexandria, right?"

"Yes. What's going on, on the mountain?"

Maggie told her. Lizzie giggled, and they both signed off.

It was two o'clock when Ted and Espinosa loomed over her desk.

"Do you have it all?" Maggie asked.

"We do. That guy Evans was a hard nut to crack, but he went along with it in the end. I hate to admit this, but I think it was the vague promise that Lizzie was going to get their money back. But it could have been the mention of the vigilantes. I just don't know. They've given up on getting the baby back, sad to say. We did our best, Maggie, but that couple is beaten down. They want to believe the paper can help. I did have to throw in the vigilantes, like I said. Mrs. Evans perked right up and said if her husband didn't agree, she was leaving him. Listen, we're going down to the cafeteria to get something to eat. It's all there. Text me if there's something you don't understand. The pictures Espinosa got will break your heart. How soon do you need me to write it up?"

"As soon as you're done with lunch," Maggie replied. "I'm not going to run with it just yet, but I want it ready in case I decide to go with a special edition. We've done all we can for the moment. Now we wait for Lizzie to see how things shake out. Check the wires while you're eating, and let me know what you think about the Christmas party at the White House."

Maggie went back to her computer and downloaded the photos Espinosa had taken. Ted was right. There was nothing more beautiful than a new baby being held in his mother's arms. In the case of the Dawsons, two babies. Absolutely nothing.

Maggie continued downloading the pictures, her eyes misting up from time to time. The babies were beautiful. The two sets of parents looked haunted. Both young mothers looked vulnerable and fragile. The fathers looked bewildered.

Maggie spread out the photos on her desk. First she lined up the babies. Then she put the pictures of the parents next to the babies. Her hands flew as she moved, shifted as she struggled to come up with a headline that would tell the story in three words or less.

A sticky pad found its way to her hand. Readers would want names to go with the cherubs' faces. The parents needed names, too. Mom and Dad? Beth and John? Rachel and Tom? Mom and Dad! Nurse, teacher, doctor, engineer? Robert, Rita, Benjy? What should she go with for her headline?

Maybe she was going about this all wrong. Maybe she should put Baron Bell's picture above the fold and go with a headline that applied to him. Like those pictures the New York papers printed about the most hated man in America: Bernie Madoff. Her reporter's instinct told her people would care, but they'd move on. No, she had to go with the babies and the parents. The headline would come to her. She was sure of it.

Eating always helped her think more clearly. How weird that she'd worked through her lunch hour. Maybe she needed to remove herself from what she was seeing for a little while. She could go to the cafeteria and get a corned beef on rye and whatever else they had that would complement the corned beef.

On her way down in the elevator, Maggie's fist shot in the air. Out of nowhere her headline hit her between the eyes. "You're toast, Baron Bell!"

Chapter 5

Lizzie Fox looked like she'd just stepped out of a salon that guaranteed the works as she gathered up her purse and briefcase. Only the flight attendant knew she'd worked through the five-hour flight. She'd freshened up twenty minutes prior to landing. Other weary passengers looked at her approvingly, but she was oblivious.

She was the first one off the plane. The time was 7:10 in the morning.

Early morning travelers took a second to admire the long-legged vision as she strode past the security lines, her gaze raking the limo drivers holding up signs. When she spotted her driver, she waved. Within minutes she was outside and settled in the backseat of the luxurious limousine Cosmo Cricket had arranged for her.

Lizzie shivered even though the heater was blowing hot, delicious air all around her ankles. Outside, a light snow was falling. She liked snow, and yet she hated snow. A long-ago memory of sitting in the cemetery, with a frozen bunch of violets in her hand, swam before her eyes. Jack Emery had saved her that awful night. She knew now that she would have stayed there and frozen to death if not for him. But that was all a lifetime ago. She had a new life now, thanks to Jack and all the vigilantes. Without them in her life, she never would have met Cosmo. Nor would she have ever married. She was almost positive of that.

Lizzie blinked away the tears that were pricking at her eyelids. She leaned forward. "Drop me off at the *Post* first, but I want you to wait for me."

"Yes, ma'am," replied the driver.

Lizzie leaned back and watched the traffic. Her mind raced through her agenda for the day, then stopped. She smiled; she had it covered. Now she could set her thoughts to what in the world she was going to get her new husband for Christmas. Cosmo had promised that when she got back, he was going to take the day off, and they were going to a forest to chop down a real Christmas tree. She'd teased him, saying Vegas didn't have any forests, and he'd said, "Oh, yes, they do. You just need to know where to look." And that had been the end of that. A big tree, he'd said. He'd even bought a pickup truck to cart it home. He was so proud of the seventy-five-dollar rusty clunker. Then he'd announced that the springs under the seats were shot. He'd called it a kidney crusher. She'd giggled all day over their newest possession, but she had to admit, she couldn't wait to go out to the forest to cut down the tree. But that wasn't solving her problem of what to get Cosmo for Christmas. Something would come to her; she was sure of it.

When Lizzie stepped from the limousine, a strong gust of wind almost blew her over. The snow was coming down heavier and in squalls. She hoped it stopped before her return flight back to Vegas later in the day.

Lizzie signed in, was given a card saying she was a visitor. She looped it around her neck as she made her way to the elevator.

Maggie was waiting for her the minute she stepped out of the elevator. "Martin called to say you were on your way up. Let's go to the kitchen. I just made some fresh coffee, and I bought some doughnuts and bagels on the way in. We'll just close the door and have all the privacy we need."

Lizzie sniffed appreciatively as Maggie poured her a cup of the fragrant coffee. She watched as the EIC toasted bagels and spread them lavishly with butter and cream cheese. "Oooh, this is sooo good. I didn't realize how hungry I was. I never eat on planes. Do you?"

"As a rule, no. I usually travel with my own snacks, but I will eat the fruit. So, tell me, do you have a game plan, or do you want to hear mine first?"

"My appointment with Baron Bell is for eleven o'clock. When I leave here, I want to go back to my house to shower and change. I'm simply going to lay my cards on the table and hope the man sees the light. I expect him to clam up and admit to nothing. If you have something you care to give me to show him, that just might make it easier for the Dawsons and the Evanses. Thank Ted for me for getting the Evanses to sign on. What are they saying on the mountain?"

"They're saying everyone in question is under surveillance. The girls are ready to move at a moment's notice. In case no one told you, you are to take pictures of Bell's office, especially that monstrosity of a safe. Charles's people managed to get the blueprints, but things can change. Not that the safe will have been moved. I understand it weighs a couple of tons. Do you think Bell will lie to you?"

"Oh, yeah. I have my ducks all in a row. When are you going to start running your articles? By the way, I saw on the Net that Bell is gearing up for his White House kids' Christmas party."

"Yeah, we blew that one up big-time. I gave him way too much press, but you do what you have to do to get where you want to go. I'm sure he was preening like a peacock when he read all his accolades. The man is vain, even though he pretends otherwise."

Lizzie finished her coffee and bagel. Maggie tidied up the kitchen, unlocked the door, and led Lizzie back to her office. Lizzie tried not to laugh at the way Maggie was balancing several bananas, an orange, and a box of Ring Dings. In the office, Maggie dumped her snacks in her desk drawer.

"You want to see Espinosa's photos in glorious color on the computer, or do you want to hold them in your hands? The guys did a great job. It's going to cost me a meal at Martin's, but it's worth it. I think you'll agree when you see what we have."

Lizzie reached for a stack of glossy pictures. She took her time looking at each one, her eyes misting as she looked down at the babies. Maggie watched the lawyer's jaw set, her eyes turning steely and hard. She felt sorry for Baron Bell.

"They're great, Maggie. Do you have a headline to go with these?"

"I do. Want to see it?"

"You bet!" Lizzie watched as Maggie clicked her mouse. She leaned over to stare at the stark headline. She clapped her hands. "That'll do it, Maggie! It's perfect! Good going, Miss EIC! Listen, I have to run. Say hello and good-bye to everyone for me."

The two women hugged each other. Maggie walked Lizzie to the elevator.

"Good luck. If I can do more, call, okay?" said Maggie.

"Will do." They hugged one more time. "See ya in the funny papers."

Maggie laughed. She stood at the elevator for a long time before she made her way back to her office. Her expression was short of dreamy, almost the same as Lizzie's expression when both of them had looked at the cherubs on the glossy prints. For the first time in her life, she gave some thought to her biological clock ticking away second by second. She rather thought Lizzie was probably thinking the same thing on her way home.

Tick-tock. Tick-tock.

The office phone was ringing when Maggie slammed the door of her office. She felt like she was going to cry any minute. "Yes," she barked into the receiver.

"That's how you answer your phone? Didn't your mother teach you any manners?" Jack Emery barked in return.

Maggie sniffed. "What? Are you calling to pick my brain, or are you calling me to tell me something I don't already know, which I find to be very unlikely? Why aren't you in court?"

"I'm not in court, because crime has taken a holiday, and I already locked up all the bad guys. Actually, I was calling to ask if you wanted to go to lunch with me and Harry. I'm on my way to pick him up. He's being a real pain in the ass with the construction guys working on his dojo. The foreman on the job pulled me to the side yesterday and asked me if there was any way for me to take him off their hands. Bring Ted and Espinosa. We'll have a regular party, you know, one of those three-hour lunches we used to do. By the time I get him back to the dojo, they'll be ready to quit for the day. Of course, Harry won't see it that way and will probably kill one of us, but what the hell. Anything for my friend Harry."

Maggie laughed, her sour, maudlin mood gone for the moment. Jack could always make her laugh. "Squire's Pub, twelve thirty, work for you?"

"It does. It would be nice if the *Post* picked up the tab," Jack said, then hung up when Maggie started to sputter.

Jack had to park more than a block away and hoof it back to Harry's dojo. He had to wiggle his way between utility trucks, cable trucks, telephone trucks, plumbing vehicles, plus the cars and trucks of the workers. Harry's Ducati was wedged in so tight in the back, he would have to physically pick it up and turn it around if he wanted to take it out. Aha! That was why old Harry had invited him over: he needed extra muscle to get his bike out to the street. Little did Harry know he was on his way anyway.

Jack made his way to what had once been the back door and was now just a big, gaping hole in the building. A dozen different people could be seen scurrying about, shouting orders to one another. Harry was leaning against a half wall, drinking tea.

"I bet you could clear this room in a few seconds if you served those guys some of that shitty tea you're guzzling," Jack said by way of a greeting.

"Eat shit, Jack. I only share my shitty tea with those near and dear to my heart. What do you think? Not that I value your opinion or anything. I'm just curious."

"I love it. So will you when it's done. Listen, I

know a secret. Well, I sort of know a secret that concerns Yoko. Nikki didn't *exactly* tell me I couldn't tell you, so I guess I can. You know me. When I give my word, nothing, not even wild horses, can drag it out of me. I pretended not to be interested so I wouldn't have to give my word so that I could have a clear conscience when I told you."

Harry set his cup with no handles down on the half wall. He raised three fingers. Jack knew he had precisely three seconds to tell Harry the secret, or the great master of the martial arts would kill him on the spot.

"Okay, okay. Look, I'm just the messenger, okay, so don't do something you're going to regret," Jack said with a straight face. "That also means you can't even *think* about doing something. It seems . . . Jesus, Harry, I don't know how to tell you this. I guess I just have to blurt it out. Yoko has had a change of heart. She doesn't like pink anymore. She's into . . . champagne colors. That means you have to get rid of all that pink shit we bought. The bright spot is it was on sale. That should take away some of your pain, and, buddy, I am feeling your pain. I thought it was beautiful, but . . . it's champagne from here on in. Nikki said all the girls agreed. It seems pink is now passé. Who knew, Harry? Certainly not me."

"I paid a thousand dollars for all that pink crap *on sale*, and now I have to throw it out. Is that what you're telling me, *Jack?*"

"Well, yeah, it's either that or Yoko is going to

throw you out. She doesn't like peonies anymore either. Women are so fickle!" Jack proclaimed dramatically. He looked at Harry and thought he'd never seen a more stupid expression in his life. "After lunch we can go shopping. You want to go to Target or Neiman Marcus? Walmart is also a possibility. Your call."

"What if all that crap isn't on sale, and I have to pay full price?"

"Then, oh, well. The cost of love is expensive, Harry. You want to kill someone right now, don't you? Stifle that feeling. Try your best to feel the love that's going to come your way with all those soft, muted champagne colors. Oh, I almost forgot. Nikki said Yoko is now into champagne-colored roses and white tulips. I didn't know they had champagne-colored roses. Did you know that, Harry?"

The stupid look was back on Harry's face. He was also speechless.

"What I would do if I were you is this . . . and may I say I'm glad I am not you. I would call some florist and leave a standing order for delivery. That's what I would do, Harry. Harry, what's wrong with you? Are you having a fit or something? Shake your head! Drink that damn tea! Ah, that's good. Your eyes are uncrossing. I never saw you cry before, Harry. I know, I know, you aren't crying. It's all the sawdust and Sheetrock dust clogging up your eye pores, or whatever it is that gets clogged up in your eyes."

Harry looked at Jack and smiled. It was the most evil smile Jack had ever seen in his life.

Jack opted to run like hell, calling over his shoulder, "We can order from a catalog or online."

Harry stopped in his tracks. "Do you have a catalog?"

"I do, Harry, I do. I swear to God I do! After lunch we can go to the house. Catalogs come by the pound to the house. I have *hundreds* of them. We can have everything shipped to my house. You feel better now?"

"I do, Jack. I really do. Help me with the bike."

Thirty minutes later they had the Ducati on the street. Both of them were huffing and puffing.

"This is your property, Harry. Why didn't you tell those guys to move their trucks so you could get your motorcycle out of there?"

"Are you kidding! They get paid by the hour. You're free."

Jack digested that information as he looked at an oil stain on his suit jacket. Good old Harry had a point.

It was still snowing when Jack parked his car two blocks from Squire's Pub. He was glad he'd changed his shoes for his Nikes. Harry managed to squeeze his cycle into the skinny space close to the passenger-side door of Jack's car. He was covered with snow. He shook his dark mane of hair and yanked it back into a ponytail. He shook himself like a wet cat and took off on the run. Jack just shook his head at the sound of Harry's sandals slapping on the wet, snowy concrete.

The pub was jammed with office workers who preferred to eat their lunch away from their desks. It was also one of the most popular watering holes in the District. Jack was glad Maggie had called ahead for a reservation. He spotted her and waved.

There was a bit of a commotion as Jack and Harry removed their jackets and shook them out to rid them of the snow that was sticking to them.

It was hot and steamy in the cozy booth at the back of the pub. Waiters, trays held high, moved quickly as they shouted to one another. Everyone knew the service was only as good as the tip you left. Maggie was known as a high tipper. A waiter appeared, listened to their order, and raced off.

"How do you like this weather?" Maggie asked.

"It sucks. I wish I were on some island somewhere, on a beach with white sand, warm breezes, and a drink in my hand," Jack said.

Harry agreed.

"It's not going to happen. This is the Christmas season, so get in the spirit." Maggie looked down at her watch. "Lizzie should be in Baron Bell's office right about now."

"How do you think that's going to go?"

"Surely you jest, Jack!" Maggie teased. "How

do you think it's going to go? We're talking about Lizzie here. He's toast."

Jack made a face. "Don't be so sure, Maggie. I've seen that guy in court. They call him Saint Baron around the courthouse. There is also speculation that he has a couple of judges in his pocket. I'm just saying."

"By chance, Jack, are those the same judges who get tongue-tied when Lizzie appears in front of them? You want to put his record up against Lizzie's?"

Jack shook his head. "No, Maggie, I don't. I just don't want you to forget that Bell has some really powerful friends here in the District. Yes, I know Lizzie does, too. He goes in and out of the White House like it's his home away from home."

Harry watched the two of them, his head going back and forth like he was at a tennis match. He decided it was time to weigh in. "Lizzie will be working at the White House come January second."

Maggie laughed. "Bell will be history by January second. Here, check this out," she said, sliding a folder across the table. "I'm sharing my headline with you. What do you think?"

"Well, damn. You're right. I think he might be toast," Jack agreed.

"Might be?" Harry said, his tone full of menace.

Jack slid the photos and the mock-up headline back into the folder just as the waiter set down a huge tray with a dozen hot dogs, all topped with "the works," along with a triple order of onion rings and french fries.

The trio dived into the food, each of them mumbling that his or her cholesterol was in the normal range.

Ten minutes into the food orgy, Jack dabbed at his mouth with his napkin. He fixed his gaze on Maggie. "Are Harry and I sitting this one out? I haven't heard a thing from the mountain."

Maggie stopped eating long enough to say, "I don't think so. The last thing I heard was you guys are going to be front and center. Stay on the alert."

"We're always on the alert, aren't we, Harry?"

Harry glared at Jack.

Jack tried for one of what he hoped was his more innocent expressions, and said, "Maggie, what do you think of champagne as a color?"

"Oh, I love it. When we were on the mountain, we were talking about interior decorating. It's all the rage. It's so clean and elegant looking. You know, regal somehow. I seem to remember Nikki and Yoko saying they liked it. Why? Are you going to do some redecorating?"

"Not right now. Down the road possibly. Maybe in the spring," Jack replied. He risked a glance at Harry, who appeared to be in a trance. He winked at Maggie and reached for his fifth hot dog.

Chapter 6

Dressed in a faux white mink coat and hat, Lizzie drew stares as she exited the luxurious limousine, wearing sunglasses to shield her eyes against the blinding whiteness all about her. She looked like a Russian spy in a popular movie as she strode toward the building that housed Baron Bell's offices. The door was thrust open by a smiling doorman. He watched as the striking woman, her every move choreographed, sailed across the ornate lobby toward the elevator, which opened as though by magic. And then the goddess was gone, and the lobby's occupants went back to what they were doing before the vision in white had graced their space.

The only occupants of the old-fashioned elevator were Lizzie and an elderly lady with blue-white hair. The grandmotherly woman carried a cane and was tapping it to the upbeat Christmas music that seemed to be piped in on the top of the elevator. Lizzie's thoughts were on what she considered the impossible task of finding just the right present for her husband. She leaned forward and pressed the number twelve.

The elevator stopped on the fifth floor, and the elderly lady moved forward. "Merry Christmas, dear. May I say you look lovely today."

"Thank you, ma'am, and Merry Christmas to you, too." Impulsively, Lizzie moved forward, and said, "Ma'am, do you remember your first Christmas when you got married?"

"As if it were yesterday. Why do you ask, dear?"

"I just got married and I'm trying to find the perfect present for my husband and I can't think of a thing. I thought . . . Oh, I'm sorry. I shouldn't be bothering you with things like this."

"No, no, that's all right, dear. If you don't mind stepping out of the elevator, we could chat for a bit. I'm a bit early for my appointment, so it's all right. There's a small bench over there," the woman said, pointing down the hall with her cane.

Lizzie stepped out of the elevator. So she would be a little late meeting with Mr. Bell. Well, sometimes some things were just more important than being on time.

"Contrary to what people think, most old people do not talk incessantly. I know you must be here for an appointment, as am I, so I'll talk fast. The year I got married, we were terribly poor. We moved into a ramshackle house that had belonged to my husband's parents. We fixed it up with spit and glue and ten dollars. It was a very small house, but at the same time so very wonderful. We lived in it until our babies came along, at which time we had to sell it. I have an old picture of the house and the outer buildings that we took on our wedding day, which, by the way, was on Valentine's Day. I knew we would eventually move, even though we had just moved in.

"There is this wonderful shop in Alexandria, the old part. There are two brothers, and now a few sons and nephews, who work there. They make replicas of buildings. Actually, they make whole villages if a client wants one. All kinds, log cabins, McMansions, although why anyone would want one of those is beyond me. My husband was so overwhelmed with my simple little gift. At the time it cost two dollars, and that was considered expensive. I took in sewing and did laundry for other folks and used that money to pay for it that first Christmas. I don't know what it would cost today, but I do know you will get a handcrafted, unique, one-of-a-kind building. They'll make it whatever size you want. I no longer have my husband, but I still have our first little house. It sits on my mantel. I hope I helped," the woman said, standing up with the aid of her cane. "My name is Elsa Shaw, and I'm in the phone book. The shop's name is Finley and Sons."

"Elizabeth Fox. My friends call me Lizzie. Yes, ma'am, that sounds exactly like what I want, a gift for all time. Thank you so much."

"Be happy, dear. I was glad to help."

Lizzie watched the lady with the blue-white hair totter down the hallway. She waited until she was safely inside whatever office she was going to. While she waited for the elevator, she whipped out her BlackBerry and called information for the number of Finley and Sons. When she stepped out of the elevator, she had an appointment at the shop for one o'clock. Her watch told her she would have to make short work of Baron Bell if she wanted to be on time to arrange for Cosmo's special one-of-a-kind Christmas present.

Her eyes sparkling with happiness, Lizzie squared her shoulders as she swept into Baron Bell's office. The dowager sitting behind the reception desk jerked to attention as Lizzie closed the door. The two women looked each other over.

"Elizabeth Fox. I have an appointment with Mr. Bell."

"You're late," the dowager said.

"Yes, I am, but I'm here now."

"Take a seat. I'll see if Mr. Bell is occupied," the woman sniffed.

Lizzie sniffed herself but remained standing. "Why would Mr. Bell be busy if he had an appointment with me? I'm only four minutes late."

"You're late. Late is late," the woman snapped. "Mr. Bell does not like to be kept waiting. He has a hectic schedule."

Lizzie Fox did not wait for anyone. "I can leave if that will make you happy," she said, turning to open the door. She had her finger on the elevator button when she heard her name being called. She turned to see Baron Bell trotting down the hall toward her.

"Baron Bell, Miss Fox. I'm sorry. Please allow me to apologize for my secretary. Sometimes she can be aggressive on my behalf. Please, come back to the office."

Lizzie waited a full minute before she gave a slight nod and followed the pudgy attorney back to his office. The secretary glared at her. Lizzie smiled and waved a finger in the woman's general direction.

"Harriet has been with me forever. Sometimes . . . never mind. Please, sit down and tell me what brings you here to my office, Miss Fox. I hope it has something to do with my children's Christmas party at the White House."

Lizzie smiled and looked around. The first thing she saw hanging on the back of the office door was a Santa Claus suit. A fluffy, curly white beard and wig hung alongside the bright red suit in a clear plastic bag. She didn't know how she knew, but she just knew that the suit was custom-made. She could see the quality of the material even from where she was sitting. In the corner a pair of shiny black boots stood at attention. The only thing missing was the sleigh and the eight tiny reindeer. Then again, maybe they were stashed in the man's private bathroom.

Lizzie continued with her appraisal of the law office. The office was clean, old, and exceptionally tidy. Everything looked worn but comfortable. The walls were covered with framed photographs of Bell with several presidents and various dignitaries. Lizzie was not impressed. She had twice as many stuffed in cardboard boxes. Lizzie Fox never blew her own horn, preferring to let others do it on her behalf.

She made a mental note of the old-fashioned safe and where it was located. She pointed to it and said, "So that's the famous safe I've read about."

Bell beamed and nodded, but he failed to elaborate. "Coffee, tea, perhaps a soft drink?"

Lizzie wondered if the battle-ax out front would be the one to fetch the drink or if there was a bar inside this office. She needed time to snap some pictures and could do that only if Bell's back was toward her. "How much trouble would that be, Mr. Bell?"

"No trouble at all. I have a minibar there behind you. I like to wait on myself and my clients and not impose too much on Harriet. Having the minibar right here is extremely convenient and less taxing on Harriet. As I said, she can be feisty at times."

Lizzie offered up a radiant smile and replied, "Then yes, coffee. Two sugars and light cream." She was off her chair and within seconds had pictures of everything in the office, including the man's Christmas gear hanging on the door. Ted Robinson would be so proud of her; she'd even gotten a shot of the floor under Bell's desk and was on her way to her chair when Baron Bell set a heavy-looking mug down in front of her.

"I do love that safe," she told him.

"I cannot tell you how many offers I've had from people and clients to buy it. It's probably three times as old as you are, my dear."

Lizzie smiled.

"I understand congratulations are in order. You must be excited about your appointment. Is it true you're serving the president pro bono? Commendable. I wish more people would do that. I'm in and out of the White House several times a week. I can put in a good word for you if you like."

"I don't think that will be necessary, but thank you for the offer. Marti and I are personal friends. We go way back. Even though my official title is Chief White House Counsel, I'm going to be more of a personal confidante to the president."

Lizzie loved the spark she was seeing in Bell's eyes.

It took Lizzie only a minute to realize just how much she disliked the man sitting across from her. She decided to take a jab at him. "Can you believe they came up with an office for me with a window, and my hours are nine to five?"

Baron Bell twitched in his seat.

"If you don't mind me asking, what is it *you do* at the White House?"

"They call on me from time to time to . . . ask my opinions. I like to do what I can for the administration."

"I find that very commendable. How do you like Marti?"

Bell continued to squirm in his chair. "I met her only once, and we shook hands," he was forced to admit. "She seems more than capable. For a woman."

Lizzie sat up a little straighter. Bell couldn't help but see the dangerous glint in her eyes. He realized his mistake and started to babble about the South Lawn, Air Force One, and something about his upcoming Christmas party. Lizzie ignored him as she opened her ostrich-skin briefcase. Bell leaned forward.

"I suppose you've been wondering why I made this appointment. I represent two of your old clients. Actually four people. The Evans family, Beth and John, and the Dawsons, Rachel and Thomas. There's no sense beating around the bush. They want their money back. They paid you for brokering baby deals that went sour."

Whatever Baron Bell was expecting, this wasn't it. Lizzie thought he was going to turn into a rocket and explode upward. His face turned red, and his eyes looked wild. "You *what?*"

"I represent the Evanses and the Dawsons. They want their money back since they no longer have the babies. I had Adel Newsom served this morning, along with the two surrogates."

"What are you trying to say here, Miss Fox? I was just a legal intermediary. Are you out of my mind?" Clearly he thought so.

Lizzie tried not to laugh. "I'm not *trying* to say anything. I *am* saying it. My clients want you to return the monies they paid you. If we can come to terms, going to court won't be necessary. If not, we'll be appearing in front of a judge. My . . . uh . . . nonpaying *new employer* has graciously consented for me to handle certain clients on my free time, so that won't pose a problem for me. For you, with all your little in-and-out visits to Sixteen Hundred Pennsylvania Avenue, it might be a problem. Then again, the exposure might be something you want. I really don't have the time today to debate the issue. I wanted to give you the courtesy of a personal visit, as opposed to sending a nasty process server. Things like that get around at the speed of light, as we both know. As you also know, things like this get ugly very quickly."

Baron Bell went from quiet to still. His folded pudgy hands finally moved as he pushed his well-oiled chair back from his desk. "I don't have to defend the way I represent my clients to you, Miss Fox. I have signed contracts from the Evanses and the Dawsons. They knew the moment they took custody of their babies that my services were over. If you like, I can have Harriet make you copies of the contracts. No judge in the land will go against my contracts. I can't be held responsible for what happened to those two families. Motherhood is something I can't pretend to understand, so I don't try. That's why I had the contracts drawn up."

Lizzie was on her feet. "I know at least three judges who will rule against those particular contracts. Now, if there was just one contract, you might have a fighting chance. But two! That I know of at the moment. My instincts are telling me there are more, and if there are more, know this. I *will* find them. It isn't necessary to give me copies. I have them right here." Lizzie pointed to her briefcase. "Because I'm an ethical attorney, and in the interest of fairness, I'll give you until the weekend to make restitution to the Evanses and the Dawsons. If that doesn't happen, you can deal with the courts and the *Post*. If that were to happen, you might want to think about canceling your Christmas party at the White House. Thank you for seeing me on such short notice. Don't get up, Mr. Bell. I can see myself out."

Bell's voice was cold and brittle when he said, "You'll never get away with this. I'll fight to protect my good name till the end of time."

"I will, too, Mr. Bell. Considering the difference in our ages, would you care to make a small wager on which of us will be left standing?"

Bell made no response, and Lizzie hadn't expected one.

Lizzie's smile lit up the dim hallway as she tripped her way to the elevator, her BlackBerry in hand. She was talking bullet fast as she entered the cranky, old-fashioned elevator. "He's scared, Maggie, but he bluffed me. I gave him three days to pay up, which he is not going to do. I threatened him with the *Post*. We need to move to phase two. Can you send Ted and Espinosa to Adel Newsom's office? I think she needs to have her feathers ruffled a little. Then will you call the mountain and tell Charles that if he hasn't already done so, he should get his people to Newsom's beach house? I'm thinking that's where she's going to be keeping records. It's far enough away, and there are no concrete ties to Bell. Just supposition on our part. My gut is telling me he keeps his stuff there, too. If it isn't in the safe in the floor. I'm on my way to Alexandria, after which I'm heading to the airport. Can you do it, Maggie?"

"It's done. Good luck and, as my mom says, fly with the angels, Lizzie."

Maggie sat at her desk, idly drumming her fingers on the smooth surface. She *should* send Ted and Espinosa to Newsom's office, but her gut reporter's instincts were telling her this was a woman's job. Maybe she could also make a pit stop at Baron Bell's office. The big question was who to go to first. Maggie's adrenaline was at an all-time high as she contemplated getting out in the field again. She was almost giddy at the mere thought of being a real live reporter again. But if she did that, Ted was going to pitch a fit, not that she cared. Then she remembered she was to call the mountain. But if she did that, she'd be getting her information secondhand. Now, if she sent Ted and Espinosa to do the breaking and entering . . . But did she want to put them in such a precarious position?

Then a second thought hit her. She could send Ted and Espinosa to Rehoboth and have them on the scene so that when Charles's people arrived, they could trail along and report back at the speed of light. The more information she had at her fingertips, the better it would be for the Sisters. She wondered if it might behoove her to see if Jack and Harry wanted to make the trip. Especially if the gated community where Adel Newsom had her home away from home had security. *What the hell. Why not?* The more sets of eyes on a mission, the merrier it would be. She called Jack and gave him his marching orders. She was surprised when he went along with her plan.

Maggie made her way to her private bathroom, where she changed out of her business suit and into more appropriate reporter's attire, namely, khaki slacks, fur-lined boots, and a down jacket. Back in her office, she reached under her desk for her backpack, which she settled over the bulky down jacket. She let loose with a mighty sigh. Now she felt like what she was, a bona fide reporter.

The last thing she did before she left the office was to tell her secretary to hold the fort and to call only in an emergency. She called Ted from the elevator, surprised that her BlackBerry actually worked inside it, and issued instructions like a general. "You can be there in an hour and a half. Hole up somewhere until Charles's people get there. Just trail along, and don't take no for an answer. If his people squawk, call either Charles or me. You got all that, Ted?"

Ted had plenty to say, mostly that it was snowing out and the roads were bad. And on and on he went. Maggie tuned him out and ended the call.

It was snowing hard, and there wasn't a cab in sight when Maggie hit the street. Since Adel Newsom's office was the closest to the *Post*, Maggie opted to jog the distance. It took her five minutes to realize just how out of shape she was. Sitting behind a desk didn't qualify as any kind of exercise, despite all the time she spent bending her elbows eating whatever she could get her hands on.

Maggie was winded when she stomped her way to a glossy-looking building that looked like it was made entirely out of black glass. She shoved back the hood of her down jacket and swept through the revolving door. She marched over to the information desk and asked for a visitor's pass. She showed her *Post* credentials and filled out a form, noting that she was going to Adel Newsom's office. *Pretty classy digs and pricey at that for a one-lawyer office,* Maggie thought as she rode the elevator up to the seventeenth floor.

Two dentists and an architect had suites on the same floor that held Newsom's office. She made a mental note to find out who owned the building when she went back to the office. It wouldn't surprise her at all if Baron Bell owned it. *Now,* she wondered, *where did that thought come from? From my reporter's instincts,* she told herself as she pushed open the plate-glass door and entered a very pleasant waiting room that smelled like freshly brewed coffee and cinnamon.

The receptionist was a glitzy dyed blonde

sporting so much makeup that Maggie knew she had to go through a car wash to get it off. Maggie handed over her press badge and identified herself. "I'd like a few minutes of Miss Newsom's time before we go to press. I don't like printing things until all parties have a chance to respond so they can be quoted as they want to be quoted."

The receptionist looked dubious. "Miss Newsom is tied up at the moment. What exactly do you want a quote on?"

Maggie grinned. "This is just a guess on my part, but I don't think she wants anyone to know. You can tell her this. It concerns Baron Bell, and I have exactly ten minutes before I have to get back to the paper to make my deadline. So, if you'll *untie* your boss, I'd appreciate it."

Maggie crossed her fingers that Lizzie was right when she'd said Baron Bell would be on the phone with Newsom within minutes of her leaving his office. She hoped Lizzie was right. She tried to hear what the brittle blonde was saying into the intercom, but all she could hear were soft murmurs.

"Miss Newsom said she can give you five minutes. She's scheduled for a deposition in a few minutes, and the clients are already here."

"Five minutes will be enough. All I want is a quote."

"Down the hall to the right, second door," the blonde said tightly.

Maggie trotted down the hall to Adel Newsom's

office, opened the door, and entered a lavishly appointed suite of rooms. She looked around to see where the secretary was. Obviously, the dyed blonde, a walking advertisement for Clinique, had relayed Maggie's words verbatim, and Newsom had sent her secretary on an errand.

Adel Newsom was probably in her early fifties but looked sixty. Some sloppy surgeon had sliced and diced, chopped and grated, buffed and puffed her until she looked like a really bad version of Joan Rivers.

Adel Newsom had strawberry blond hair that had been dyed and fried. Maggie almost laughed out loud when she thought of the Chinese restaurant where she always ordered something called the Birdnest, which was a crackly fried noodle affair that you could see through. Newsom's hair looked just like the Birdnest. Her nose was small and pointy. Her lips looked unnatural and barely covered the woman's blinding white capped teeth. She was wearing a bright red Chanel suit. Botoxed out the kazoo. She didn't bother to get up or even offer to shake hands. Her voice was husky and sounded coarse. Too many cigarettes and too much whiskey, Maggie decided. She looked wary, which told Maggie that Baron Bell had probably called her the minute Lizzie left his office.

"I don't have much time. I have a deposition scheduled in a few minutes, but I always try to take time for the press. What can I do for you, Miss Spritzer? I don't understand what kind of quote I can possibly give you." Long, scarlet nails filed to points drummed on the desktop. Other than that, not a muscle moved on the woman.

This was the part Maggie loved. She sat down, looked the lawyer straight in the eye, and said, "Can you tell me what your relationship with Baron Bell is? Is it professional, or is it romantic? My sources are telling me it's both. Did you aid and abet him with the surrogate mothers who took back their babies from the adopting parents? I'm referring to the Dawsons and the Evanses. Again, my sources are telling me that the answer is yes in both cases. I also understand you are the attorney of record for a second, and possibly a third, placement of the babies.

"I also understand you were served this morning, along with Baron Bell. Do you care to confirm that? Before coming here, I met with Lizzie Fox. She's going to be the attorney of record on these lawsuits. Do you care to confirm or deny that she is the attorney who had you served this morning? I think I used up my five minutes, so if you'll just respond, I'll be on my way, and you can get to your deposition."

Adel Newsom would make a good poker player, Maggie thought.

"I have no comment at this time, Miss Spritzer," Newsom said in her husky voice.

"When *will* you have a comment, Miss Newsom? This is going to get ugly. I think you know that. Not only is it going to get very ugly, Miss Newsom, but there is a rumor going around the District that the vigilantes are on this case. Now it's just a rumor, which I have been unable to confirm, but in my experience, where there's smoke, there is usually fire."

Adel Newsom stood up. Maggie was surprised at how tall the Lizzie Fox wannabe was, how perfectly proportioned. The lawyer did her best to smile, but it came off as a frightened grimace. "When I have a comment I wish to share, I'll call you directly. Now, if you'll excuse me, I have a deposition to take."

"Don't worry about me. I can see myself out. Thank you for seeing me. I'll be sure to quote you verbatim." Maggie scampered to the door and opened it. She walked away from the door, then doubled back. She tiptoed to the door and pressed her ear to it. She could hear a voice but couldn't hear what was being said. She just knew Newsom was on the phone with Baron Bell. Then she did hear something. "What the hell do you think I said, you idiot? I said I had no comment."

Maggie sashayed down the hall. At the receptionist's desk, she leaned over and whispered to the blonde. "I think you should start sending out your résumé. Like right now, as in today."

Outside, Maggie checked the busy road. The snow hadn't let up in the slightest. She grimaced as she tied the strings to her jacket hood and started once more to jog down the street. Next stop, Baron Bell's office.

Chapter 7

After twenty minutes of wrangling, the quartet decided that Ted, Espinosa, Harry, and Jack would make the trip to Rehoboth together in Espinosa's secondhand Range Rover. Espinosa swore that he could drive through anything but tire-high mud.

A trip that should have taken no more than an hour and a half turned into a four-hour trek with the bad weather. Even though Espinosa claimed they were making good time considering their current circumstances.

Harry grumbled and mumbled as he tried to figure out why Maggie wanted them in Rehoboth. "It doesn't make sense to me if Snowden's people are going to be there to do the breaking and entering. Are we going there because we don't trust Snowden and his people? Or are we going because Maggie thinks Bell and Newsom are going to head there to get whatever Maggie thinks is hidden there? Ted and Espinosa I can understand. Photos and the like. I don't like going somewhere blind, with no concrete plan of action. Been there, done that. Pumpkins," he said ominously.

Ted struggled against his seat belt to turn around. "I don't like driving in snow any more than the rest of you, but you should know by now that—and this goes for you, too, Jack—*Post* employees, never, as in ever, question Maggie Spritzer. That goes for you, too, Harry. If Maggie thinks something is there that we need to either see or find, that's what we're going to do. Maggie trusts us. So why don't you just sit there and be quiet or else sing us some Christmas songs in one of your languages? It is the Christmas season, you know."

Jack sighed. It was clear to him that he had to come up with some witty dialogue before Harry went nuclear. Harry hated to be confined to small spaces, and while the Range Rover was relatively spacious, it was still a box, however large, on wheels, and Harry still felt confined.

While Jack was thinking, Ted bellowed that he had just gotten a text from Maggie. "She said Baron Bell was out of the office when she got there. She said the dragon manning the office said she had missed him by five minutes. Being as smart and astute as she is, Maggie hotfooted it back to Newsom's office and got there in time to see the two of them getting into a chauffeur-driven Town Car. She was on foot, so she couldn't follow them, and there were no taxis available. She thinks they might be headed to Rehoboth, which—by the way—is getting more snow than the District."

"Then they must be worried," Jack said. "What does she expect us to do, Ted?"

"To act independently and do whatever needs to be done. And not get caught doing it," Ted responded.

Jack offered up a few choice words of disgust.

"We're about fifteen minutes away from our destination according to the GPS," Espinosa said, one eye on his GPS, the other on the road.

Harry mumbled something that sounded terrible to Jack. Hoping to diffuse whatever Harry was about to do or say next, he literally bellowed, "So what are you guys getting the girls for Christmas?"

A spirited dialogue followed and ended with what every woman in the world knew already—none of the men had a clue what the *in* Christmas present was that year.

Since Jack considered himself an authority on women and their wants and needs, he said, "You can't go wrong with diamonds."

"Diamonds cost money," Ted growled. "Lots of money. More than I have, that's for sure."

"That depends on the carat weight," Jack said knowledgeably. "I bet none of you know that women consider their ears as storage vaults. These days women have two holes in each ear. That means four earrings per woman. The translation to that is it frees up room in their jewelry boxes for even more gems. You getting my drift here? I also know that women love and adore earrings. They like to pick their own rings and bracelets. Do *not* ever buy them a necklace unless it is a string of matched pearls like the kind Myra wears and none of us could afford even if we bought it on the installment plan. It would take forever to pay it off. So, it's earrings. I'm open for discussion, gentlemen."

Espinosa sounded like he was going to cry. "Four earrings at a carat each is four carats. That's got to be a year's salary at least."

Jack sniffed. "There are half-carat earrings and quarter carats, but women are embarrassed to wear them. Jill and Patsy at Dorchester Jewelers told me that in confidence. I don't think they'll mind me sharing with you. Maybe if we all go there and buy the earrings, they'll give us a discount."

Harry leaned over and reached for Jack's ear. "I'm going to kill you! First, you tell me I need to change my decor, and now you're telling me I have to buy *four* earrings. Is that what you're telling me, *Jack?* Considering my precarious financial situation, that is not what I want to hear."

Jack moved closer to the window. "It was a suggestion. Now, if you want Yoko to be embarrassed, well, that's your business. You already screwed up with all that pink crap you bought . . . on sale, I grant you. You might be able to get away with a quarter carat, because Yoko is so tiny, but I don't think so. You know what, Harry? I'm tired of helping you. You are so ungrateful, I can't stand it. I'm going to talk to Jill and Patsy, and I'm getting two sets. I'll get a part-time job to pay for them. What about you guys?"

"Yeah, I'm in. I don't want Alexis to be embarrassed. She's too beautiful, and she deserves four earrings," Espinosa said generously.

"Good thinking," Jack said, smacking his hands together. "What about you, Ted?"

"Yeah, yeah, count me in," Ted said.

"Harry?"

"Shut the hell up, Jack. I'll buy my own present."

"You dumb shit, you couldn't even come up with a good color scheme. Oh, I feel so sorry for poor Yoko. Now, gentlemen, you have one more decision to make. Gold or platinum? Jill and Patsy said platinum, but the choice is yours."

Further discussion stopped on a dime when Espinosa said, "Okay, we're here. There's a guardhouse, and you have to show a pass, or the owner has to call and say a visitor is expected. What do you want to do?"

"Harry, get out and put the guy to sleep. How long, guys?" Jack asked.

"We can ask the guard if anyone else has come through for Newsom. If Snowden's men aren't here already, I'd say two hours," Ted said.

Harry rolled his eyes in disgust. "And you think that *schmuck* stopped here and asked for directions! He probably dropped from a helicopter or rode in on a horse to confuse the guard," Harry said.

"You think?" Jack said airily.

"No, I don't think. I was making conversation, so I don't go with my instincts and kill you on the spot. Stay here. I will take care of matters."

Harry was out of the vehicle and walking around the front of the Rover before Jack could get his wits about him. The guard opened the door, and Harry motioned him back inside.

Harry turned on his charm, or what he hoped passed for charm. "Sir, how many people have come through here in the past two hours? I don't want you to lie to me, because if you do, I'll have to kill you. Do you understand what I just said?"

"Yes. Who are you looking for?"

"Never mind. I ask the questions. Articulate, sir."

"Mr. Donaldson came through about an hour ago. It's all on the sheet. Just look at it. Are you going to hurt me? Are you going to rob someone?"

Harry scanned the log-in sheet. "No, I'm not going to hurt you, and no, I am not going to rob anyone. I'm looking for some people I lost track of during the storm. This is a nice, cozy little place you have here. You appear to be comfortable. Can you lock this door?"

The guard's head bobbed up and down.

"What time do you go off duty?"

"Eleven. But if my replacement can't get here, I might have to put in a double shift. I have food, and there's a bathroom. Why?"

Harry ignored the guard as he looked at a huge map hanging on the wall. Each little square had a name on it. His finger raced over the map until he found the square that said Newsom. Mentally he calculated where the house was in relation to where he was currently standing. When he was certain he could find the house, he told the guard to sit down. He asked for his beeper, his cell phone, and his keys; then he cut the landline. "Can I trust you not to remember I was here?"

"My lips are sealed, sir."

A moment later the man was sound asleep in his chair. Harry turned out the light, checked the lock on the door to make sure it would lock when he closed it. Outside, he checked the knob and found that it didn't budge, then wiped it off.

He barreled around the back of the Rover and got inside. "Go down this road, make a right, then another right, then a left. The third house on the left belongs to Newsom. No one suspicious has come through, according to the log sheet."

"You're the man, Harry," Jack said happily.

"For a high-end bedroom community, you'd think these roads would be taken care of. We're all over the road," Espinosa grumbled.

"Pretty, though," Ted said, leaning out the car window to take pictures of the winter wonderland. "I'm surprised the snow is sticking, since we're so close to the water."

Espinosa let the Rover slide to the side of the road. He parked and looked around. "Now what?"

Jack pressed the button on the window and

peered out. A dim yellow gaslight at the end of the Newsom driveway glowed dully in the flying snow. He strained to see the other four houses on the cul-de-sac. The houses were as dark as Newsom's house, but the gas lamps were lit. "Doesn't look like anyone is home. It's possible these are second homes of the owners and no one is in residence. I can't see any tire tracks anywhere. If Snowden's people are here, where the hell are they, and how did they get here?"

"They might have come in from the back on snowmobiles. See that copse of trees in the back? This street backs up to the main drag. I'm just saying . . . ," Espinosa said lamely.

"Snowden's people aren't going to be turning on any lights," Ted said. "I'm game to go around the back and see if we can pick a lock. I don't see myself sitting in this truck for hours on end and freezing my ass off. We are also going to need some gas on the way back and don't want to waste what we have. I'm talking about our getaway here."

Jack had his cell phone in hand. He hit the speed dial, and within seconds Charles Martin was on the line. The connection was crackly, and he could only distinguish every third word. He knew the call would drop within seconds. "We're here on Maggie's orders. Me, Harry, Ted, and Espinosa. We think Bell and Newsom are on the way. Took us four hours to make a ninety-minute trip. We aren't seeing any sign of Snowden's people. The snow is getting worse. What do you want us to do?" Jack strained to hear Charles's response, but after the first few words, the call dropped. He knew he wouldn't be able to get Charles back. He shoved the cell back into his pocket. "I think we're on our own, guys."

"Shhh," Ted said. "Tell me what you want us to do, Maggie. Yeah, yeah, I have one in my backpack. Tell me again. Do we take what we find if we find something, or do we just photograph it? Yeah, yeah. No sign of Snowden's people, but that doesn't mean they aren't inside. Those assholes probably dropped down the chimney, or else they're stuck up there. Yeah, sure, we'll leave them stuck in there if it turns out to be true. No problem. Hey, hey, we have Harry with us. Don't worry. What's the bonus on this?" Ted asked, hoping it would make a dent in the four earrings he was going to have to buy. "That's not enough. This is dangerous. Higher, much higher. Come on, you can do better than that." Whatever Maggie's response was, Ted clamped his lips shut and opened the car door.

"I guess that means we're going to crash this place," Jack said, hopping out of the Rover, Harry and Espinosa right behind him. He was glad he was wearing his desert boots when he stepped into cold, slushy snow.

"I guess you know we're going to be leaving footprints," Espinosa fretted.

"Only if visitors can see the footprints." Ted reached up and turned off the gas lamp. "Everybody hit one of the houses on the street and turn off the lamps. The gizmo is right there below the flame." The guys sprinted off to do Ted's bidding.

"If Bell and Newsom show up, their headlights will pick up on the tracks," Espinosa mumbled, continuing to fret. "I think we should turn around and park at the house next door and walk across the backyard. The way it's snowing now, the tracks will fill in pretty quick. It won't hurt to pray that the people who own these houses are summer bunnies. Hop in, guys."

"I have an idea," Ted said. "Let's pick the lock on the neighbor's house, light it up from top to bottom. If, and I say if, Newsom and Bell show up, we can come up with some kind of story as to why we're in the neighbor's house. Assuming they knock on the door to find out why their gas lamp isn't working. I'm sure the gas connection is somewhere around the back door. Like a gas leak or something. Since all the lamps are now out, it will hold water. I think."

Ten minutes later the house next to Adel Newsom's was lit up like a football stadium. Five minutes after that, Ted let loose with a grunt of satisfaction when the kitchen door to the Newsom house opened. A blast of cold air rushed outward as snow swirled inward. "Okay, let's split up and work as fast as we can. We need to get out of here as soon as we can. Espinosa, take pictures of *everything*. The house isn't all that big, so we should be able to zip through it in no time. Wonder where Snowden and his people are."

"Who cares?" Jack snarled. "Before we go off half-cocked here and waste time, let's think. If you were going to put a safe in a place like this, where would you put it? In the floor? Built in a wall behind a picture? Where? Now, we split up and look everywhere. If you see something, whistle. This place only has a crawl space. No basement and no attic. Let's move, guys."

The foursome split up, Jack and Harry taking the first floor, Ted and Espinosa covering the second.

It took only fifteen minutes for the guys to meet back in the kitchen. "There's nothing on the second floor. We even tapped the walls and crawled across the floor, looking for loose boards and such," Ted said.

"I have wall-to-wall pictures. We can upload them and blow them up. There's nothing there, Jack. What did you guys find?" Espinosa asked.

"Zip. There's nothing in the garage except the hot-water heater. I'm thinking Newsom never even used this house. Maybe it was strictly an investment."

Ted opened the refrigerator. "Weird that they leave this plugged in. It's empty." He opened the freezer section of the refrigerator and said, "Whoa! Guess you were wrong, buddy." Ted peered into the freezer. "Eight trays of lasagna, baked ziti, manicotti, and spaghetti and meatballs. Eight trays, two each. She must like Italian food."

"What did you say?" Jack said as Ted stepped out of the way for him to get a better look at the contents of the freezer. Jack reached in to pick up one of the oversize trays. "Lasagna, my ass. Grab these and head next door. This isn't food! These are the records. I tried a case not too long ago where these drug dealers hid their money and records in dummy food containers in the freezer."

"Oh, shit!" Harry shouted. "Car lights arcing through the front window. There goes the garage door. Move! Move!"

Jack tossed the freezer trays to the guys. "Don't slam the kitchen door. Ted, did you turn the gas off over there?"

"Yeah. I told you the gas connection is back there by the back door. I did it when we broke in. There won't be any heat, and I didn't see wood anywhere for the fireplace. They aren't going to be able to stay in that house. Who turned the breaker off?"

"I did. I ripped that box to hell and back," Harry said. "I dumped those nuggets behind the hot-water heater. No gas, no electricity. If the temperature drops any lower, the pipes are going to freeze and burst. That happened to me once at the dojo when I first bought it and we had a ten-day freeze. You have to let the water drip."

"How soon before there's a knock on this door?" Espinosa asked.

"Any minute now," replied Jack. "C'mon, guys, close the drapes and blinds. Espinosa, you're the one who will open the door if it happens. They might recognize Ted from some of his articles and bylines. Harry and I can't be seen. Just say you're the owner's nephew and you came down here at his request to turn the heat up and . . . drip the water. Shit! We don't know the owner's name. Newsom might know the owner."

"The name is Michael Otis. The house on the other side is owned by Kevin and Joan Holmes," Harry said.

"Man, I love you!" Jack said, hugging his friend.

"So, what's our game plan?" Ted asked. "Are we staying here, or are we leaving? When is that guy at the guardhouse going to wake up, Harry?"

"We're good for now. What do you want to do, Jack?"

Harry's deferring to him was such a rarity, Jack was stunned. "I say we wait thirty minutes to see if anyone knocks on the door. If it doesn't happen, we split, head for town, get rooms at a motel, and sack out."

Ted pointed to the stack of freezer trays he'd piled up on the washing machine in the mini laundry room. "You backed up the Rover, right?"

"You're losing it, Ted. You were in the damn truck, guiding me. Yeah, I backed it up. Why?"

"We have to get this stuff in the truck. Four guys. Their stuff is gone. What do you think those two are going to think? Too bad we weren't smart enough to back into the garage. If you had done that, we could have barreled out, and if they are watching, they wouldn't know there are four of us. Four means robbery!" Ted snarled just as the front doorbell rang.

"Espinosa, you're up! We'll hole up here in the laundry room. Make it good!" Jack said.

Espinosa raced to the front door and took a deep breath before he opened it. "Yeah?" he barked.

"You aren't Mike Otis," Adel Newsom said, suspicion ringing in her voice.

"Thank God!" Espinosa said dramatically. "I'm his nephew. By marriage. He asked me to come down to check the pipes so they don't freeze. Not that it's any of your business, ma'am. Who are you anyway?"

"Your neighbor. I just got here but have no heat. There's something wrong with the breaker box, too. We . . . I don't have any electricity either. Do you have heat?"

"No heat, but the power is on. The gas lamps are out on the street. Could have been the wind. It is pretty *squally* out there right now."

"When did you get here?" Newsom asked.

"You sure are nosy for a neighbor. About an hour ago. I'm just getting ready to leave. You got a problem, take it up with my uncle. I'm outta here."

"Did you . . . did you see anyone on the street when you got here?"

"Lady . . . I don't even know your name . . . You can't get in here unless the guard allows it. You should be talking to him, not me. I've never been here before, so I can't help you."

"What's your name?" Newsom asked.

"What's yours?" Espinosa parried.

"Adel Newsom. I'm a lawyer. And you are?"

"Mike Otis's nephew, Fabio Garcia. I'm a plumber. A good one, by the way. Before you leave, you better let the faucets drip, or the pipes will burst. Then you won't have any water either. That's the problem with having a vacation home. You need to live in a house and keep up with it from time to time. If you don't mind, I was just getting ready to leave. Call Mike if you have any problems. Check your car radio for the weather. Nice meeting you, Ms. Newsom."

"Do you have any wood?"

Espinosa leaned against the door frame. "Nah. Mike didn't order any. If he had any, I'd sleep by the fireplace. I'm not looking forward to heading into town. Doesn't look too good out there. You be careful now. I want to check everything one more time before I leave." He yawned elaborately. "Hey, why don't you try calling the guardhouse or whomever you call for maintenance around here? Sorry I couldn't help you."

"I'm sorry, too," Newsom said as she tried to peer past Espinosa and into the house.

"Well, if there's nothing else . . ."

Newsom shrugged and hugged her down coat tighter to her chest. "Be careful on the road. Good thing you have a four-wheel drive," she added as an afterthought. At least that was the way it sounded to Espinosa.

"Yeah, I wouldn't have attempted this if I didn't have four-wheel drive. That's why Mike asked me to make the trip. Maybe we'll meet up again when Mike has his annual Fourth of July party."

"Maybe," Newsom said, turning around and heading across the narrow porch to the steps.

Espinosa couldn't resist a parting shot. "Don't be foolish and try staying in the house. You could freeze, and with gas, you never know. Carbon monoxide," he said dramatically. He slammed the door shut and raced to the laundry room.

"Does she suspect something?" Jack demanded.

"Hell, yeah, she suspects something. Suspicion was flooding out of her pores. I'm going out through the garage. I'll back in the back end of the Range Rover. You guys jump in and we're outta here. I'm thinking that staying in town is *not* a good idea. I'll head out to the highway and stop at the first rest stop I find. Ted, work that GPS. Maybe we should take our chances and head back to the District."

"Temperature is dropping," Ted said. "This crap on the ground is going to ice up real fast."

"Stop at the guard hut," Harry said.

Espinosa obliged.

Minutes later, keys in hand, Harry entered the guardhouse and woke up the guard. "Listen to me, sir."

The guard jerked upright. "I'm listening, young man," he said groggily.

Harry felt momentarily flattered at being called a *young* man. "I want you to pay attention to what I'm saying. I am not going to tell anyone you sleep on the job. Your secret is safe with me."

The guard shook his head. "Oh, thank you. I guess I was just exhausted. I swear to you, I have never, ever slept on the job."

"I believe you. The weather does strange things to people. Now, the second thing is, I was never here, okay?"

"You were never here. Right."

"If you say I was here, I will come back, pull your brain down through your nose, then send it back to your head through your ears. Clearly, your brain will be scrambled. When I leave here, I want to leave knowing you and I have a clear understanding. Do we, sir?"

"You betcha we do, young fella. You were never here. I will never, ever sleep on the job again, and my brain will remain intact."

Harry reached over and patted the guard's cheek. He smiled. "You have a nice night now, you hear?"

"You betcha, young fella."

"Business has been taken care of, gentlemen. We can now leave this snowy paradise," Harry said, jumping back into the Rover. "Quickly, because I can see headlights back in the distance."

Espinosa did his best to burn rubber.

Chapter 8

"Something is wrong," Yoko whispered to Nikki, who was sitting next to her. "Watch Charles. Whatever he's hearing is not good for us. Harry has not called. Did you hear from Jack? Alexis said Joseph has not called her either. I just checked the weather, and they are driving into the storm. We should have heard something by now, don't you think?"

Nikki's heart fluttered in her chest. She was worried; so was Alexis. She could tell by the frown lines between her lustrous brown eyes. She took a deep breath and moved to the side, but not before she whispered to Yoko, "I'm going to call Maggie. She has her finger on the pulse of everything."

A second later Maggie's voice came through, crystal clear. Maggie didn't even give Nikki a chance to say anything before she started to rattle off what was going on. "The guys' phones aren't working. No one knows what happened to Snowden's people. They were a no-show. The guys persevered and prevailed. They have the *goods.* It was in the freezer, disguised as frozen food. They're on the turnpike now, on their way back home. They were going to stop in town, but they had to do a little . . . construction work, so that means Newsom and Bell will be heading to town to spend the night."

Nikki sucked in her breath. "What kind of 'construction'?"

"They turned off the gas and threw the knob into the snow. They ripped out the breaker box. No heat, no electricity. No wood either. The guys almost got caught but got out in time. Talk about some foresight . . . Ted and Espinosa picked the lock on the house next door, turned on all the lights, so they skedaddled over there the minute Newsom and Bell arrived. Newsom knocked on the door, and Espinosa answered and said he was the nephew of the owner and was just there to check on the house. He said he didn't think she bought his story, but there was nothing she could do. Five minutes later they were out of there."

"Do you know where they are right now?" Nikki asked.

"Somewhere on the turnpike, headed this way. Ted called about fifteen minutes ago and said they're playing it careful and staying behind a sanitation truck that is salting the road. That's it for now. I'm going to stay here at the paper until they get here. Do you know anything?"

"No, nothing. Charles is on the phone with someone, and whatever he's hearing isn't looking good. I'm thinking it's Snowden. I'll tell him the guys pulled it off the minute he gets off the phone. I'll call you back. Thanks, Maggie." Nikki ended the call and shoved the phone into the pocket of her sweatpants. Charles was doing the same thing, the frown on his face getting more pronounced by the second.

Charles motioned for the Sisters to take their seats at the round table. "Avery Snowden just called. There was an eleven-car pileup on the turnpike. He and his people were in cars eight and nine. The northbound lane was and still is blocked solid with an eighteen-wheeler that went over on its side. Ambulances and fire trucks have been trying to get to the scene. They can't even cross over the lane to head back south. Southbound is moving at a snail's pace, but it is moving. It's the weather, and no one can control Mother Nature."

Nikki held up her hand. "The guys scored, Charles. They're on the way back with the evidence, which was hidden in Newsom's freezer." She quickly related all that Maggie had shared with her.

"Have they looked through the records?"

"Maggie said no. All they wanted to do was get out of there. She said she's going to stay at the paper to wait for them. Not much you can do when Mother Nature takes a hand. All we can do now is wait."

Charles nodded. "Let's all go over to the dining room. I made some pizza for a late-night snack. I have things to report and discuss, and we need to make plans to get you all down off the mountain. Mr. Bell's children's Christmas party is in a few days. Your window of time is going to work against you because of Mother Nature."

The Sisters donned their down jackets and headed for the door, Charles bringing up the rear. The minute they were in the toasty warm dining room, they shed their outer gear and clustered around the fireplace. Before long the wonderful smell of baking pizza wafted into the dining room.

Charles joined the Sisters and made his announcement. "There's something wrong with the cable car. Tee said his heart was in his throat on the way down. I watched the car come back up, and even I could tell something is wrong. I can't put you at risk, so you're going down the mountain on snowshoes. Myra and Annie will be on one of the snowmobiles. Transportation will be waiting at the base of the mountain. You leave tomorrow, as soon as it gets light."

"Where are we staying, and will the things I ordered be there when we arrive?" Alexis asked.

"I took care of everything, Alexis. You're going to be staying at the *Post* apartment. It's in a corporate building for companies to house overnight guests, and Maggie assures me no one pays attention to anything, as most of the apartments are rarely used and rarely for more than an overnight stay at any one time. What that means is there won't be any curious neighbors paying attention to you or the deliveries that will take place tomorrow morning.

"The offices, firms, and Bell's office pretty

much are locked up by six o'clock. My intel tells me that on occasion an architect on the second floor stays as late as eight o'clock. And he uses the stairwell to get to the underground garage and doesn't go through the lobby. We already discussed the security guard, so there's no point going over that again. You want to be in and out."

"What makes you so sure Bell wasn't keeping his records at Rehoboth, where Newsom kept hers?" Kathryn asked.

"Instinct. With Bell keeping his records separate, Newsom has no hold on him other than a possible personal relationship. I suspect when caught, both of them will try to blame the other to get out from under. It's the survival instinct. Storing such incriminating records in a freezer tells me Newsom is not the brains of that duo. Bell, now, has thought this through and prepared for it. I can almost guarantee it. I suppose I could be wrong, but I don't think so."

"If you're wrong, and Bell has moved his records from the office, where does that leave us? With no proof of wrongdoing, our hands are tied. The guy is a lawyer and knows how to cover his butt," Kathryn said.

Charles laughed. "Girls, a little matter like no proof has never stopped you before. It's a given that he won't willingly give up anything, but Newsom will."

Isabelle was about to voice a question when the timer on the oven went off, signaling that the pizza was ready. At the exact same moment, Charles's cell phone chirped. The girls rushed to the kitchen, while Charles moved out of sight to talk in hushed whispers.

Alexis poured root beer into frosty glasses from the freezer while Annie and Myra sliced the pizza with kitchen shears. Plates rattled, napkins were unfolded, and silverware was placed on the table just as Charles slipped his phone into his pocket. "I have news."

"Tell us, dear," Myra said. "The pizza is too hot to eat at the moment."

"One of my people has zeroed in on the surrogates. They're waiting for word from you as to when and where you want them taken. The original adoptive parents are standing by. Right this moment, we do not know where the babies are. That information, I'm sure, will be in Ms. Newsom's records. I have a small cadre of nurses on standby who will bring the babies to a designated safe house, at which time the original adoptive parents will be brought in to claim their babies. It seems all the surrogates are third- or fourth-year college students, recruited from Georgetown, George Washington, and the Catholic universities. The ones we know about all filed suits to reclaim their babies."

"So what you're saying is, we're going in blind. Everything will go down in real time, and there is no margin for error. Is that what you're saying, Charles?" Nikki asked.

"That's about the size of it. I'll choreograph it down to the last chord, but the rest will be up to you." He reached for a slice of pizza, bit down, and rolled his eyes. "Delicious!"

"The only thing I'm worried about is the babies," Annie said. The others agreed with her.

"I'm working on it, Annie. No matter what, the babies are our first priority. I want to stress, as strenuously as I can, that no matter what happens or what goes down, the babies come first. Tell me you all agree. I want to see a show of hands."

Seven hands shot upward.

"Good! Now, I think we're ready for our second pie. I'll do the honors this time," Charles said, getting up from his chair.

"Does that mean what I think it means?" Isabelle asked. "If it comes to a crunch, and it's either us or the babies, the babies win?"

"Yes, dear, that's exactly what it means," Myra said.

Seven very sober faces looked up at Charles as he set the second pizza in the middle of the table. "Pepperoni and sausage," he said cheerfully.

As Charles prepared to serve the pepperoni-and-sausage pizza, Adel Newsom and Baron Bell were quarreling bitterly. Bell was driving a silver Mercedes, which was supposed to be good in bad weather conditions. It wasn't. He was driving at a snail's pace and all over the road. He tried to ignore his companion, but it wasn't working. She was shrilling at him at the top of her lungs. "You're a fool. You said this was a foolproof operation. Not only are you a fool, you're stupid. It was your idea to drive here, instead of having Douglas drive us here in the Town Car. Look at you! Just look at you! You never drive in snow and don't know what the hell you're doing. You're all over the road. You're going to kill us!" she shrieked.

"Shut up, Adel. I didn't tell you to store your records in the freezer out here in the boondocks. That was your own brilliant brainstorm. I told you it was stupid, but did you listen to me? No, you did not, and this is the result. I must have had my brains in my ass when I got involved with you. I *thought* you were smart. I was wrong. You're just a greedy bitch." Then he added insult to injury and said, "An *old* greedy bitch."

Adel Newsom continued to screech. "Don't tell me to shut up, Baron. You turned green when I told you that reporter, the one who runs the *Post,* came to my office. You almost wet your pants when that old harridan that works for you told you the same thing. *They know.*"

"Who are *they,* Adel?" Bell demanded through clenched teeth.

"They are whoever you want them to be. Lizzie Fox, the reporters, that Hispanic guy back at the beach house. And I wouldn't be one damn bit surprised to find out that those goddamn vigilantes are in on this. I never believed for one minute that they got away from Lizzie Fox when they made their escape. She's too smart to let something like that happen. What that means, Baron, is she's involved with them. You said this was foolproof. I believed you. Now we're a hair away from getting caught. Goddamn you, Baron, say something."

"Shut up, Adel. I'm thinking." And he was thinking. But he was thinking about the children's Christmas party at the White House. He was reasonably certain he'd covered all his tracks. What Adel did, she did on her own. The worst thing that could happen to him, he thought, was he'd be a three-day story about an extramarital affair. He might be banned from the White House for a while, but all things blew over sooner or later in Washington. No matter what, he had to pull off the Christmas party. No matter what.

Bell wondered if he could get away with killing Adel Newsom.

"Lizzie Fox did not file the suits yet. She said she wanted to make a deal. She just did us the courtesy of letting us know what she had. She's in the *Post's* pocket, and that's how they know. Legally, Lizzie will cut a deal. She's probably the most ethical lawyer in the District. For God's sake, she has the president's ear. The *Post* is just interested in headlines and selling papers. In case you aren't getting it, Adel, this is about those babies you've been selling to the highest bidder. I warned you. This is what you get for thinking you're smarter than I am. I'm going to enjoy watching them dragging you off to jail."

"You miserable son of a bitch! Do you think for even a nanosecond that I won't tell them all those surrogates and adoptive parents were referrals from you?"

"If you're dead, you won't be able to tell anyone anything," Bell snarled.

Adel Newsom clamped her lips shut and started to wail. "What are we going to do, Baron?"

"I don't know. I need to think this through. There's a motel up there on the right. I'm going to stop. Let's just hope they have available rooms." Bell hunched over the wheel to see better out the window, between the wiper blades. His cell phone took that moment to ring.

"Don't answer it, Baron. They can tell by the pings where you are. I saw that just recently on television, in some kidnap case."

Like he was going to answer the phone. He knew without looking at the phone that it was his wife checking on him, the way she did every night before she went to bed and he wasn't home. Right now, right this minute, he'd give up everything he owned if he could turn the clock back and be sitting in the den with his wife, in front of a nice cherrywood fire, eating popcorn. His wife always gave him the fluffies right off the top. She was such a good woman. She was also a wonderful mother. She was also a wonderful wife in all ways except the bedroom.

Bell had to physically restrain himself from knocking Adel silly when she said, "This looks like a fleabag, one of those places that charges by the hour."

Bell stopped the car. "You go in and register. I'm too well known. Pay cash. Try to get an outside room."

Adel looked like she was going to protest, but in the end she opened the car door and got out.

I should just drive off and leave her here, Bell thought. The moment the thought entered his mind, he had the car back in gear and was headed around the circle that would lead him back to the turnpike.

Now he could think.

The Mercedes's taillights were just a pinpoint of red light when Adel Newsom exited the lobby of the Blue Jay Motel, room key in hand. She knew instantly that she was on her own. "You miserable, lousy, rotten piece of crap," she shouted, her words carried off by the swirling snow. Tears rolling down her face, her high-heeled leather boots soaking wet, she walked around the side of the building to room twelve.

The only thing that could be said for the brown and yellow decorated motel room was that it was warm. Very warm. Maybe she was having a hot flash. All the plastic surgery she'd had was external. Internally, her body was way over fifty and allowed for hot flashes, along with a host of other female problems. She shuddered as she slipped out of her fluffy down coat and tossed it on the bed.

Newsom's thoughts were all over the map as she paced the sleazy room. *How dare that bastard go off and leave me like this! How dare he!* Well, he'd dared, because here she was in this puky room, with no vehicle at her disposal and the possibility of prison looming on the horizon.

Newsom's pacing took her into the ratty bathroom. She looked at herself in the mirror and cringed. She looked awful, and every single day of her over fifty years glared at her from the worn-looking mirror. *Over fifteen years of my life I've given to that bastard,* she thought, *and he drives away and leaves me in this rat hole.*

She leaned closer and rubbed her fingers over the mirror to see if the film would disappear. It didn't. She should look better, but she didn't. She wanted to cry, but she was too scared and angry.

Back in the bedroom, she rooted around in the huge Chanel bag for the throwaway, untraceable cell phone she'd bought six months ago. Somehow or other she'd managed to program the stupid thing, a feat in itself since she was not electronically inclined. The first call she made was to the Dawsons' surrogate, Donna Davis. She crossed her fingers that the call would actually go through despite the bad weather. She almost fainted when she heard her client's familiar voice. "No names, please."

The voice came through as high and shrill. "I tried calling the office, but they said you were gone. Someone is watching me. Two men have been asking questions about me at the university and here in the apartment building. Someone knocks on my door on the hour. I was going to leave, but the weather is really bad. On top of that, my car won't start. I spoke to Joan Olsen earlier this morning. I called from the school cafeteria. Is it the . . . you know who?"

Newsom sucked in her breath. Her worst nightmare was coming true. She tried to calm her voice, but she sounded jittery even to her own ears. She knew Donna Davis was picking up on it. "Right now I'm stuck in Delaware, with no car at my disposal. I'm trying to get back to the District, but that probably won't happen till tomorrow morning. I want you to sit tight. Do not talk to anyone, and refer all queries to me. Where is—"

Anticipating the question, Donna Davis said, "Safe. Look, if I see a chance to get out of here, I'm gone. I'm not stupid. When I was a little kid and did something wrong and my father found out, he would say, 'The jig's up, girlie.' Well, I'm telling you the same thing: The jig's up, Ms. Lawyer. The handwriting is on the wall. Joan Olsen agrees with me."

"Don't do something you will regret. I'm working on getting back to the District. I'll take care of things the minute I get back. Please, give me your assurance that you will do as I've asked."

"Well, guess what, Ms. Lawyer? I'm not giving you any assurance. I'm outta here the first chance I get. I know Joanie feels the same way I do. Find some other suckers to fund your designer wardrobe." Newsom blinked when she realized the surrogate had hung up on her.

A glutton for punishment, she hit the speed dial and waited to see if Joan Olsen would answer the phone. The call immediately went to voice mail. She cursed under her breath and threw the cell phone on the grungy yellow bedspread.

Her breathing was so ragged, she thought she was going to black out.

Adel Newsom sat down on the edge of the bed and dropped her head into her hands. *How the hell did I get into this position? Is Baron right, and it was my own greed? Oh, God!*

A sob caught in her throat. She squeezed her eyes shut as she hoped for a lightning-bolt solution to hit her between the eyes. All she had to show for her life was a mediocre law practice, a pricey house in Georgetown with an uncomfortably high mortgage, a high-end car that she was upside down on, scars all over her body from all the exorbitantly expensive plastic surgery, and another woman's husband three times a week.

There was no doubt in her mind that Baron Bell would throw her to the wolves to protect his nice cushy life. She also knew he'd covered his fat ass all along the way.

"Well, we'll just see about that, you little toad."

Newsom pulled on her puffy coat and slogged her way through the snow over to the lobby of the motel. There had to be someone heading into Washington who would give her a lift into town.

Fifteen minutes later she was sitting high in the cab of a truck headed to the nation's capital with a delivery for Starbucks. For a measly five hundred dollars, the trucker had agreed to drop her off near the White House. Newsom was no fool. "Half now, and the other half when you drop me off," she told him. "I think I should warn you, I'm a lawyer and an officer of the court. I have a pistol in my bag, and I'm licensed to carry it."

She fished around in her bag and finally scraped together all her loose bills. He could just whistle "Dixie" for all she cared when it was time for her to get out. Unless he took credit cards, he would be out of luck for the second half of his transportation fee. She let him see the pistol, then leaned back to listen to Willie Nelson blaring from a CD. Her mind raced. Should she cut and run? If she did that, she would have to go back to the house in Georgetown to take what little money she had stashed under her mattress. The thought made her blood run cold. *A lawyer with money under the mattress! What is wrong with this picture?* Maybe she should go to the office on Nebraska Avenue, tidy up, and leave from there.

She had several changes of clothes in the small closet, and her car was in the parking lot. That meant she would have to pay someone to shovel it out. Once she paid off this hick driver, she would have only coins left. The petty cash in the office would barely get her a cup of coffee. Talk about being between a rock and a boulder. Unless . . . she could get to Baron's office before he did. She looked down at the Rolex on her wrist. She knew the security guard's routine, only because of the late-night trysts in Baron's office back at the beginning of their affair fifteen years earlier. She knew the combination to the ugly safe, too. What Baron didn't know was that she knew about the safe built into the floor under his desk. While she didn't know the combination, she knew where he kept the secret numbers. At least she thought she knew where he kept the numbers. Men were so predictable.

Once, during some heavy-duty pillow talk, Baron had blurted out about the cash he kept in the safe. At the time he'd said it was to whisk her away to some exotic getaway where no one would ever find them. While she had never seen the brochure to that exotic getaway that he'd boasted about, he'd said it was in the safe, to be utilized at the proper time. Well, this sure as hell was the proper time. Too bad he wouldn't be accompanying her on the junket. The only thing she didn't know for sure was how much cash Baron kept in the safe. For the most part, Baron wasn't a liar, so she had to assume the amount would be robust. And he'd once bragged about a fortune in bearer bonds that had come his way via the death of a wealthy client with no heirs.

All she had to do was get in and out of his office, make her getaway, and the world would be her oyster.

Not once did she think about any of the babies or their well-being as a result of her and Baron Bell's activities.

Sometimes life was a stinking bitch.

Chapter 9

Charles looked down at his coffee cup and was surprised to see that it was empty. He wondered how many cups he'd consumed. Not that it was important in the scheme of things. He knew that however many cups he'd consumed, he'd consume that many more before dawn broke over the horizon. He raised his head to look up at the wall, at the bank of clocks that gave him the time all over the world. For some strange reason, looking at the clocks always calmed him down. As much as he hated to admit it, he was nervous. Sending the Sisters down the snowy mountain and into the waiting arms of Snowden's people was unnerving him for some reason.

Charles moved his neck from side to side, hoping to alleviate the kinks that were bothering him. He knew what his problem was, and worrying wasn't going to help solve it. Anytime 1600 Pennsylvania Avenue came into play, things became problematic. He poured himself a cup of coffee and walked over to the window. The snow had stopped about an hour ago, and he could see that it had not started again. The white world outside the window was bathed in a golden glow from the lamps in the courtyard. It looked eerie, ominous somehow.

Charles looked down when he felt something brush against his legs. Murphy on one side, Grady on the other. Absently, he reached into his pocket for the treats that he always carried with him. They were man's best friend, and as such, both animals deserved everything he had to give for their love and loyalty. Both dogs waited expectantly to see if there would be a second treat, and there was. This time the dogs carried their chew bones over to the hearth and lay down. A sign that their world was just fine. At least for the moment.

Break time was over. Charles walked back to his bank of computers. He saw two incoming e-mails at the same moment the fax machine whirred to life. He was about to click on the e-mails when his special encrypted cell phone rang. It was Avery Snowden. Charles felt his stomach muscles bunch into a knot. "Avery, just give me the short version and the resolution," he said briskly.

"Donna Davis, the Dawsons' surrogate is on the move. She sneaked out the basement door of the apartment. Right now she's standing in the doorway. I think she's waiting for someone to pick her up. I removed the distributor cap of her vehicle hours ago. She went back inside.

The lights are on in her apartment. I assume the babies are still in her apartment, but in checking earlier, she leaves the babies with a woman on her floor from time to time. Do you want me to tail her or snatch her?"

Charles didn't even hesitate. "Snatch her and take her to the *Post* apartment. The girls will be arriving later today. Find a female operative and take the babies someplace safe. Make sure the babysitter is fully aware of the repercussions should she . . . talk to anyone."

"Understood. Do you want us to snatch the Olsen woman? As a reminder, the baby she sold is not with her, but we know where he is. She's in for the night. Apartment is dark, so I assume she's sleeping."

"Yes, take her to the *Post,* too. Don't do anything about her baby. We're still working on that. Check in on the hour, Avery. Good luck."

Charles sipped at his coffee as he scanned his e-mails and the incoming fax. Satisfied that things were moving at the speed of light, he sat down and proceeded to fire off e-mails.

Hundreds of miles away, in the nation's capital, Maggie Spritzer jerked to wakefulness when Ted Robinson shook her shoulder. "Wake up, Sleeping Beauty. We come bearing gifts. And food," he added as an afterthought. He plopped down two steaming pizza boxes, along with a six-pack of Corona that he'd bought from an all-night pizzeria around the corner.

Jack and Harry were busy removing their winter gear and kicking off their boots. "Can you turn the heat up, Maggie? Espinosa's heater conked out halfway here. We're frozen," Jack said.

Maggie eyed the foursome before she ran into her private bathroom for a bundle of wool socks. She tossed a pair to each of the four before turning the heat up all the way. "My mother always said if your feet are warm, you'll be okay. They're unisex socks, so don't be shy about putting them on. What'd you get? Tell me you got everything that will give me a drop-dead headline."

Ted turned defensive. "We got everything there was to get. We didn't take the time to go through it. We were too busy trying to stay alive on the damn highway. We all deserve a monster bonus for putting our lives at risk. How much?"

Maggie bit into a slice of pepperoni-and-sausage pizza. She rolled her eyes in happiness. "Whatever you want," she mumbled.

Ted and Espinosa lit up like Christmas trees. "Do you mean it?" Ted asked.

"No!"

Four slices of pizza later, Maggie came up for air. "Okay, let's get to it. We need to copy every single sheet of paper. Then we have to fax each and every sheet to the mountain. By the way, the girls will be leaving as soon as it gets light. That's about three hours from now, so chop-chop, boys."

Exactly one hour later Maggie sat back on

her heels and looked at the others. "This is a gold mine. I have to give Adel Newsom credit: She kept impeccable records. She was smart, too. She outsourced some of her clients and got kickbacks from other lawyers. The main thing is that there is a complete list of the babies put out for adoption after being reclaimed from the parents who arranged for a surrogate through Baron Bell. This has to go to Charles right away so he can put his people on it. The only thing that matters is getting those babies back to their original adoptive parents."

"Kidnapping babies is a federal offense," Jack said.

"Possession is also nine points of the law," Maggie said. "Charles told me if we were successful in finding the babies and snatching them, Nikki's old law firm has agreed to take all the cases on a pro bono basis. Lizzie will be in charge behind the scenes. If it looks like it isn't going to go our way legally, he is prepared to, ah . . . relocate the babies and their adoptive parents to a more friendly environment. That's not our problem right now. Freeing up the information and getting it into the proper hands is our end of the job. And the headlines and story, of course. 'Tis the season of miracles, and the public will be on our side. Trust me."

"Like we have a choice," Ted muttered.

"Look!" Espinosa said. "There are pictures of the babies, along with foot- and handprints on each adoption. This should make the lawyers' work a little easier."

The time was 3:10.

At 3:45 the fax machine shut down, forcing the foursome to head out to the main office to finish up. At 4:05 they had three copies of each file, and one set was safely on the mountain. The second set was packed into three packing boxes to be sent out to Nikki's old law firm by private messenger as soon as they could arrange a pickup.

"I'm feeling pretty good about this," Maggie said. "Anyone want to go out to breakfast? Our job here is done."

Harry looked pointedly at the two empty pizza boxes and shook his head. "I'm going home."

"Me too," Jack said as he pulled on his boots. "Did they say anything about the closings? This town shuts down when it flurries out, especially government."

"You lucked out. Court's closed. Schools, everything. Listen, guys, thanks. I'm going to stay here and see what else I can do before the girls get here. By the way, they will be going to the *Post* apartment on their arrival."

"You want me to stay, Maggie?" Ted asked, hoping she would say no.

"No. Go home and take care of Mickey and Minnie. You can bring me some warmer clothes when you get back. What about you, Espinosa?"

"I'm going to catch some z's at Ted's. I'll plan on getting here around noon, weather permitting, if that's okay with you."

"That'll work." She blew the guys a kiss and

started picking at the crumbs in a pizza box. The moment the door closed, she dived into the files stacked up on her desk.

She felt her eyes start to burn as she stared at first one baby, then another. She rubbed her thumb over the chubby faces of the babies and whispered, "I'm going to get those bastards, and that's a promise. I'm going to make sure you go back to your real parents, so you can grow up in the loving home that was supposed to be yours. I'm going to make sure you little gals get to play Little League and you little guys get to take guitar lessons. I'm going to make it my mission in life to follow your lives. From here on in, I'm Aunt Maggie, and *I* will not let you down. That's a promise."

Maggie swiped at the tears rolling down her cheeks as she realized the commitment she had just made to two dozen babies and their adoptive parents. Well, she'd have a lot of help by way of the guys and the vigilantes to make it all come to pass. She crossed her fingers the way she had when she was a little girl and she was making a wish for something. Her expression turned stubborn. Wishes did come true. Sometimes.

On the mountain, Charles Martin's face was just as stubborn and grim as Maggie's as he pulled sheet after sheet from the fax machine. He scanned them with one eye as he picked out the pertinent data on each sheet, while his other eye was on his cell as he called Avery Snowden and the other operatives, who were standing at the ready to do his bidding.

Feeling eyes on him, Charles turned to look over his shoulder. His chicks, as he thought of the Sisters, along with Myra and Annie, were standing in the open doorway, fully dressed, coffee cups in hand.

The time was 4:02. He smiled and motioned with a slight tilt of his head that they were to take their seats at the round table. Just as he finished his last call, the final sheet of paper from Maggie flew out of the fax. He held up his hand for silence even though no one was speaking.

"This intel just came to me from Maggie. We owe the boys a huge vote of thanks for securing all this valuable information. By the time you reach your destination, all of this," Charles said, pointing to the twenty-inch stack of papers, "will be waiting for you at the *Post* apartment. What I have here belongs to Adel Newsom. She kept impeccable records, which is good for us. From a quick glance, there appear to be at least two dozen babies whose real parents arranged for a surrogate birth but were reclaimed by the surrogate mothers, then disposed of in a privately arranged adoption, with big bucks changing hands. What a scheme. Consider it. The cost to produce the children, every penny of it, fell on the couples who arranged for the surrogate mothers, with Baron Bell richly rewarded for his efforts.

"Ms. Newsom did not handle all the surrogates after the birth of the babies. She outsourced some of them and received fees from other lawyers. Quite a bit of money changed hands.

"There is a bit of a problem, and it is this. For now, we are only going to concern ourselves with the current year. Once this matter is brought to light by all of you, the authorities will step in and go back over the past ten years and bring to light how long this scheme has been in operation. I see no reason at this point in time to disrupt all those children's lives or their current parents' lives, especially at this time of year. Maggie and the *Post* will be on it. So for now," Charles said, waving a thick stack of papers, "we're just going to work on this year's adoptions. Time will take care of the others.

"The two surrogates, Donna Davis and Joan Olsen, are being taken to the *Post* apartment and will be held there by Snowden's people until you get there. The babies will be taken to Maggie's house in Georgetown. Nurses will be on the job, along with Snowden's operatives. As much as the weather is a detriment, it is also a blessing for all of you. Everyone will be too busy with the snow to pay attention to any of you. At least that is my hope."

"Do we know if Bell and Newsom made it back to town?" Kathryn asked.

"At the moment, we know nothing about either one of them. We have people watching Bell's home and office as well as Newsom's home and office. I don't know why I say this, but

I doubt we'll see activity once it gets light out. Having said that, Bell will brazen it out. Newsom, from what Maggie tells me, could very well cut and run."

"We need them both," Nikki said as she stared down at the pictures of the babies the others were passing around. "This is one punishment I am really looking forward to."

The other Sisters agreed with Nikki.

"Are we going to allow Baron Bell to follow through with his Christmas party at the White House?" Isabelle asked, an innocent smile on her face.

The Sisters hooted with laughter, to Charles's dismay. Then he remembered the discussion they'd had around midnight. He allowed a small smile to tug at the corners of his mouth. "Absolutely," was his response.

"I just have one question," Alexis said. "Will my Red Bag have everything I asked for?"

This time Charles offered up a full smile. "And then some!"

Yoko got up and poured fresh coffee for everyone just as Charles's phone pinged to life. Everyone stopped what they were doing to listen to his end of the conversation. They knew immediately that Adel Newsom had just shown up at Baron Bell's office. Not only had she shown up, she'd eluded the night guard and managed to get into Bell's office.

"Either Adel Newsom is a very resourceful lady, or she's one desperate lawyer. My money is on the latter," Kathryn said.

* * *

Three hundred miles away, Adel Newsom let herself into Baron Bell's office. She congratulated herself on her sneakiness in having made a wax impression of his office keys while Bell slept after a rousing evening of sex. She hoped that she would never have to have sex in a bathtub again. Ever.

Newsom waited for her eyes to adjust to the darkness of the office before she made her way to her coconspirator's desk. She pushed the chair aside, dropped to her knees, and slid the sheet of hard plastic to the side, revealing the false floor. She moved the panel aside, too, and tried the knob of the safe. No such luck that it was open. She managed to get to her feet and rushed into the old-fashioned bathroom. She opened the medicine cabinet and took out a can of shaving cream. What looked like an expiration date on the bottom of the can was really the code to the safe. She ran the numbers through her brain until she was sure she had them down pat. She ran back to the desk and again dropped to her knees. *Four turns to the right at 5, three turns to the left at 44, two turns to the right on 26. Turn until safe opens.* The safe didn't open.

Newsom rocked back on her heels and tried again, this time her hand steadier. The safe still wouldn't open. She cursed as she heaved herself to her feet again and walked back into the bathroom. This time she brought the shaving cream can back with her. She tried every variation of the numbers she could think of. The safe's heavy steel door refused to budge. She cursed ripely. The son of a bitch must have changed the combination. She wanted to cry, but she was too angry.

In the end, all she could do was put things back where she'd found them. She returned the shaving cream can to the medicine cabinet. She bumped into the ugly safe standing in Bell's office, the obvious safe, which he was so proud of. Well, she knew that combination by heart. Her hands were rock steady when she twirled the knob. It took all her strength to open the heavy door. She knew there was nothing of importance in this particular safe other than old files. It contained a small wad of cash in case anyone ever had the audacity to break in and force Baron to open the safe. Baron had once told her he kept eleven hundred dollars in the safe because it sounded like the amount someone would expect to find. She grabbed the money and shoved it into her purse. She closed the safe and looked around, listening for any sound from outside that would indicate the guard was making his rounds. The building was totally silent, eerie actually.

If nothing else, she at least had enough cash to check into a hotel.

In the small reception area, Newsom looked around. *Petty cash.* The thought came to her out of nowhere. Lightning quick, she was poking through Harriet's desk drawer, and there it was, the small box that held petty cash and Baron's corporate card. She had no idea how much she was dumping into her purse; she just upended the little box. The corporate American Express card went into her pocket. She could hoard the cash and use the card until such time as she thought she might get caught, or until Baron or Harriet reported the card as stolen. Her gut instinct was that Baron wouldn't open that can of worms.

She saw the Santa suit hanging on the door and had the insane urge to rip it to shreds. She probably would have, but she heard a sound from the hallway and saw the shadow of the guard outside the glass door leading into the reception area. She ducked behind the reception desk, hardly daring to breathe. She almost fainted when she heard the antique doorknob rattle. She let her breath out in a long sigh as the steps she'd heard moved away. It was a short hallway, so either he was going up to the next floor or down to the one below this one.

Within minutes she was up, out the door, and running toward the exit that would take her down to the basement, where she could make her way out to the street.

The minute the frigid air hit her, Newsom realized how cold and wet and hungry she was. Her head down, she trudged forward, fighting the swirling snow that was still battering the District. Numb with cold, she stumbled into the first all-night eatery she came to. She looked around to see tired sanitation workers with hot mugs of steaming coffee warming their hands. She walked over to one of the empty booths and sat down. When the coffee appeared without being ordered, Newsom viewed it as nectar of the gods. She ordered pancakes and bacon with a glass of orange juice. When the tired waitress moved off, Newsom leaned her head back against the wall and closed her eyes.

She knew without a doubt she was in some deep doo-doo, and it was only going to get worse. She needed a plan. A plan that would work for her and screw Baron Bell. The urge to cry again was so strong that she bit down on her bottom lip hard enough to taste her own blood.

Sometimes life was a real bitch.

Chapter 10

The Sisters peered out the huge bay window as they dressed for their trip down the mountain. In the end, by popular vote, it was decided that while Annie and Myra would double up on a snowmobile, as per Charles's plan, the others would ski to the bottom. The Sisters agreed with Nikki's point that snowshoes would take too much time and rob them of their stamina. Since they were all accomplished skiers, even Yoko, Charles was outnumbered, something that seemed to be happening to him more and more of late. He took the decision with good grace, however, and trekked with the Sisters out to the utility shed that housed the snowmobile and all the ski equipment.

Skis and poles were handed out, along with boots, as Annie fired up the snowmobile and cruised out to the snow-covered apron in front of the cavernous shed that held all manner of seasonal equipment needed to reside on the mountain.

A bit of confusion ensued as the girls squabbled over the boots and whose was whose. Finally, the matter was settled, boots were snug on their feet, their snow goggles in place. Annie, Myra, and Charles watched them make their way to the ski trail at the edge of the mountain.

Snow flurries that had been sparse were by then heavier and swirling in all directions. The worry in Charles's eyes did not go unobserved by Myra and Annie. Myra patted his arm and said, "Not to worry, dear. The girls are excellent skiers. They'll watch over Yoko, as she is the novice of the group." She walked over to her snowmobile. "I think we're ready, Annie," she said.

Annie hung back for a moment. "Ah, Charles, I think I know what I want for Christmas this year. I was wondering if it would be possible to have it in place when we come back from our mission. I realize the timing might be a tad off, but you did say you had people coming to the mountain today to work on the cable car."

"And that would be . . . what?"

Annie told him.

Charles didn't think anything could surprise him at this point in his life, but Annie's request made him blink. "Well, I . . . are—"

"I don't need a dissertation, Charles. A yes or no will suffice. I'll even settle for a maybe. Well?"

"I . . . uh . . . uh . . ."

"I'm going to take that as a yes," Annie snapped as she lowered her snow goggles and moved toward the snowmobile, her back ramrod straight, which meant her Christmas present better damn well be in place when she got back, or there would be hell to pay.

Before Annie cranked the gears and revved the engine, Myra said, "I heard that, Annie! Are you out of your mind?"

"Actually, Myra, my mind is just fine and clicking away on all cylinders. It's your mind I'm worried about. Now, hang on and keep quiet. One more peep out of you, and I'm going to strangle you with your own pearls. I have to concentrate on getting us to the bottom of the mountain. In case you haven't noticed, because you were too busy minding my business, it's snowing harder, which means there is virtually no visibility. You getting it, Myra?"

Myra thought about responding to the question but opted not to, since she had no desire to be strangled by her own pearls. She wrapped her arms around Annie's waist and closed her mouth so tight, she thought her jaw was going to crack.

Myra thought the high-pitched whine of the snowmobile ricocheting across the mountain was equal to a dozen chain saws felling monster trees. She knew that when Annie finally brought the machine to a halt, her ears would ring for hours. She did marvel at how Annie handled the powerful machine and knew she couldn't do it half as well. As Kathryn would say, Annie had it going on, which meant that she, Myra Rutledge, did not have it going on. She felt irritated at the thought that she wasn't measuring up in the girls' eyes.

And then there was silence as their conveyance came to an abrupt halt. Annie hopped off and tied her helmet to one end of the steering mechanism. "Hustle, Myra. We beat the girls! We need to break off some of these pine branches to cover the machine until someone takes it back up the mountain. You can talk now if you want to."

"You remind me of the Gestapo, Annie. Guess what? I have nothing to say," Myra said as she hung her helmet next to Annie's. She immediately went to a low-hanging pine and snapped off a tiny branch. She flicked the snow at Annie and took a perverse delight in seeing her old friend falter. "Sorry," she said sweetly.

"My ass you're sorry, Myra. You did that on purpose. I forgive you because you are such a poop. There are times, like right now, that I don't want to admit I know you. So there," Annie sniped.

Wounded to the quick, Myra felt tears spring to her eyes. "I *am* sorry, Annie. But a pole! What will the girls think?"

"Myra! It was *their* idea! I heard them talking, so I eavesdropped. When you eavesdrop, that's when you hear the *good* stuff. I'm just making it happen. We aren't getting enough exercise. And I need to brush up on my dancing for when I meet up with Tee to go dancing. I just thought of something. I'll call Charles later and ask if he can light up the pole from the inside.

Incandescent. That kind of thing. This is exciting, isn't it, Myra?"

Myra was so excited, she could barely contain herself. Not. She sighed. "Annie, pole dancing isn't dancing. Dancing is waltzing and fox-trotting. Don't you remember all those dance classes and recitals we had to attend? We didn't have incandescent lights then. All I can see is you getting a broken or fractured hip."

"Why do you always rain on my parade?" Annie broke off enough branches from a dead pine and dragged them over to the snowmobile. After carefully arranging them, she decided that anyone who was not looking for a snowmobile would not know that there was one beneath. "That should do it! There is dancing, and then there is dancing. I'm talking about *limbering* up. Moving all your body parts, not just your feet. For your information, there is a tutorial on the Net for pole dancing. I have to say, I think it will be challenging, but I think I can do it. *You, now,* that's another story."

"What is it with you, Annie? You're not the same person you used to be. How did all this happen?" Myra asked fretfully as she envisioned herself being urged by the others to give pole dancing a shot.

"I'm alive, Myra. I want to experience everything life has to offer. Just wait till we get our pardons. You watch my dust then."

"Oh, Annie, I don't see that happening anytime soon. If you're counting on that happening . . . what will you do if it doesn't happen?"

"It's going to happen, Myra, and it's going to happen soon. I'm ready to go out into the world under my own steam. I am going to blaze a trail that will scorch the earth. You are way too negative for me. I can see it now. You and Charles will go back to the farm, and from time to time, maybe once a week or so, you'll have dinner with Nellie and Elias or Pearl, if she can find a way to sneak back into town. You might go riding a few afternoons a week. You and Charles will undoubtedly go into town to dinner on the weekends. I suppose you might take up gardening or something equally silly. Maybe finger painting. Think about it, Myra. What are you going to do with all the rest of the hours? Watch TV? Wait to hear from the girls, who will be so busy with their own new lives, they won't have time for you or me? That sounds pretty damn deadly to me."

Myra had to agree that it did sound deadly. Even though she didn't want to ask Annie what she would do if a pardon was forthcoming, she found herself saying, "And what are you going to be doing, Countess de Silva?"

"Well, I can't go home to the family homestead, since I more or less turned it over to Joseph Espinosa's family, and no, I do not regret that for one moment. My mountain in Spain has a tenant, but I imagine once we vacate Big Pine Mountain, Pappy might return with his family.

"I thought I would stick my nose into the *Post*'s business and pester Maggie. I can just see several rip-roaring headlines with my byline underneath. Now, that's a goal to aspire to, Myra. I think I'll make an excellent roving reporter. I'll go dancing with Tee and blow his socks off. When I get bored with him, I'll head to Vegas and take a shot at running my casino. Cha-ching! I'll dally around with Fish and teach him a thing or two, assuming I learn something along the way. If nothing else, Myra, I'll be *limber,* and I'll be living, not stagnating. Ah, here come the girls!"

Myra digested Annie's dialogue and had to admit Annie's new life, if she managed to make it happen, did sound exciting. She wondered when her old friend would sleep. Knowing Annie as she did, she'd probably go on the Net and find a tutorial about power naps. She smiled at the thought.

A flurry of activity followed as the girls shed their ski boots, skis, and poles and stashed them under the mountain of dead evergreen limbs that now housed the snowmobile.

"It's snowing harder. I thought by the time we got off the mountain, it would have let up," Nikki said, worry in her voice. "Someone call Charles and tell him we got down safely."

"I'm doing it now," Alexis said.

"Our ride is here," Yoko said, pointing to a white van that was almost impossible to see through the swirling snow.

The Sisters climbed in the van and settled back for the ride to the nation's capital.

* * *

Martine Connor, the president of the United States, Marti to close friends, Madam President to those who worked for her, and POTUS to the Secret Service, with the code name Chick, stood at the window, coffee cup in hand, staring out at the snow. It was a winter wonderland for sure. She wondered how much snow had fallen during the night. Six inches, she surmised. And it had just started to snow again a short while ago. In a way she was glad it was snowing, because it would make the annual children's Christmas party hosted by Baron Bell and herself that much more exciting for the little ones.

Martine had already performed her early morning presidential duties and had a few free hours to herself. Her secretary had told her that, because of the inclement weather, cancellations were coming in for all the ten-minute interviews and photo ops that had been scheduled for the day. That was fine by her. She needed some downtime.

She walked back to her kitchen and poured more coffee and returned to the window. She liked to stare out the window at the outside world and just let her mind wander in whatever direction it wanted to go. Just then, it was going in Baron Bell's direction. She had met the man only once and hadn't really formed an opinion of him. Lizzie Fox hadn't seemed enamored of him, that was for sure. Yet the man was in and out of the White House on a regular basis. Or so Lizzie had said. As Martine sipped her coffee, she tried to remember what she'd read about the lawyer over the past months. Nothing earth-shaking. A philanthropic attorney in the District. A lover of children.

An itch settled itself between her shoulder blades; then her eyes narrowed. Had Lizzie been trying to warn her about Bell that day she came to lunch? Had she missed the signal, whatever the signal was? Her eyes narrowed in thought. Before she could think twice, she moved over to the in-house phone and buzzed her secretary, Connie Quintera. "Connie, I want you to stop whatever you're doing and go through the visitors' logbook. I want to know how many times Baron Bell has been to the White House this past year. I want times logged in, times logged out, and who he met with while he was here, and I want it ASAP. I'm in my quarters, so bring it to me as soon as you have it. Thanks, Connie."

The president went back to the window to stare out at the falling snow. Always when she was in a reflective mood, she thought about how she'd gotten to this place in time. And then she thought about who it was that had put her here at the eleventh hour. She knew without a shadow of a doubt that she was in some deep trouble if she didn't come through with the promise she'd made to the vigilantes. She shivered at the thought of what could and would happen if she didn't make good on that promise very, very soon.

It wasn't that she hadn't tried. She had, but she'd been shot down from so many directions, she'd had to fall back and regroup. She was still too green, too new at her job, to fully appreciate that, within certain limits, she could do whatever she wanted.

No matter what anyone said, no matter how much they professed to be on her side, Connor knew she was dealing with the good ol' boys, and the good ol' boys still didn't cotton to a woman president. Especially her chief of staff, Aaron Lowry. In private, she called him a pit bull. He always showed just the right amount of respect for her position, but she knew he didn't like her. How she'd become saddled with him was still a bit of a mystery to her.

Not coming from the world of Washington, a virtual outsider to politics in a year when the public was demanding that the foxes guarding the henhouse be put out to pasture, she found herself having to create an administration from scratch. And, somehow, when Lizzie had at first refused to come on board, she had acquired Lowry as her chief of staff. It was one of so many things here in this exalted house that were mysteries to her, and that was another reason she wanted Lizzie Fox in the White House to watch her back. Her eyes narrowed again. She was a woman of her word. Always had been, always would be. She'd grant those pardons or die trying.

Connor walked back to her little private desk and pressed the button that would summon Aaron Lowry. Her back stiffened when she heard his voice. "I'd like you to come up to my quarters now, Aaron."

"Madam President, if it's not an emergency, can the visit wait an hour or so? I'm up to my neck in some tricky—"

"I said *now,* Aaron." She broke the connection before the COS could utter another word.

Fresh coffee in hand, she sat down on one of the chairs she'd arranged in a small informal setting. She waited for one of the Secret Service detail to fetch the COS.

When Lowry finally bustled in, huffing and puffing, he looked at her with disdain. "Did something happen? Is there some emergency I'm not aware of?" he grated.

"No. Please, Aaron, sit down. You appear winded. We have an excellent gym here. You should take advantage of it."

"I would if I had time. Unfortunately, I work sixteen hours a day, so that leaves little time for gyms. What did you want to see me about?"

"Several things. One being your long hours. That's going to stop the first of the year, when you will work nine to five. Lizzie Fox will be here by then to lessen your workload. I'm also going to switch up your assistants. By the way, none of this is negotiable. If there's anything I'm about to tell you that you don't like, feel free to tender your resignation. Now, tell me what you and Baron Bell have in common."

Whatever Aaron Lowry had expected to hear, a question about Baron Bell was not it. "He's got the ear of just about every politician on both sides of the aisle. One of the Joint Chiefs is his cousin. He knows everyone. Always offers sound advice. A good man to have in our corner. Why are you asking?"

"Because I can. I'm the president. Did you forget that?"

"No, Madam President, I did not forget that."

Connor looked at the little toad of a man and felt herself wince. She was almost certain he had a Napoleon complex. "You don't like me, do you, Aaron?"

Lowry pretended horror. "What? Why would you ask me something like that, Madam President? Of course I like you. I'm here to serve you. I try to do it to the best of my ability. If there's something I've done or something you think I should have done and didn't, you should tell me."

"I don't like you, Aaron." *Good Lord, did I just say that?* Obviously, she did, because the man's face turned brick red. Connor leaned forward to pick up a cigarette and fired it up. She blew a perfect smoke ring upward. The look of horror on Lowry's face made her take a second puff from the cigarette she didn't even want.

"I'm sorry to hear that, Madam President. Do you want me to resign? Is that what this is all about?"

"No. I am more than capable of working with people I don't like. I realize this is not a perfect world. I just want you to know where I stand. From this moment forward, you will clear *everything,* and I mean everything, through me. If you so much as order a roll of toilet paper for the staff bathroom, I want to know about it. Are we clear on this?"

"Yes, Madam President."

"Good. Now, how are we doing on the presidential pardons for the vigilantes?"

The COS immediately bounced up off his chair and looked down at the president. "We aren't doing anything on the pardons. We discussed that months ago. If you do that, if you even try, it will be political suicide for you and this administration."

Connor stood up and towered over Lowry. "That's what *you* said. I said to proceed. I admit to a certain laxness where the matter is concerned, but now I want it done. As far as you are concerned, however, it no longer makes a difference, since Lizzie Fox will handle the matter. That will be all, Aaron."

"But, Madam President—"

"I said that will be all, Aaron."

After a shocked and dismayed Aaron Lowry left, Martine Connor walked back to the window, minus her coffee cup. The cigarette was still in her hand, however. She stuck it between her lips and dusted her hands together. "I think that went over rather well," she muttered to the steamy window. She used her index finger to trace the word *vigilante* on the window. "One pardon coming up, ladies. Just be patient."

Chapter 11

Kathryn Lucas stared out of the van window at the snowy landscape. She was sitting next to Nikki, who was texting Jack. At least that was who she thought she was texting. In actuality, Nikki was texting the office manager at her old law firm to get the latest update via Lizzie Fox.

The driver of the van leaned his head back and shouted, "We're forty minutes out of the city. Pick your drop-off spots, ladies."

The van came alive with sound as the Sisters started to jabber to one another. In the back row, Myra and Annie sat upright to try to get their bearings.

Annie's voice was cheerful when she said, "I don't know about you, Myra, but I'm getting a certain sense of déjà vu here. This is like the last time we came into the District, were dropped off, then made our way to the apartments of credit-card thieves Bonnie and Clyde."

Myra chewed on her lower lip. "We made it

happen, Annie. There's no reason to jinx us now with that kind of talk."

Annie's voice was still cheerful when she said, "I'm just saying, Myra. I always like to go on the record with things like this."

Myra fingered her pearls. "Yes, I know, dear. Annie, about that . . . uh . . . lighted dancing pole. Why do you want it to be lighted?"

"Myra, don't you read? It's not just a light. Well, it is, but it changes colors. You know, like in one of those disco dance halls. It just makes it more . . . *official* somehow. I'm all atwitter just thinking about it. You should be all atwitter, too, Myra, but I understand you're busy thinking about your wedding and all. We have time, so don't fret about it."

Myra blinked. "I'm not fretting. Time for what?" she asked nervously as she plucked at her pearls.

"To get into the swing of things. This is your chance to show off your tat."

"Tat?"

"That's the lingo for tattoo. You are so not with it, Myra." Annie patted Myra's arm the way she would if she were consoling a child. "We're partnering up, Myra. That's because the girls think we're old, and we are, but I so hate to be reminded of my age. Each of them is going off on her own while we partner. If you don't feel comfortable with me, you can go with one of the others, and I'll go alone."

"Don't be silly, Annie. I wouldn't dream of

leaving you to your own devices. Besides, I feel very comfortable with each of us watching the other's back. We work well together. Sometimes you are just so outside of the box, I don't know what to think."

"Your answer is don't think. Just go with the flow and the moment. Everything is instinctive, you know." Annie dropped her voice to a whisper. "Myra, we can do anything the girls can do. We really can."

"No, we can't, Annie."

"Okay, we can't. But we're wizards at improvising. Can you accept *that?*"

"Yes, dear, I can accept that. Now, put on your boots. We get dropped off first. I wish Charles had called."

"Yes, Mama," Annie said, tongue in cheek. "I imagine he has his hands full at the moment, Myra. We know what to do, and, like you said, we can think on our own if things go awry."

"First stop, ladies. Dupont Circle," the driver said thirty minutes later. "Careful now. That step has ice on it."

Annie shot the driver a withering look as she jumped down into almost a foot of snow piled on the side of the road. She reached for Myra's hand, but Myra shook it off as she, too, landed in the snow in an upright position. They waved airily to those left behind in the van. They managed to cross the road, holding on to each other for safety's sake.

It was beyond a winter wonderland. Annie

kept mumbling over and over that it was the North Pole, and it was going to be a white Christmas, after all. Myra ignored her as she concentrated on slogging through the snow.

There were few people out and about, though; as always during a storm, a few hardy souls braved the elements. The few cars that could be seen were slipping and sliding on the roads, which the sand and salt trucks couldn't keep up with. The nation's capital appeared to be in lockdown mode. A few more daring souls were ahead of them, trudging through the snow, their heads burrowed into the collars of their coats.

Annie pulled Myra into a vacant doorway with a canvas canopy that looked like it would collapse any minute from the weight of the snow. Her teeth chattering, shivering inside her down jacket, she said, "Myra, I think, but I'm not sure, because I can't really read the street signs through the snow, but I think we're about two and a half blocks from Baron Bell's office. We're a block west, possibly a block and a half, from the *Post* apartment. Take a look around you. Bell is not going to be in his office today. He just isn't. How about we go there now, just you and me? If the weather gets any worse, we might not be able to get over there once it turns dark. And, when it gets dark, law enforcement will be out watching over things. If the weather lets up, we'll be more noticeable. I'm thinking right now is the perfect cover. What do you think, Myra?"

"I suppose it makes sense, and I'm game, but I think we need to tell the others what we're doing."

"That would work if it was a perfect world and cyberspace cooperated, but alas, dear heart, we lost all reception on the cells. Even Charles's handy-dandy, one-of-a-kind, no-one-can-penetrate phone isn't working. We'll be on our own. Are you worried that Bell *might* be there? Don't be. Between the two of us, we can render him helpless in . . . in whatever time it takes us. Decide, Myra. I'm freezing here."

The last thing Myra wanted to do was go to Baron Bell's office in the middle of a raging snowstorm with inoperable cell phones. "I'm your girl," she said sprightly.

Annie grabbed Myra's arm, and off they went. "Sometimes you just rock, Myra," she said as she got a mouthful of snow.

Forty-eight minutes later Annie announced that they had arrived at their destination. "I say we go around the back and through the door that leads to those first four floors that Charles told us about. The one where the architect has his offices. If we make it that far, we can then take the elevator to the twelfth floor and pick the lock on Bell's door. I'm an expert now, Myra."

Myra sighed. All she wanted was to get warm, and if it was in Baron Bell's office, picking his door lock and breaking into the man's safe, so be it. "Let's do it, partner!"

"I love you, Myra."

Myra wasn't sure if she loved Annie at the moment or not. She was too cold and tired to care much about anything. "Aren't you just a little worried about the guard downstairs, Annie?"

"Not one little bit. He probably worked a double shift, and his replacement didn't make it in. There doesn't appear to be anyone in any of the offices. Relax, Myra. If he shows up, we'll just . . . uh . . . take him down and truss him up like a turkey. After we turn up the heat in Bell's office. Look, Myra, we're in. Now all we have to do is make our way to the twelfth floor. Pay attention, dear. I'm locking the door behind me. That means we're safe. Check your cell phone and see if you can get a signal."

Myra did as instructed. She shook her head. "Maybe Mr. Bell's landline is working. We can call Charles from here. What do you think, Annie?"

"Sounds like a plan to me. Let's see if we can make it work for us."

Within minutes they were on the twelfth floor. The elevator swished open, and they stepped out into the dimly lit hallway.

Myra reached for Annie's arm and pulled her backward. "Look!" she hissed as she pointed downward with her finger. "Water. And it's leading to . . . Baron Bell's door."

Both women tiptoed forward to the suite of offices that was down one suite from the elevator.

"There aren't any lights on inside. You can see through the opaque glass," Annie said thoughtfully. "There are several possibilities, Myra. One is the guard was outside, then came in, but that sounds pretty lame even to me. The other is either Bell or Newsom was here and left. Or maybe the secretary made it in and left early. I say we give the door a try."

"I wouldn't have it any other way. First, though, why don't you try the knob to see if it's open before you start destroying property?"

Annie thought about Myra's comment and tried the knob. The door opened without making a sound.

Myra rolled her eyes.

"I'm going to give you that one, my friend," Annie whispered. "The fact that this door is open tells me someone other than Bell was here and didn't care about locking the door when they left. Damn it, Myra, someone beat us here." Annie stepped into the dimly lit office. "Yoohoo!" she trilled. "Anyone here?"

"I don't think anyone is here, Annie. Look, there are wet footprints leading across the reception area and, it looks like, across the hall to that office where the door is half open. Some light would be a good thing."

"Turn on the lights, but be sure to lock the door. I don't have any bad feelings about this little break-in, Myra. The weather is in our favor today, and I for one don't know how we got so lucky. Try calling Charles or the boys while I check out this huge safe."

Annie dropped to her knees and flexed her fingers as she roll-called everything Tee had taught her. "Someone was definitely here, Myra. The carpet is wet where I'm kneeling, and whoever it was opened this safe."

When there was no response from the reception area, Annie pressed her ear to the safe and twirled the knob. It took her three tries before the massive door creaked open. She blinked at the jumble of papers shoved onto the shelves. Folders were scrunched, with corners sticking out every which way. It took her only seconds to see that the contents of the huge safe were years old. She twirled the knob to read zero and closed the heavy door, using her shoulder.

Off in the reception area, Annie could hear Myra talking to someone. *That's good,* she thought. *She's made contact with someone.* She moved over to Baron Bell's tidy desk and again dropped to her knees. She pushed the swivel chair aside and was about to slide the heavy sheet of plastic that protected the floor from the rollers on the chair when her hands touched cold water. Someone had been here also, and not that long ago.

Annie sucked in her breath and slid the hard plastic sheet to the side. She tapped at the floorboards until she found the one that would pop out. She lifted the panel and peered down at the secret safe and went to work. She wanted to shout at the top of her lungs when she got it right the first time. She opened the door of the safe and stared down at the contents. Small bundles of money. She flipped through the bills and estimated there was twenty-five thousand dollars, give or take a few dollars. Quick-getaway money, nothing more. She riffled through the files but couldn't find anything related to baby adoptions. A huge file about a road project in Bowie, Maryland, took up one shelf in the safe. The second shelf held personal papers, including birth certificates, passports, and other assorted papers pertaining to Bell's family. It also housed other files, one for a senator and some young boy charging him with things he shouldn't be charged with, at least according to the senator. She shrugged, then almost jumped out of her skin when Myra tapped her on the shoulder. She whirled around, her eyes big as saucers.

"Someone is out in the hallway. I could hear voices. What did you find, Annie?"

"Nothing, but if you want the skinny on Senator Lantzy, I can give it to you. There's some money, not a lot, but that's it. Someone beat us here. The carpet was wet by the big old safe, and there was a puddle on the plastic before I moved it. What did you hear?" Annie asked as she closed the safe, slid the hard plastic back into place, then pushed the chair under the desk.

"Just voices. Sounded like men to me. There's a dentist and an insurance agency on this floor, but I can't believe someone came out in this weather to go to a dentist or to buy insurance. We can't leave until they leave, whoever they are. I was going to turn the lights out but decided to leave them on. The light might be reflected on that funny-looking door."

"Good thinking, Myra. Who did you get hold of?"

"Jack. Harry is with him, and they're at the house in Georgetown. Jack said it took him almost three hours on foot to get home. The babies are supposed to be taken to Maggie's house. They're there to help. Ted and Espinosa are on the way. Jack said he's been trying to call Nikki and Charles, but there's no signal. He did get hold of Maggie, who is still at the paper. She is sitting tight and doesn't want to attempt the trip home. Jack says we should stay put for a little while since this phone is our only means of communication."

"Well, I don't agree with Jack on that. I think we need to get out of here, and the sooner the better," Annie snapped. "Sit tight, Myra. I'm going to see if I can find out what's going on out in the hallway."

"Annie, don't!" She might as well have saved her breath. Annie was up and running to the reception area, where she cracked the door and peered out. She clamped her hand over her mouth and ran back to where Myra was waiting for her.

"It's the police. Three officers and two other guys. Not the guard, though. They're arguing about something, but I couldn't hear what it was all about. Shit! Shit! Shit! That's what Kathryn would say, isn't it? Myra, what are we going to do if they come in here?"

"Do I have to remind you this was your idea?

Bearing that in mind, I do have a solution. Look!" Myra said, pointing to the Santa suit hanging on the back of the door. "Get some pillows off that chair, and let's get dressed. Move, Annie!"

Annie stared at her old friend. "But, Myra, there's only one Santa suit!"

"There's an elf outfit behind it. Stop talking and get dressed. Hurry. I'll tie the pillow around your waist with my scarf. We can do this, Annie," Myra said when she noticed Annie's glazed eyes. "Damn it, Annie. I said, *'Move!'*"

Within minutes Myra and Annie were zipped, stuffed, and Velcroed into the Santa and elf suits. Annie was pulling on the shiny black boots when the door to the office opened. Five men, three of them police officers, stood in the doorway.

Myra whirled around and said, "Baron, your beard needs some more latex. I left it on the sink. Hurry, or we'll be late." She whirled back around and asked, bold as brass, "What can I do for you, Officers? We're running late with the snow and all, but we did promise the kiddies over at Georgetown Hospital we would be there. Now, where did I put that green sack? Oh, here it is."

"Sorry, Miss Harriet, but Mr. Bell called a while ago and said he thought someone broke into his office," a man dressed in a mackinaw said.

"It wasn't Mr. Bell. We've been here all morning," replied Myra. "Actually we spent the night here because Mr. Bell's car wouldn't start and I live too far away and today was so important and you know how Mr. Bell is when it comes to Santa and not disappointing the children. Feel free to look around. Baron, what *is* the problem? Excuse me, gentlemen, while I help Santa with his beard. The dry cleaners cleaned it, and it just isn't feeling and fitting right."

"No problem," one of the officers said as he looked around while a second officer took Myra up on her offer. The guard, who was out of uniform, was busily explaining to the third officer about Baron Bell and his Christmas schedule. The fifth man, who said he was an insurance agent, remained mute.

"A day doesn't go by during the Christmas season that Mr. Bell and Miss Harriet aren't parading around in those outfits. The kiddies love it," the guard said happily.

The officer who was checking out the suite of rooms moved closer to the bathroom. "Sorry to have bothered you. Merry Christmas!"

Annie gave her beard a jerk and, managing a rumble from deep in her gut, replied, "Ho! Ho! Ho!"

The guard laughed and said, "Mr. Bell is such a card. He gets right into the spirit of the holidays."

When the office door closed behind the men, Annie sagged against the old-fashioned sink. "That was way too close for comfort, Myra!"

"You think? Try this on for size, Annie, dearest. That cop who was making the rounds looked at me a little too close. Didn't you hear what the guard said? Mr. Bell called them. That has to mean Mr. Bell thinks Adel Newsom is or was coming here. Don't ask me how that could have happened, but it's the only thing that makes any kind of sense. I have a feeling they're coming back.

"That cop's eyes were a little too sharp for my liking. It was almost like he thought he knew me but didn't know where he knew me from. For all we know, those officers might be calling Georgetown Hospital right now to see if we're scheduled to make an appearance. We're going to have to take the stairs all the way to the basement level and make our way in these outfits to the *Post* apartment."

Annie didn't have to be told twice. She was at the office door before Myra could turn around. "We're going to freeze out there in these getups."

Myra tossed her the down jacket as she slipped into her own.

On the way down the steps in the oversize black boots and Santa outfit, Annie managed to come alive. "Tell me our sleigh with eight tiny reindeer will be waiting for us when we open that door."

"Will you settle for a SWAT team and assault rifles?"

Hours before and hundreds of miles south as the crow flies, Charles Martin found himself in the unenviable position of trying to come to a decision. He looked at one of his old friends, Reginald Clapper, a comrade from the old days when he, Avery Snowden, and Clapper worked for the queen. Retired now, like Charles and Avery, he was just glad to be back in the game no matter how small the job.

Reginald Clapper, Reggie to Charles and Avery, looked worried. "Don't even think about it, Charlie. Conditions are beyond horrendous. The fact that you couldn't get that damned snowmobile started ought to tell you something. It's an omen, I tell you.

"You'll kill yourself if you try skiing down that mountain. When was the last time you were on skis? A lifetime ago, I'd wager. I don't care how good you were back in the day. This is now and you're a hell of a lot older and your bones know it. There's no visibility out there."

"I don't have a choice, Reggie. All our communication has been wiped out. I'll take the dogs. Just tell me where you left the Hummer."

Reggie Clapper stood with his back to the fire as he did his best to plead his case. "If you kill yourself, what good are you going to be to the women? Think about the dogs. Give it a few more hours, Charlie. This storm can't go on forever. Please. Look, my friend, you don't have to keep proving yourself to Myra and the ladies. You hit a bad patch a while ago. They understand. If they didn't understand, Myra wouldn't be marrying you. I hate to think Myra will be standing at the altar, waiting for a groom who is a no-show because he was too damn stubborn to listen."

Charles just shook his head. "I've given it too many hours already. It's up to you, Reggie, to hold the fort. Keep trying to raise someone on the phones. The generators are working, so you aren't going to freeze, and the firewood is stacked to the ceiling. There's plenty of food. After you install that . . . that contraption and make damn sure the bolts are solid, then you can bring in the Christmas tree and set it up. We cut it down the other day, and it's sitting on the porch outside the kitchen so the branches would loosen up and drop into place. If we . . . if things go awry . . . you know what to do."

"Damn it, Charlie, can't you wait just a little while?"

Charles clapped his old friend on the back. "No. I have to go. The dogs will lead me to the bottom. Just keep trying to raise someone and tell them I'm on the way."

"You have a good six hours to go once you hit the bottom, Charlie. That's if the roads are in a drivable condition, which we both know they won't be. We're looking at ten hours here. The women might come up with alternate plans and implement them in ten hours' time. As you've said time and again, they're very resourceful."

"I don't think Mother Nature is interested in resourcefulness today for some reason. Sorry, Reggie. I have to go." Charles whistled for the dogs, and they came on the run. He was surprised that they allowed him to outfit them in

Yoko's wool sweaters. It was almost as if they knew what they had to do and were cooperating. Treats in his pockets, a water bottle in one of his vest pockets, flashlight in another, Charles clapped Reggie on the back. "You'll see me when you see me."

Reggie Clapper stood at the window and watched until the snow swallowed Charles and the dogs. He offered up a prayer, dressed himself to cross the front courtyard, where he first built a fire, then got to work on installing the heavy pole in the center of the big room. He took a moment to wonder how the ladies were going to decorate the pole. Women had such strange ideas when it came to decor. It never once occurred to him that what he was installing was a stripper pole.

His heart thundering in his chest, Charles started his descent down the mountain, Murphy and Grady in the lead.

Thirty minutes later he was at the base of the mountain. He offered up a prayer before he made his way to the military Hummer that guaranteed to take him anywhere he wanted to go in any weather condition. He used up another twenty minutes storing the skis and his boots and drying off the dogs. He turned on the engine and cranked the heat as high as it would go before he climbed back out to clear off the ice and snow from the front and back windshields. By the time he got behind the wheel, the heater was spewing out warm heat. He handed out chew bones to the dogs, talked to them a minute or so before he shifted into reverse, and headed out to the highway, where Lady Luck smiled on him a second time with a stretch of highway that had just been plowed and sanded. The huge tires of the Hummer gripped the road, and Charles was on his way, the dogs sleeping peacefully in the backseat, curled up next to each other.

Charles prayed that the sanitation workers along the route he was driving were as on top of the storm as the North Carolina road crews.

"I'm coming, Myra," he muttered over and over as he blasted down the road.

Chapter 12

By the time Myra and Annie made their way to the *Post* apartment building, both women were exhausted, physically as well as mentally. Myra held the door open with her shoulder as Annie trudged past her. "I have never, ever in my life been this cold or this exhausted. These damn boots have given my blisters other blisters."

"My feet feel like two blocks of solid ice in these ridiculous elf slippers," Myra said wearily as she pushed the elevator button.

Both women sighed with relief when the elevator door swished open.

"Look, Myra, there's the door. I can see it from here. All we have to do is walk twenty feet, and we'll be warm again. You don't think we'll get pneumonia, do you?" Annie asked fretfully as she took Myra's arm and clomped her way to the door, where she pressed her thumb to the doorbell and held it there. When it didn't open immediately, she screamed, "Open this damn door right this minute!"

A heartbeat later the door was opened by Kathryn, with a gun in her hand. Another heartbeat later both women's feet left the floor. The black boots stayed by the door, as did the elf slippers.

The Sisters were rushed to the two bathrooms in the apartment, stripped down, and shoved into steaming showers.

"Who are those women tied to the table legs?" Myra asked from behind the foggy shower door.

"The two surrogates. Snowden's people brought them here. We took over and they left," Nikki said.

"What about Baron Bell and his paramour?" Myra asked.

"I don't know, Myra. Our only contact with the outside world is through Maggie. None of our special phones are working. The cable isn't working either. It's a good thing there's a landline in this apartment, which, by the way, is not too shabby for a corporate overnight stop. It works for a while, goes dead, then comes back on. Right now it isn't working. This apartment is no frills. You know what I mean. No pictures, no doodads, no green plants. But it has two bedrooms, two full baths, and the fridge has food in it thanks to Snowden's people." Nikki knew she was babbling but couldn't seem to stop herself.

"Does this place have a washer and dryer?" Myra asked.

"It does. One of those stackable apartment things. Why?"

"Dry the Santa suit and beard and the elf suit. We might be needing them."

"Okay. Do you want hot coffee, hot chocolate, or hot tea?"

"Coffee, dear. Thank you."

When Nikki made her way to the kitchen, she found the Sisters huddled up against the refrigerator. She waited until the swinging door settled into place before she spoke. "Myra said to dry the outfits, and she wants coffee."

Isabelle pointed to the dryer, which was humming softly. She then pointed to the coffeepot.

"What now?" Kathryn asked. "I haven't heard a word from Bert. It's like we're caught in a time warp, and there's no way out. There has to be a way to get in touch with the guys. Do any of you have any ideas?" She walked over to the window and looked out at the storm, which was blanketing everything in sight. "I don't mind telling you I'm worried. All of this," she said, pointing to the snow outside, "is beyond our control. I don't like it when we have no control. Way too many things can go wrong."

"Shhh," Yoko said, her finger to her lips. "I'm calling Maggie. The line just started working again."

The silence in the kitchen was deafening as Yoko listened to Maggie's latest update. When she hung up the kitchen phone, she said, "She can't get anyone on the mountain. She can't reach Ted, Espinosa, or Harry and Jack, but she does know that Harry was with Jack, and Ted and Espinosa were on their way to her house to help with the arrival of the babies. But she said that was hours ago. She assumes they're in position. No news as to whether the babies arrived or not. She spoke to Bert a little while ago, and he's still in the Hoover Building. But he did make arrangements to have a snow truck with a plow break down in front of this building. That's how we get out of here, assuming we get out. That's it! She did want to know if Myra and Annie were okay. I said yes."

As if to prove they were okay, Annie and Myra appeared in the doorway. Both women reached for the steaming coffee cups Isabelle was holding.

"I see our supplies arrived," Annie said, motioning to the outer room.

"Everything was here when we arrived. This is going to be one giant fiasco if Snowden's people don't find Baron Bell and Adel Newsom," Nikki said. "What time is it?"

"It's after eight. And it's still snowing," Yoko said, her voice sounding ominous.

Annie thought Yoko looked like someone who was holding a lit stick of dynamite with only an eighth of an inch to go before the explosion. "I think it will taper off soon, honey. Let's all just try to think positive. Have the two . . . uh . . . ladies tied to the dining-room table said anything?"

"When we got here and they saw us, they were screaming and yelling, but once Snowden's men left, they clammed up and haven't said a word. Although they have been fixated on *our supplies.*

They can't seem to take their eyes off that delicious-looking stuff," Kathryn said. "However, they only whisper to each other."

"So at the moment we have no plan. Is that everyone's understanding?" Myra asked as she peeled a banana.

"At the moment, Myra," Nikki said. "But you know things can turn on a dime in a heartbeat." As if to prove the truth of her words, the two surrogates screamed as the front door flew open and all hell broke loose as four snow-covered people stumbled into the room.

The Sisters watched, bug-eyed, as Baron Bell slid across the polished wood floor, Adel Newsom right behind him. Both cursed loudly and ripely at the indignity they were undergoing. Avery Snowden, Charles's man in charge, gave Bell a swift kick. Bell slid farther across the floor. Newsom curled into a ball and whimpered as the two surrogates clutched fiercely at one another, their eyes full of fear.

"They're all yours, ladies!" Snowden announced.

Myra followed the two men to the door and whispered to Avery, "Has there been *any* word from Charles?"

Snowden shook his head as he squeezed her arm. "No, I'm sorry. I can't even raise my people. We're all flying blind here, sad to say. I have my people scattered, so to that extent, everyone is where they're supposed to be. It's the getting from point A to point B that is our immediate problem. I want to commend you on making it here at all. I can't ever remember being on a mission with weather conditions the way they are right now."

"Where are you going now, Avery? How is it you managed to capture those two?"

"Dumb luck on our part. I had a man on Newsom. He told us where Bell usually holes up when he spends the night in town. We got there just as he arrived. We snatched him before he could blink. Right now we're going to do our best to get to the *Post,* and from there we'll head to Georgetown. I have two of my people trying to scrounge up some snowmobiles. If they're successful, we'll do what we can for the crew bringing in the babies. For all we know, they might be safe and sound in Ms. Spritzer's house. Since we don't know what the situation is, we have to forge ahead and do what we can. Be careful, Myra, and don't take any unnecessary chances. Charles will draw and quarter me if anything happens to you and the other ladies."

Myra did her best to smile, but it was a lame attempt. Snowden squeezed her arm again and left the apartment. Myra felt like crying, but she stifled the feeling as she made her way back to the dining room, where she dropped to her haunches and brought her face to within an inch of Baron Bell's ruddy face.

"Listen to me very carefully, Mr. Bell, and you others, listen, too. Because of your nefarious activities, a great many people have been put in harm's way this evening. It's short of a miracle that all of us are safe for the moment. Outside, fighting the elements, there are dozens of people who are trying to make things right because of all the wrongs you four committed. We know there are more of you, and we will find them, maybe not today or tomorrow, but we will find them. If I were you, I'd start praying right now that the babies, all two dozen of them, are safe and ready to be returned to the parents who helped bring them into the world, their rightful, real, adoptive parents."

"I want a lawyer," Baron Bell bellowed.

The Sisters burst out laughing before Kathryn stomped her foot on Bell's neck. "You aren't getting it, are you, Mr. Slimeball? You don't get a lawyer. What you are getting is seven judges who make up a seven-panel jury who will decide your fate. Are you getting it now?" She raised her foot slightly, just enough to allow Bell to speak.

Bell, faster than a snake, grabbed Kathryn's ankle and was about to topple her when Yoko reached down to send him airborne. Bell landed with a thud against the far wall. A picture with a glass frame crashed to the floor, shards of glass flying in all directions.

"Oh, my God! You killed him. You people are insane!" Adel Newsom screeched. A second later she was lying on top of Baron Bell.

Yoko smiled.

The Sisters scooted over and peered down at the dazed couple.

"You were saying . . . ?" Kathryn said.

"What do you want?" Newsom whined.

"Shut up, Adel," Bell snapped. "In case you

don't know it, these women are the vigilantes. You should know what they're capable of. They've been splashed over the papers for years. You even told me once you admired them. Do you admire them now, you stupid bitch?"

One of the surrogates took that moment to come alive. "The vigilantes!" she screeched.

"We're all going to take your . . . discomfort, your tart mouth as a compliment," Kathryn said as she eyed Newsom. "From you, we want nothing. We went to your house in Rehoboth and took all your files from the freezer. That was so . . . Stupid doesn't even cover it. Even low-level drug dealers know about hiding stuff in freezers. It's what Mr. Bell has that we want. We opened his safes—that's plural—earlier this evening, and there was nothing of value in either one. However, someone other than ourselves also opened them, because there were puddles of melted snow in front of the safes. And, Mr. Bell, yes, we knew about the safe in the floor under your desk. You can say something now."

"Like I'm going to tell you anything! Ha! Wait till my friends at the White House hear you kidnapped me," Bell blustered. "They'll be all over you like fleas on a dog. I'm part of the current administration."

Isabelle dropped to her knees and tweaked Bell's nose. "That's not what we heard. You're about to be banned from the White House on orders from President Connor. You can thank Ms. Fox, the new chief White House counsel.

Get used to the idea that no one, and I mean no one, is going to come looking for you."

"Oh, Isabelle, that's not true!" Alexis singsonged. "The FBI and the local police are hot on his trail. The *Post* is set to run an exposé of him and Newsom and those two college girls over there. They're going to be famous household names!"

"More famous than us?" Yoko pretended to pout.

"Never!" Annie said dramatically.

Nikki tilted her head to the left to indicate that the Sisters should relocate to the kitchen. She turned and called over her shoulder, "Move, and we'll kill you!"

Newsom started to sob; the surrogates continued to cling to one another as they sniveled and mewed like sick kittens. The Sisters turned a deaf ear to all of them as they entered the kitchen.

"What now?" Nikki asked. "It's almost ten o'clock. We need to make some plans. We can't just sit here with those scuzzy people and do nothing. Maybe we should try and make our way to Georgetown. If the snowplow truck is really out front, we could take it and take those creeps with us. It's better than sitting here doing nothing." Nikki turned to Kathryn. "Since you drove an eighteen-wheeler, do you think you could drive that kind of truck?"

"Absolutely," Kathryn said.

"We need to vote," Yoko said.

"No one wants to leave here more than I do,"

Myra said. "If we leave, no one will be able to reach us. At least if the phones come back on, they know they can reach us here. This is where we're supposed to be."

"Myra has a point," Annie remarked.

"We could split up," Isabelle said. "Three in the truck, four stay behind."

"Then the four who stay behind have no means of transportation from this location," Alexis said.

"Another good point," Annie said, "which means as much as we don't like it, we have to stay put. At least for now."

"Well, then, let's make good use of our time by grilling our guests," Nikki said.

Myra chewed on her lower lip. "Annie, I have the strangest feeling that Charles is trying to get in touch with me. I don't mean on the cell phone. I mean," she said, whispering in Annie's ear, "the way Barbara gets in touch with me."

"Good Lord, Myra, don't say something like that!" Annie cried. "Getting in touch . . . that way would mean Charles is dead."

"No, no, Annie, he's not dead!" Myra assured her. "No, he's doing that thought transference thing. I know how . . . silly that sounds, but I *feel* it. I really do. It's a good feeling, Annie."

"Oh, well, in that case, home in on him and maybe he'll get a message to you. I'm going to take the clothes out of the dryer. I wonder if the Christmas party is still on tomorrow," Annie mumbled.

* * *

Myra wasn't wrong in what she was feeling. Charles Martin, less than a mile away, was saying over and over, "I'm coming, Myra. I'm coming." He stopped his litany just long enough to stare at the building he was approaching. At first he thought he was seeing things, possibly becoming delusional, but within seconds he knew Lady Luck was riding on his shoulder. The *Post* building!

Charles steered the Hummer as close as he could get to the curb, which was piled high with snow. He turned off the engine and got out, then climbed and waded his way over the mountain of snow to the sidewalk, where the snow was thigh deep, then to the door, the dogs alongside him. He pushed and shoved and finally got it open. He literally fell through the revolving door onto the marble floor, the dogs jumping over his prone body. He got up and ran as fast as he could to the elevator, which, magically, was working. He pressed the button for Maggie's floor and sucked in his breath. The moment the elevator door opened, he bellowed at the top of his lungs, *"Maggie!"*

Hearing her name ricocheting around the empty newsroom, Maggie blinked, then blinked again. "Charles! Oh, my God! Charles, is it really you? How did you get here? What's going on? Are the dogs all right? Is everyone okay? I can't believe you're here! Come with me. I just made some coffee. No one is here but me. I sent everyone home so they could be with their families. Oh, Charles, I haven't heard from anyone," she said breathlessly. She gave each of the dogs a stale doughnut and watched as they gobbled them down. She then filled a bowl with water and set it on the floor. Both animals drank greedily.

"I know. That's why I'm here. I have a vehicle. How far is it to the apartment where the girls are?"

"Six blocks. Here, drink this hot coffee, and we can leave. I was afraid to chance it, or I would have gone myself. Where did you get a car?"

"I had one of Avery Snowden's men doing some work on the mountain. He stayed behind, and I used his Hummer. I got lucky and managed to get behind a snowplow and followed it on the interstate. I thought I would never get here," Charles said wearily. "I'm ready. Can we go now?"

"Just as soon as I put my boots on. I'm so glad you're here, Charles. This is all going to work out, isn't it?"

"I hope so, Maggie. If it doesn't, it won't be for lack of trying."

Maggie shivered as she thought about Murphy's Law.

Chapter 13

Jack Emery threw an extra log on the fire and watched the flames shoot upward. "Stand by the fire, Harry. You'll warm up in a minute. I cranked the heat up to ninety. God, I have never been so cold in my entire life. I'm going to heat up some chicken soup. We'll both be good as new in a few minutes. First, though, I'm going to warm up some socks in the dryer. My mom always used to say 'If your feet are warm, you're good as gold.' Maggie says that, too, so it must be true." He was babbling, but he couldn't seem to stop himself. Moreover, he didn't care.

Harry had his backside to the fire, a look of pure ecstasy on his face. "You talk too damn much, Jack. Just do it before we die of hypothermia."

Like Harry even knew what hypothermia was. Jack hustled. He tossed two pairs of socks in the dryer and within minutes had two cups of chicken soup heating up in the microwave oven. He carried the socks and soup into the living room and handed Harry's over to him. "Once our insides are warm, we'll be okay. I think," he said.

Harry sat down on the raised hearth and pulled on the warm socks. His eyes rolled upward in sheer delight at the delicious warmth. "The damn weatherman said to expect snow flurries. What's going on out there is not snow flurries."

"I know, Harry. I know," Jack said soothingly. "Sometimes they don't get it right."

"They never get it right," Harry snarled. "What are we supposed to do now? Do you have any *food?*"

Sensing a Harry meltdown, Jack said, "I do, Harry. You just sit here, and I'll pop some dinners in the microwave. While I'm doing that, see if you can get in touch with anyone on the landline." The words were no sooner out of his mouth than the doorbell rang. "Shit! Who could that be?"

"Try opening the door, and you'll figure it out," Harry said as he plucked at the numbers on the phone in his hand.

Jack threw open the door to see Ted and Espinosa covered in snow. "Why are you standing there? Get in here, and take off your boots and socks. I know just what to do. Go on in. Harry's by the fire."

From that moment on, Jack was busier than a posse of squirrels storing their food for the winter. When he returned to the living room with warm socks, heated blankets, and a tea cart loaded down with food, he said, "Your goddamn paper said we were going to have snow flurries. There has to be ten inches of snow out there. Maybe more."

Ted bellowed in outrage, his teeth chattering, "So, you're blaming me for all this snow! Is that what you're saying?"

Jack sniffed. "Well, it *is* your paper!"

"No one is answering, Jack. Annie and Myra obviously didn't listen to you and left Bell's offices. Maggie is the only one who answered, and she hasn't heard from anyone." Harry narrowed his eyes and stared across at Jack. "That means we do not have a plan. We need a plan."

Jack opted to take the high road. "Then come up with a plan, Harry. I'm all ears. And, it goes without saying, I am at your disposal. I think I speak for Ted and Espinosa as well. So, Harry, let's hear it."

"I'm working on it, Jack. I sure as hell can't do worse than you did with those stupid pumpkins in Utah."

"Well, Harry, those pumpkins, stupid or not, worked, now didn't they?" Hoping to divert Harry and erase the murderous look on his face, Jack looked over at Ted and Espinosa. "Did you guys decide about your Christmas gifts for the girls?"

"I did!" Espinosa said. "I e-mailed the ladies, and they're going to gift wrap the earrings in a white satin box and send them by overnight mail. I'm done, and twenty tons have been taken off my shoulders. Gold wrapping paper with a green satin bow. I gave my credit-card number, and bing, bing, bing, it was done. Patsy e-mailed me and said it was a pleasure doing business with me."

"Me too," Ted said. "Jill said I get silver paper and red velvet ribbon. Maggie is going to love it. I'm done. How about you, Harry? What did you decide? What about you, Jack?"

Jack decided it was time to play host. He stacked the TV dinner trays on the tea cart, along with the empty cups. "I haven't decided," he mumbled.

"You know why the son of a bitch hasn't decided? Because he's probably going to get a discount on his gift for sending the ladies new customers. Ain't that so, *Jack?*" Harry said through clenched teeth.

"No, that ain't so," Jack sniped. "For your information, I am buying Nikki ten one-pound boxes of See's Candies. She loves their milk-chocolate orange creams. Ten boxes, gentlemen!"

Ted let loose with a loud guffaw. "Candy! Tell me you aren't serious? Even *I* know candy won't cut it. Women want something of substance, something they can pawn if things go awry. I know this because Maggie explained it to me. She also told me something else. If you value your life, do not ever, as in ever, give your girlfriend something with a plug on the end. Presents with plugs on the end are the kiss of death to a relationship. I thought you knew everything there was to know about women! Ha!"

Harry looked like he was in agony as he

turned first to Ted and then to Jack and Espinosa as he tried to make sense of what he was hearing.

Jack was saved from making a comment when the phone on the end table rang. All four men looked at each other, and yet no one made a move to answer it.

"I think you should answer that, Jack," Espinosa said. "It might be Charles—you remember Charles—who just might have a plan we can implement."

Jack picked up the phone. "Yes, sir, I can hear you just fine. Yes, sir." He mouthed the words *my boss* for the others' benefit. "I don't know what I can do, sir. I had to leave my car in town and walked home. Georgetown hasn't been plowed. I don't have snowshoes, sir. I understand every police officer, every reserve officer, every retired officer has been called in to help. Even the FBI? I didn't know that, sir. CIA, too. That leaves the Secret Service, and you know how those guys hate us locals. I don't understand why the Secret Service boys would think a terrorist attack might be in the offing with this weather. Well, yes, sir, there is paranoid, and then there is paranoid. The Christmas party at the White House is still on, and they have to deal with Santa Claus. Yes, I understand Santa Claus and the kiddies are a top priority. What do you want me to do, sir?"

Jack's eyes went from wild to glazed as he listened to his boss. "I have three friends here, sir. I suppose . . . Yes, sir, I am an officer of the court and will do exactly as you say. I will deputize all three of my friends. I'm happy to be of help, and I'm sure they . . . my friends will be just as happy." Jack wondered how his boss would know they would understand, because Harry was going to kill him, and Ted and Espinosa would bury him in the snow, and his body wouldn't be found till the spring thaw.

Jack looked at his friends, who were staring at him with deep hatred. He sucked in his breath and held it for a moment. "Sir, there are no vehicles to commandeer, and if there were vehicles to commandeer, they wouldn't be able to move in this snow." He listened again, his face turning white. "That does sound rather like a plan, sir, but how will you get them here? I'm not sure my friends know how to ride horses."

Harry, his own eyes glazed over, balled his hand into a fist and drove it into one of the logs sitting on the hearth. Splinters of wood shot in every direction. Jack tried not to look at Ted and Espinosa, who were dancing in all directions, waving their hands and shaking their heads. He took their antics to mean they were not going to ride horses no matter what he said.

"Yes, sir, I'll wait for your call as to the delivery of the . . . the animals." Jack broke the connection and said, "Boy, it's hot in here, isn't it?" And then he was on the floor, being pummeled and pounded to within an inch of his life. "Damn it, hold on. You're choking me. Let me catch my breath. After that, you can beat the shit out of me for all I care. It wasn't my order. It was the

DA's order. Look at me, all of you! You are officially deputized as of this minute. Now, go ahead and kill me. They'll execute you for killing me. You know that, right?"

"What? You think we're stupid? You have to read us something official. Then you have to give us a badge or something," Ted said.

"In normal circumstances, yes, you're right. However, as my boss pointed out, these are not normal circumstances. You'll get a commendation and an official deputy badge when this is over. So will your . . . uh . . . horse."

Espinosa rolled over on the floor. He looked to Jack like he was going to cry. "I've never been on a horse."

"So what! You say giddy-up, and the horse does the rest. How hard can that be?" Jack demanded.

"Where do we get weapons?" Ted asked.

"Who said anything about weapons?" Jack replied. "I have one, and I'm the full deputy. You do not get a weapon. Harry, now, is different. Harry is his own weapon."

"Let me make sure I have this right," Ted said. "Number one, we're deputies who are going to ride horses. Number two, we will not have a weapon to fight whatever crime and Santa Claus we're assigned to fight because your asshole boss gave you the authority to deputize us. Number three, we have nothing at all to say about this. Is that what you're telling us? Oh, and one other thing. Number four, what about the elves? Do we get to fight the elves, too?"

"Yeah, that's what it means. But I'm just the messenger. I bet if you call Maggie, she'll order you to do what I say."

Espinosa got up and walked into the kitchen. They could hear him rummaging in the kitchen drawers. When he came back, he said, "Take your pick, Ted. It's either a corkscrew or an ice pick. Harry doesn't need anything. Good old Jack here doesn't need anything, because he has a gun. Personally, I think we should just shoot good old Jack right now."

His face absolutely inscrutable, Harry finally decided to speak. "All of this for some damn Christmas party at the White House that those morons refuse to cancel. Remember Kalorama and how we dumped those Secret Service agents in the Dumpster? I'm thinking we might not have much of a welcoming committee. When do our trusty steeds arrive, *Jack?* I guess this is part of the plan we don't have. Sometimes, not often, but sometimes, I admit to being stupid. I thought we were here to help with the babies who are being transferred to Maggie's house. See, that was a plan, *the* plan, actually. So, if we're galloping off somewhere, assuming horses can gallop in snow, who is going to work or help out on the *real* plan?"

"I don't know, Harry. I guess we'll find out when the mounted patrol shows up at our door. *The* plan is illegal, first of all. There is no way in hell the DA could know, can ever know, I'm involved with the vigilantes. That's a whole other ball game. I have a job, a career, I get paid on a regular basis, and in order to keep getting paid, I have to do what my boss tells me to do. Obviously, we need to figure out some things. Ted, for starters, call Maggie, since she's the only one we can reach, and see what she has to say."

Harry sat down, assumed the lotus position, and stared off into space. Espinosa twirled the corkscrew round and round in his hands. Jack sighed and started to gather up the splintered wood, which he promptly threw into the fire.

Talk about being between a rock and a hard place.

Later, when the kitchen was tidied up and the guys were dozing in front of the fire, Jack stirred and walked into the kitchen. He was too antsy to sleep. He popped a Bud, turned, and bumped into Ted, who was opening the refrigerator.

"It's still snowing," Jack growled.

"And this surprises you why? Cable went out. So, guess it's campfire stories from here on in," Ted said.

Jack moved his beer bottle from one hand to the other. "Uh, listen, Ted, about that plug business. Were you serious about that . . . plug business, or were you jerking my chain?"

Ted whirled on a dime. "Are you admitting that right now, right this minute, I know more about women than you do? Ah, there is a God!" he said dramatically.

"Cut the bullshit, Ted. This is when guys have to stick together. I solved your problem with the diamond earrings, didn't I? Well, turnabout would be nice here as a show of good faith."

Ted lounged back against the refrigerator and grinned. "I like it that you're so desperate. What did you have in mind?"

"Maybe a Kindle, an iPod, something along those lines. They don't have plugs. Maybe a charger or something. I hardly think a charger would count. Batteries?"

Ted was in his glory as he contemplated his answer. This was a moment in time when he had one-upped his buddy, and he wanted to savor every minute of Jack's discomfort. He shook his head vigorously. "Patsy of Dorchester Jewelers said she had a one-of-a-kind diamond tennis bracelet as an alternative to the diamond earrings. It comes in a white velvet box with a white satin lining, but it was out of my reach dollarwise. Gift wrapped, of course. Snowflake paper. The snowflakes are dusted with glitter, and she said she would use a fine-mesh silver bow. Aren't you damn lucky I remember all this?

"Espinosa said Jill mentioned a diamond-studded cross on some kind of special chain, in case he didn't go with the earrings. So, you have two choices. Here is the way I see it. You *could* sell your car to pay for it. I don't think you have enough time to hold a garage sale, but it's a thought." Ted's expression turned solemn. "I worry about you sometimes, Jack."

"Eat me!" Jack snarled.

Ted let loose with a loud guffaw.

Back in the living room, Harry was still in the

lotus position, staring at something no one else could see.

Jack bent over, snapped his fingers, and said, "Earth to Harry. Look alive here. We need to confer. Like now."

Harry unwound his legs, stretched, and in one fluid motion was on his feet. He stared at Jack and observed in a hushed voice, "My ancestors tell me they have grand plans for you, Mr. Emery. That's the only reason you're still standing."

"Yeah, well, tell them to hold off on whatever they're planning, because we need to plan. This time I'm turning the floor over to the three of you since you never like my plans. So, let's hear it, hotshot! You're up, Harry!" Jack said, waving his arms magnanimously.

Chapter 14

Murphy and Grady hippity-hopped through the snow as they did their best to lead Charles and Maggie down the street and around the corner.

Charles was fuming. "I was gone only ten minutes, and they plowed in my Hummer! Unbelievable!" he snorted.

"Save your breath, Charles. I know for a fact there's a shovel in the closet at the apartment for just this reason. I bought it myself when I was living there temporarily and my car got snowed in. They were selling shovels on every street corner at the time."

"That doesn't help us at the moment, but I've made a mental note to bring the shovel with us when we leave. Are we even close, Maggie?"

"Up ahead," Maggie gasped as she concentrated on putting one foot in front of the other in the thigh-high drifts of snow. Not that she exercised, but if she did, she wouldn't have to do it for a week with the workout she was getting.

And then they were there. Murphy and Grady barked in relief as they raced toward the lobby door. Charles knew without a doubt that they were picking up their mistresses' scents inside the building. Inside the lobby, the shepherd and Lab did a crazy dance as they shook themselves to get rid of the snow. Charles thought it uncanny as they ran to the elevator and waited. Both were panting, anxious to get where they were going.

Maggie had the key to the apartment in her hand as they rode the elevator. The moment the elevator door slid open, the two animals raced down the hall and stopped in front of the *Post*'s apartment door. Maggie inched past the jittery dogs and inserted the key in the lock. She shoved the door open as far as she could, and the dogs did the rest.

"*Whoa!*" Maggie shouted, her hands shooting high in the air as she came face-to-face with seven women, drawn guns, their hammers clicking back in sync.

"For God's sake, Myra, take your finger off the trigger, and put the safety on before you kill someone!" Charles bellowed, knowing Myra couldn't hit a bus at ten feet if it was at a dead stop right in front of her.

"Maggie! Charles!" the Sisters cried in unison.

"Ooooh, I love you, too," Kathryn blurted out, laughing aloud as she cuddled with the huge shepherd while Alexis rolled around on the floor with Grady.

"What? How? What's going on?" The Sisters all started to babble at once as they helped Charles and Maggie with their outer gear. Yoko gathered up the pile of wet clothing and ran to the dryer as Nikki motioned everyone into the kitchen.

Myra ran to Charles and hugged him. "I *knew,* Charles. I knew you were trying to reach me. I just didn't think you'd come in person. It was like when Barbara comes to me," she whispered. "Oh, I feel so much better now that you're here."

Charles leaned over and kissed Myra's cheek. "Old girl," he said affectionately, "do you think for one minute I would let anything happen to you? I've been after you for thirty-five years, and you finally agreed to marry me. I'd go to the ends of the earth to find you." And that was as romantic as Charles Martin was going to get in front of an audience.

"That works for me, dear." Myra's eyes twinkled.

Kathryn cleared her throat and pointed to the trussed-up foursome, then looked at Murphy. "Guard, Murphy. If they move, if they sneeze, do what you have to do."

Alexis ordered Grady to do the same thing. Both dogs moved closer to their quarry, where they sniffed each of the four, walked around them, sniffed some more. Then both dogs sat back on their haunches, their teeth bared.

In the kitchen the Sisters, along with Charles and Maggie, brought each other up to date.

"Charles has a vehicle, but we need a shovel to dig it out. I saw the truck that Bert left for us. What's the plan?" Maggie asked.

Everyone started to jabber all at once.

Suddenly Nikki squealed, "Look, it's stopped snowing! That means we're going to be good to go by morning. Someone check the phones. How much snow do you think is out there, Charles?"

"More than a foot," Charles said as he squeezed Myra's arm.

"The way I see it, we have to make all that snow work for us," Kathryn announced. "Let's sit down and figure out how to do that."

"Cells are still out. Landline is up," Yoko said. "I'll try Maggie's house first, then Jack's. Just because ours is working doesn't mean theirs will be."

Five minutes later Yoko had her report. "Landlines still down in the District. I'm waiting for Lizzie to pick up now. Cosmo said she was showering." She held up her finger for silence when Lizzie started to talk. Yoko listened raptly, her tiny head bobbing up and down from time to time. She was smiling when she hung up.

"What? What?" the Sisters asked the minute Yoko hung up the kitchen phone.

"For starters, Nellie called Lizzie and told her how bad the weather was. She won't be heading to the mountain till next week, or whenever she gets plowed out from the farm. They are literally stranded, but she has a generator and plenty of food.

"Lizzie said she got through to Jack and Harry around eight o'clock our time. Ted and Espinosa had just gotten there. Harry said transportation was being provided for the four of them. By whom, she didn't say. She said she didn't know if the babies got to Maggie's house or not, but that they were traveling by ambulance. A whole fleet of them. They would get top priority on the roads and highways.

"The Christmas party is still on at the White House. Lizzie said the president called her at six o'clock, which would be nine o'clock our time. The party for the children will be in the Blue Room, whatever that is. The sleigh arrived this afternoon and is on the South Lawn, with a cover over it. She didn't know anything about the reindeer.

"She also said Cosmo cut down a giant tree, and they were getting ready to decorate it. She sounded incredibly happy, girls. Oh, she also said that just before she headed to the shower, she tried calling Maggie, but there was no answer. She knew about Bert sending the truck that's sitting outside. She said he is fine and will be at the White House tomorrow for the party. You all heard my end of the conversation as I told her about Bell and Newsom." Yoko laughed. "That's it."

"That means everyone is present and accounted for," Annie said. "I think we're all relieved, so it's time to crack those four nuts in the dining room. Let's rumble, girls!"

Myra raised her hand. "Since Charles has

never been . . . privy to what we do, and since he looks dead on his feet, I suggest that we send him off to bed before we commence our activities. I want to tuck him in personally, so while I'm doing that, girls, you can . . . warm up our guests."

"That'll work, Myra. Tootle on and don't be too long," Annie said, an evil glint in her eye as she advanced toward their four guests.

Myra led Charles down the short hall to one of the bedrooms. "You look exhausted, dear. I'll turn on the bed warmer while you get ready. The medicine cabinet has everything you need. Everything is new, so don't be afraid to use it. Thank you for coming, Charles. I was so worried about you."

Charles was so weary, all he could do was nod as he trotted off to the bathroom. When he was snug under the covers, he said, "Don't let me sleep too long, Myra. Keep my phones with you just in case they start working. Updates will be coming in quick and fast. I want your promise, old girl."

Myra moved her hand out of sight and crossed her fingers. "Okay, my dear. Sleep tight."

"Myra, are you really going to . . . learn how to use that . . . pole?"

"Of course. Go to sleep now."

"Will you tell me when the recital is?"

Myra giggled. "Absolutely."

"What are you going to wear?"

Myra really hadn't gotten that far in her

thinking. "Oh, a little of this and a little of that." She leaned over to kiss Charles good night, but he already appeared to be sound asleep. "I don't know what I'd do without you, my darling."

"I don't either, old girl."

Myra laughed out loud and closed the door softly behind her.

Back in the dining room, Myra stood to the side to watch the grilling of the foursome, which was already under way. Kathryn was in the lead at the moment and demanded that all four strip.

"You can't make me do that," Baron Bell blustered. Across from him, Adel Newsom had her arms crossed across her breasts, while the two surrogates were wailing at the tops of their lungs.

"You need to stop that infernal wailing, or I'm going to take a bat to those pricey porcelain caps that decorate your mouths," Isabelle said menacingly. The two surrogates sniffed, choked, and went silent. "And as for you, Madam Lawyer, none of us here care whether you have boob implants or not, so do as Kathryn says, and do it quick."

Apparently outraged, Baron Bell literally screamed, "Implants! You have implants!"

"Oh, shut up, Baron."

"She's right. Everyone just shut up and do what I tell you. Now strip!" Kathryn ordered.

Only Newsom started to unbutton her shirt. The two surrogates started to plead and beg to know what was going to happen to them.

"Well, for starters, tell us everything we need to know about these two sleazebags," Nikki said. "Tell us how you were recruited, how much you were paid, whose idea it was to take back your babies. The whole ball of wax. Talk slowly and distinctly. Each pearl that drops from your lips will be recorded." Nikki pointed to the recording machine sitting on top of the dining-room table.

"This might also be a good time to tell you that we already have all of Ms. Newsom's records, but there are a few gaps we need to fill in. Mr. Bell here hasn't seen fit to turn over his records to us. Yet. But he will. Say your name, give today's date, and talk like your life depends on what you say. Which, by the way, it does." Nikki's voice sounded so cheerful that Bell cringed.

"My name is Joan Olsen. Today's date is . . . It was him," she said, pointing to Baron Bell. "He had regular seminars at Georgetown, and that's how he recruited us. He pretended to be interested in all us female law students. In the guise of helping us, promising us internships when we graduated, he'd take us out to dinner, for coffee, for drinks, that kind of thing. A few times that woman, Adel Newsom, was there. She was nice to us, too. They got us to confide in them. They were like a big brother and sister. At first.

"About three months after our first meeting, we were all having dinner at some fancy restaurant in town. The two of them had a flurry of calls. From time to time they would get up from the table and go outside to talk. One would go, then come back, then the other got a call, and so on and so on. Then they started to talk about these adoptive parents and how badly they wanted a baby. One thing led to another, and Newsom pulled out this yellow sheet of paper with a list of names. There had to be at least fifty names on the list. Next to each name was a sum of money. It was a lot of money. *She* said that was how much a surrogate got if she would agree to have a baby for a particular set of parents. She kind of offhandedly asked if I was interested. At first I said no. Then I thought about how much easier my life would be with that money. I'd been working two jobs, trying to study, getting by on little or no sleep. The bills kept piling up. They let it drop right there, and they both acted like they were disappointed in me. Dinner was over, and we went our separate ways.

"A few days later, Newsom called and asked if I had thought about the offer and did I want to change my mind. I said that I did. Then things kicked into high gear, and we were off and running. I met the people who would adopt the baby. They were a nice young couple, and I actually felt good about what I had agreed to do. They paid for everything, made sure I got all the prenatal vitamins, saw an ob-gyn once a month. They even took me to the doctor. They gave me a food allowance to make sure I ate properly. They bought me maternity clothes. They gave me presents. When I had the baby, they filled my room with flowers. They kissed and hugged me.

And then it was over. I went back to my life, a little sad, but I was happy I had done something nice for the Evanses. I thought that was the end of it, but it wasn't.

"I was leaving the law library one evening a few months later and waiting for me outside was Adel Newsom. She said she wanted me to sue the Evanses for the return of my child. I said no. She said yes. We argued right there on campus. I wanted to knock her silly, but I kept my temper. She gave me a card and said I was to go to that office the next day and that the lawyer there would represent me. She told me how much money I would get for filing the suit, and that then we would . . . privately place the baby for adoption with other, more suitable parents. That's what she said, 'More suitable parents.' The Evanses were more than suitable, and they had been very kind to me. She said they didn't have the money to fight a lawsuit, and the courts always gave the birth mother the baby. I held my ground for a few days, and she kept threatening me. She said she would post all kinds of garbage on the Internet and no one would hire me once I took the bar exam. I caved in and did it. I cried for days and days." She jerked her head in Donna Davis's direction and said that the same thing had happened to her the same way.

"This is a stupid question, but what did you do with the money?" Alexis asked.

Joan Olsen started to cry. "I spent the first money paying my tuition and rent. I never touched the rest. It's in the bank. I just couldn't bring myself to spend it. I was going to try and send it back to the Evans family. I didn't do that, though. I'm sorry about all of this. I really am."

"That's it! Or is there more?" Kathryn demanded.

"There's more. That bitch said she wanted me to have another baby and that the pay would be doubled. I ripped her a new one and shoved her out of my apartment and told her never to come back or I'd report her to the police. She threatened me with the Internet again, said she knew all the judges and lawyers in town, that kind of thing. I said I'd kill her if she did that, and I meant it at the time."

"And now?" Annie asked quietly.

"I'm hoping you do it for me," the surrogate said bitterly.

"Give me your bank account information," Nikki said. "If you really haven't spent the money, we'll go easy on you. If you lied, oh, well!"

"Don't believe a word she says!" Adel Newsom sputtered. "She jumped at the money. She tried to hold me up for double what she was offered."

"Yeah, right. The money's in the bank. Be my guest. Take it and give it back to the Evanses."

"You're up next!" Yoko said, prodding Donna Davis.

"My story is the same as hers. I spent the money. I bought a car." Donna Davis rattled off her bank account information, then said, "I have eight hundred fifty dollars in the account. Take it if you need it."

Myra motioned to the other Sisters that they should all head for the kitchen.

"Guard," Kathryn and Alexis said in unison. Both dogs barked as they circled the foursome, their ears straight up, tails between their legs, the ruffs on their necks on end. Murphy growled deep in his throat. Not to be outdone, Grady showed his teeth, which were pearly white and awesome looking.

"If the surrogates are telling the truth, I say let them go," Myra said. "My gut feeling is they got caught up in this and couldn't find a way out. If Newsom and the other lawyers she sicced on them threatened them with the Internet and exposure, the Olsen girl was right. No one would hire them. I've read horror stories about how things that are posted can ruin a person's life. They got caught up in a web. We could take the Davis girl's car, sell it, give the money to whomever it belongs, confiscate the Olsen girl's account, and be done with the two of them. I can almost guarantee they'll both take the bar exam and disappear forever. That's my thought. Do any of you agree with me?"

Seven hands, including Maggie Spritzer's, shot into the air.

"Let's go back in there and crack Newsom. She's the key, and she'll turn on Bell in the blink of an eye," Nikki said. "At least I hope she will."

Annie was an avenging angel as she marched into the dining room. She stood tall and hovered over their guests, who were reclining on the floor, their eyes full of fear. "Listen up! You've already seen what this little stick of dynamite is capable of," she said, motioning to Yoko. "Now, let me tell you what the rest of us are capable of. Myra, dear, will you do the honors? Our guests need to see what's in store for them. First one who talks gets a pass."

Before Myra could even begin her demonstration, Newsom pleaded, "You have my records. I don't have anything more."

"I'm not telling you anything, and I don't have any records. I've done nothing wrong. I demand you let me go. I'm due at the White House to play Santa in a few hours. They'll send out a search party for me."

"You are a pathetic little wimp, Mr. Bell," Kathryn said. "First of all, give it up. No one is going to come looking for you, and when we do get around to notifying someone to come get you, after we're finished with you, you will be in no condition to do or say anything. So, tell us where your records are right now, give us your bank account information, and we'll rethink that Santa Claus bit."

"Screw you and the horse you rode in on," Bell bellowed.

"I thought you were going to say that." Kathryn sighed. "Myra, he's all yours!"

Chapter 15

Jack Emery bolted upright, unsure what had awakened him. He looked around, but Ted, Espinosa, and Harry were still sound asleep under mounds of covers and pillows in front of the fireplace. He looked down at his watch: 4:00 AM. He looked over at the fire, which was still burning nicely but could use another log or two.

What was it that had woken him up? The landline hadn't rung. None of the guys were snoring. There were no animals in the house to make noise. Was it the total quietness? Did the house creak? Old houses, and this was an old house, made strange noises from time to time; settling, the old-timers called it. Jack looked toward the bay window and realized what it was that woke him. Blue and red flashing lights were arching off the walls. "Shit!" he groaned. The flashing lights could mean only one thing, the locals were out, and he was certain four horses would be waiting for him outside his front door.

Careful not to disturb the others, Jack untangled himself from the pile of blankets and padded over to the window. He blinked at the long line of ambulances he was seeing. He counted six. He looked around for the horses but couldn't see any. What he did notice other than the flashing lights was that it had stopped snowing. "Thank you, God!" he whispered.

After checking to see if the landline was back in operation, Jack made his way back to his sleeping buddies. He whistled sharply between his teeth, then bellowed, "Look alive, guys! I think the babies are here! There are six ambulances that I could see. There might even be more. C'mon, c'mon, up and at 'em, gentlemen!"

Harry sat up and did his best to smooth down his spiky hair. "You better not be telling me those goddamn horses are out there. Do we have time to shave and shower?"

"There are no goddamn horses out there that I could see," Jack answered. "That doesn't mean they aren't out there, Harry. I don't want to lie to you and have you grind me to a pulp over an error. No, you do not have time to shower and shave. You can, however, *freshen up* if you feel it's absolutely necessary. Chop-chop, guys."

"Eat shit, Jack," Harry snarled as he looked around for his boots and outerwear.

"This is a hell of a way to start the day," Ted grumbled. "Are the phones working?"

"No, nothing's working yet, but it stopped snowing, so that's a plus," Jack replied.

"I hate to ask this, but do we have a plan?" Espinosa inquired.

"Nope! Well, maybe we do, but I don't know what it is. Yet."

"I want to know where the horses are," Harry said, petulance ringing in his voice.

"Well, guess what, Harry? I do not have the answer to that question, and I don't give a shit if you like my answer or not. Get your ass in gear and let's go. Those people are waiting for us over there. We have a job to do, so let's just grit our teeth and do it."

"I never thought I would hate you at four o'clock in the morning, but I do. Do not come near my person at four in the morning ever again. Do you hear me, Jack?"

"I do, Harry. I really do. You have my solemn promise that I will never go near your person at four o'clock in the morning. Ever again. Right now you are not my favorite person either, but I am willing to put that all aside and overlook your surly attitude considering our current circumstances and the hour. The translation to that, Harry, is, you can eat shit, too."

"Will you two just knock it off already before one or the other of you kills someone, and Espinosa and I have to be witnesses," Ted said, stomping his way to the door. "I can't believe these damn phones are still out," he mumbled and muttered to anyone interested in listening to him.

"Whoa! Hey, be careful out here. I can't find

the steps! Damn, the drifts are over the tops of the cars. Tread lightly, boys!"

It took them a full twenty minutes to slog their way three doors down to Maggie's house, where they were greeted by the leader of the caravan of ambulances. He introduced himself as Archie Trumble, one of Snowden's men. "Mate, I am so happy to meet up with you. They're all yours now, and I can't say I'm sorry to get rid of this particular delivery. We just unloaded the last of the supplies. Good luck, mate!"

"Hey, hold on. Don't we need a little more information than you're not sorry to unload this particular delivery and all the supplies are in the house?" Jack asked, a worried frown building on his face.

"Nope, that's it. We just deliver. We have to get these ambulances back to where we . . . uh . . . borrowed them from. You following me, mate?" At the stupid look on Jack's face, Trumble said, "There's a crisis here in town, the ambulances are needed, and we stole them. Now, are you getting it?"

"Yeah, yeah. So are the nurses inside? They have it under control, right?" asked Jack.

"Not exactly, mate. Like I said, there is a crisis here. That means when all the power went out, we weren't able to arrange a pickup of the nurses. We're damn lucky we got the babies. They're all safe, and now they're your responsibility. No more time for chitchat, mate. See you in the funny papers."

Jack's jaw dropped as he watched first one ambulance, then the ones behind it, peel away. "Oh, shit!" He ran as fast as he could to Maggie's front door, where the boys were waiting for him.

There was panic in Harry's voice when he said, "I don't see any nurses, Jack. Where in the damn hell are the nurses?"

"So you're going to blame me for that, too! That schmuck in the lead ambulance said they just deliver. He kept saying there was a crisis and didn't we know it. They stole those ambulances, and now they have to take them back. Open the damn door already, Ted!"

Once Ted got the door open, the men dashed inside the house and skidded to a stop when they stared into Maggie's living room. Row after row of babies of indeterminate age were laid out, tied in bundles like papooses. All but one were wailing at the top of their lungs. Jack wanted to sit down and cry. Ted just gaped and chewed on his lip. Harry, Jack could tell, was somewhere in outer space.

Espinosa, however, was grinning from ear to ear. "I think I probably qualify as the person with the most experience where babies are concerned. I grew up in a family of eleven kids. I had to change diapers, bathe, and feed the little ones. So, for starters, let's get the heat turned way up, square away the diaper supply and the food, which in their case is formula since we have no breast-feeding surrogates in attendance."

Jack reached for Harry when it looked like he was going to black out. "Okay, Espinosa, you are officially in charge. Tell us what to do. How the hell do you get them to shut up?" he bellowed at the top of his lungs.

"You feed them!" Espinosa yelled. "We'll heat the bottles in the microwave. I think you can do that if you take the nipples off the bottles."

"You THINK!" Jack bellowed again. The babies continued to squall, even the one who had been previously quiet. "Their faces are red. What's wrong with them?"

"They're pissed off. That's what's wrong. They want to eat. Babies eat on a schedule," Espinosa explained. "I thought everyone knew that, even you, Jack. Come on. We have to warm up this milk. We'll worry about changing their diapers later. They squeal when they make messy poo poo."

"Poo poo?" Harry said, sliding to the floor, his eyes glazed.

"That's what you call it in polite company. Wouldn't want the little ones to hear nasty words," Espinosa answered.

Shaking his head in disbelief, Ted ran to the kitchen, his hands and arms full of bottles. "How long, Espinosa?"

"Thirty seconds," Espinosa called. "Then you squirt it on your arm to see if it's too hot or not hot enough."

"Yo, Harry, either you look alive here, or I'm telling Yoko you are *not* father material!" Jack said. "Just do what Espinosa says, and we'll get through this. C'mon, Harry, you can do this. Okay?"

Ted ran into the living room with the first batch of warm bottles.

"Lesson one-oh-one. Listen up. This is how you do it. The bigger babies at the ends of the lines can have their bottles propped up," Espinosa instructed. "Go, gentlemen!"

The ear-piercing din in the room lessened by six as the babies sucked greedily.

"Here's six more bottles," Ted shouted, getting into the swing of things. "Oooh, next batch coming up!"

"This one is finished," Harry said, getting into gear. "Oh, my God, I think it wants more! He's making a fist, and his face is getting red."

"He might be making messy poo poo," Espinosa commented. "Kind of soon, though. He probably just has gas. You have to burp him. Put him over your shoulder and pat his back. When he burps, lay him back down and give him more. He's not a sack of potatoes, Harry. Hold his head. Yeah, yeah, that's it. Good going, gentlemen! I am so proud of you!"

The only sound to be heard in Maggie's living room was the sound of contented babies burping.

"Hey, Espinosa, how often do you have to feed babies?" Jack asked.

"At the rate we're going, after the diaper change, they'll be ready to eat again. You have to wait ten to fifteen minutes so they can do messy poo poo. It's pretty warm in here now, so the bottles might get to room temperature and we won't have to warm them up. When a baby wants to eat, he wants to eat. Mothers can anticipate their child's hunger. I don't know how they do it, but they do. Mothers are the most wonderful people on this earth."

"Kill him now, Jack, or I will. Why can't you just say after they crap in their pants? Huh? Why can't you say that? We're grown men. We understand about crapping in your drawers. No one says messy poo poo. No one!" Harry bellowed.

"Because, Mr. Wong, that's what my mother used to say, and to repeat, your terminology is offensive sounding. I hope you get a really smeary one," Espinosa sniped. He walked along the rows of wide-eyed babies, who were staring up at the four giants towering over them. "Did we all burp?" he asked cheerfully.

"Mine all burped," Jack responded just as cheerfully.

"So did mine," Ted said proudly.

"Harry?" Espinosa said threateningly.

"All but this one," Harry said through clenched teeth. "Why is he holding out?"

"Shift him a little higher so his belly is on your shoulder. Pat him just a little harder," Espinosa replied.

Grimacing, Harry did as instructed. The loud belch ricocheted around the room. Harry looked at the little bundle in awe. He nodded to Espinosa to concede that he was indeed the undisputed authority on babies.

"How old do you think these kids are, Espinosa? How are we going to know which kid belongs to which set of adoptive parents?" Jack asked.

"They range from about two months to maybe six or seven months. The ones here at the end can almost hold their own bottles. They're all wearing ankle bands. See, the kid's name is on each one. It will be up to the girls to figure the rest out. Maggie has the list, and she knows who belongs to whom. She was supposed to call all the adoptive parents earlier today. I don't know if she did or not, since our phones went out."

Suddenly all the cell phones in the room rang, pealed, chirped, or sang, as did the phone in the kitchen. The babies as one started to howl their displeasure at the invasion of their solitude. And there was no shutting them up.

When the four giants moved off in different directions, the babies howled louder.

"I have to go, Nik. I'll call you back," Jack shouted.

"I had it under control until you called, Alexis," Espinosa shouted.

"What? What? I can't talk now. I have to clean up messy poo poo," Harry cried. "You heard me!"

"Wow! That took guts, Harry!" Jack said before he danced out of the way.

"Listen, Maggie, I don't care how big the bonus is, this sucks. Cats I can handle. Cleaning a litter box I can handle. I cannot handle shitty diapers. Good-bye and do not call me again," Ted said, slamming his cell shut.

"Suit up, men, it's diaper time!" Espinosa announced. "Look alive here. These are onesies. They're for the young little ones. These are threesies, these are sixies, and these bad boys are for those chunky ones at the end. Take your pick. For those of you who are not experienced in this endeavor, pay attention. Boys pee up, girls pee down, so unless you want a snootful, cover the boy's doohickey until you are ready to button him up. I'll give you a brief demonstration. These are called Wet Ones. You wipe their bums and their . . . privates with them. You then discard all the Wet Ones in this bag right here. Messy poo poo stinks after a while. Watch!"

Ted, Jack, and Harry watched in awe as Espinosa carefully undid a baby's diaper and reared back. "This is what I mean by a smeary one. You use your wrist, making sure you get everywhere you're supposed to get, and then you lift up this end, slide the diaper down, tug it into place, peel the tabs, and wallah, the baby now has on fresh pants."

"Oh, God, I don't want to do this. I can't do this!" Harry pleaded.

"Just breathe through your mouth, Harry," Jack said as he swiped and wiped and peeled. "Two down. You need a bigger sack here, Espinosa," he said when he was finished with his fourth diaper.

"Coming right up! See, that wasn't so bad, now was it?"

"I bet we could streamline this process," Ted said.

"Shut up, Ted. If it ain't broke, we ain't fixing it. We did it. And it only took us twenty-five minutes. That's one minute per baby. Well, maybe nine-tenths of a minute, since there are twenty-six babies here," Jack said. "When do they go to sleep?"

"Usually after they get their bath, but we aren't going to be doing any bathing, so relax, gentlemen. Although, I have to say, it is a very rewarding and bonding experience. That's why I am so close to my brothers and sisters. So, to answer your question, any minute now they should be nodding off." Espinosa pointed to the two babies at the end of a row who were already sleeping peacefully.

"Why do I feel like I just did fifty laps around a track?" Jack said, lying down on the floor. "A baby is a lot of work. Twenty-six babies is a hell of a lot of work. How much time do we have before they wake up again?"

Authority ringing in his voice, Espinosa said, "Well, if they were in their own beds, in their own environment, I'd say three hours. Here, I'd say we're going to be lucky if they sleep for ninety minutes. I have all the bottles lined up on the kitchen table, since that's the warmest room in the house. We can fluff out the diapers now so they'll be ready for the next change."

"Yeah, why don't you do that, Espinosa?" Harry said, lying down next to Jack.

"I'm calling Maggie to see what's going on," Ted said, walking to the front of the house. He took one look out the front window and raced back to the living room. "Hey, Jack, you better come see this. Our transportation is here!"

Harry started to swear in all his seven languages. Jack started to laugh and couldn't stop. Espinosa continued to fluff open diapers. One by one the babies started to howl, until there was a crescendo of noise.

Chapter 16

Martine Connor swung her legs over the side of the bed, wondering what it was that had woken her. The silence that surrounded her told her there was nothing going on. Her throat was dry, and she needed a drink of water. She looked at the red numerals on her bedside clock, which glowed like beacons in the dark room: 4:10. She would have gotten up in another twenty minutes anyway.

Martine rummaged around on the bedcovers until she found her old robe, a chenille one that she'd had forever and a day. It was worn, frayed, an old friend she would never part with. It even had matching slippers, which were just as old and worn, and just as comfortable.

She brushed her teeth, then shuffled her way to the kitchen, where she made her own coffee. She'd always been an early morning, two-cups-of-coffee-and-one-cigarette kind of person. Just because she was the president of the United States didn't mean she couldn't remain that kind of person. It was this quiet time that she liked, "being alone with the universe time," as she called it. While she sipped at her coffee, she reflected and made decisions.

While she waited for the coffee to drip into the pot, Martine walked over to the huge window that overlooked the White House lawn. It looked like daylight outside. She blinked when she saw the blanket of snow that covered everything. She didn't think she'd ever seen anything quite as beautiful as what she was looking at right at that moment. And it had stopped snowing. She wondered if she'd be able to make the trip to Camp David after the children's Christmas party this afternoon. Right after Thanksgiving, she'd made the decision to go to Camp David to spend the holidays. She wasn't sure if it was a good or bad decision; she just knew she had made the decision and was stuck with it.

Where was the sleigh? Martine ran from window to window to look out at the winter wonderland but could see no sign of the sleigh that had been there when she'd retired for the night. Was it covered with snow? Surely not. A deep frown built itself between her eyebrows. The fine hairs on the back of her neck seemed to be moving. Without stopping to think, she ran to the door, opened it, and asked the Secret Service agent standing outside what had happened to the sleigh.

"I'm not sure, Madam President, but I did hear some talk early in the evening that a crew was coming for the sleigh to take it back to the horse barn so the wheels could be removed. The sleigh has to be put on a lift so the undercarriage can be taken off. Wheels won't work with all this snow, which—as you know—was unexpected. I can call down to the office to find out for sure. Do you want me to do that, Madam President?"

"No, that makes sense. I just don't want anything to go wrong for the children's party today. Some of the kids are already here from neighboring states, so we can't disappoint them."

"No, you can't disappoint children at this time of year, Madam President."

"Thank you, Agent Morales."

Martine closed the door and walked back to the kitchen, where her coffee was ready. She poured a cup and carried it back to a deep, comfortable armchair by the bay window. She curled her legs up under her and sipped at her coffee, her mind going in all directions. The fine hairs on the nape of her neck still seemed to be at attention, which meant all was not well. She immediately thought of Lizzie, then Baron Bell. Well, after today Baron Bell would be just a memory. And come the first of the year, her chief of staff was just going to be a memory, too. She should have given him his walking papers the minute he defied her regarding the pardons, but because it was the Christmas season, she'd convinced herself the beginning of the year would be soon enough. She'd always deplored businesses that fired or laid off people during the holidays all because of the corporate bottom line for the end-of-the-year accounting.

Martine walked back to the kitchen, looked at the clock on the stove before she poured her second cup of coffee of the day. This was when she had a cigarette, something she was going to give up the first of the year. It was the only resolution she was willing to make. At this point in time.

Forty minutes later the president of the United States was sitting at her desk in the Oval Office, the fine hairs at the nape of her neck still dancing to their own tune. POTUS shivered.

Less than a mile away, at the horse barn in Georgetown, the missing sleigh was being raised on a lift as Avery Snowden's people prepared to remove the wheels that allowed the sleigh to move on asphalt. Waxed and oiled runners would be installed by competent hands. When the work was completed, the sleigh would be loaded onto a custom dolly, which would be wheeled out onto the snow so that the runners didn't touch the concrete floor of the barn.

The sleigh was huge, a beautiful, one-of-a-kind construction, specially ordered and crafted in Russia and shipped to Baron Bell some twenty-odd years ago. Once every five years, at his own expense, Bell paid to have one of the craftsmen come to the United States to repair the paint, redo the gilt, sand and wax the steel runners. They even tuned the bells that hung on strips of leather and adorned the horses' necks as they pulled the sleigh.

The inside of the sleigh held portable, battery-operated foot warmers. It was lined in plush red velvet; the seat covered in soft, buttery leather.

A sleigh fit for a king.

"How much longer?" one of the men shouted, the sound bouncing off the walls of the huge barn.

"An hour, tops. I've never seen bolts like these. Whoever did the work on this baby knew what he was doing. This sleigh is a work of art, that's for sure. It's big enough to hold ten people, maybe more. By the way, where are all the horses that live in this place? I counted sixteen stalls, and they're all empty."

"Out on patrol would be my guess," said a man bigger than an oak tree, who was busy on his BlackBerry, texting. The gist of the message was, what time do you want the sleigh to leave the barn? When will the horses arrive?

The text went to Charles Martin, who was sleeping, but it was Myra Rutledge who called for a break in Baron Bell's interrogation and responded by sending the text on to Jack Emery, who sent it to Bert Navarro, who sent it to Lizzie Fox, who stopped her Christmas-tree trimming to send the text on to POTUS, informing her the sleigh was ready for the Christmas festivities and would arrive on time. Then she sent the text on to Maggie Spritzer, not knowing Maggie was with the Sisters in the *Post* apartment.

The answer to the original text to Snowden's men was short and concise: Sit tight.

"We just got our orders, boys. We sit tight until told otherwise, so take your time with those bolts."

Maggie Spritzer looked down at her watch the moment she received the incoming text. She felt uneasy at the silence surrounding her. Even their captives were silent. Nikki motioned to the kitchen. Once again, the Sisters trekked into the kitchen to confer.

"It's almost six o'clock. We still haven't cracked Bell and Newsom," Nikki said. "We also need to make a decision on the two surrogates. Olsen was telling the truth. She didn't touch the money in the bank. It's been sitting there a few months. Davis, now, she bought a high-end car, when a much cheaper model would have served her purposes. If we put that aside and just take the car, I think we can turn them loose. I'll have them sign confessions of their parts in all this. Knowing that it will be hanging over their heads, I think they'll both stick to the straight and narrow. I wish we had the others in our sights."

The Sisters agreed, but it was Myra who said the surrogates weren't to be turned loose until the Sisters were safely away from the apartment. Once again, everyone agreed.

Maggie looked up from her furious texting to say, "If Newsom doesn't have the list, then Bell does. Drag it out of him. This is a first!"

"What?" Annie asked, alarm ringing in her voice.

"Ted isn't answering me," Maggie replied. "I just tried Jack and Espinosa, and they aren't responding either. Harry never responds to anyone but Yoko."

Nikki laughed so hard, she had to hold her sides. "That's because they're taking care of twenty-six babies. Snowden's men didn't deliver the nurses. They dropped the babies off, along with their diapers and formulas, and left. It was left up to the guys to take charge. I don't think it's going too well. Maggie, what's the story on the adoptive parents? What kind of arrangements did you make for the pickup?"

"It's been tricky since the cells went out," Maggie reported. "Before it happened, I did manage to get in touch with your firm's office manager. She did a lot of the calling. I did some, and there are only two sets of parents we weren't able to reach. We need a meeting place. Logically speaking, my house is the choice since the babies are already there. That gives me visibility, Jack as well, when everyone shows up at my house. The neighbors, for the most part, are a mind-your-own-business group, but something like this might whet their curiosity. Considering the current circumstances, I don't see us having much in the way of choices. What we need now is a time, so we can make our calls. Bear in mind the weather, the roads, and anything else that can go wrong. I don't care how busy he is. He should be texting me," she grumbled.

"Okay, girls, we've wasted enough time. Maggie is handling her end of things. Charles is sleeping, so let's get back to doing what we do best," Myra said.

The girls trooped back into the dining room. Both dogs barked as they released their prisoners to the women. While they both moved away, they remained alert and ready to be called to duty with a one-word command.

"Our guests don't seem to like obeying our orders," Kathryn said. "I find that rude, don't you, girls?"

"I certainly do," Isabelle said as she ripped at Adel Newsom's shirt. "The lady told you to strip, and you're suddenly going all prudish on us! What's up with that?"

"You're up, fat boy," Annie said as Bell tried squirming back against the wall. "I don't have any patience for this nonsense. Yoko, help this man out."

Yoko danced her way over to Baron Bell, leaned down, and squeezed his nose. He closed his eyes and went limp. Alexis and Nikki proceeded to undress him.

Kathryn eyed Adel Newsom. "We said to take *everything* off. That means the bra and panties. You can do it yourself, or we'll do it for you."

"What are you going to do to us? You have my records. I don't have anything else to give you. Please, this is so humiliating. What more do you want?" Newsom wailed as she removed her bra and panties.

"We want Bell's records," Kathryn said. "We want his bank accounts. If this was all his idea, you might get some leniency if you help."

"If I could, I would. For God's sake, why won't you believe me? I'm the one who was in his office. I have the combinations to both safes. I'm the one who left the puddles. I took some money, but there were no records. I swear to God, there were no files in either safe. That son of a bitch," Newsom said, jerking her head in Bell's direction, "left me stranded outside Rehoboth Beach. I had to hitch a ride with a trucker to get back here to town. I hate his guts. It was his idea, all of it. I did go along with it, I'm not denying that, but he got the bulk of the money. He even shortchanged the surrogates. We, the other lawyers and I, had to give him a percentage of everything we took in."

"So where does he keep his records?" Kathryn asked.

"I don't know. Probably home. Maybe a safe-deposit box. He led me to believe everything was in the safe built into the floor in his office. I know now that was a lie, like everything else he told me. That's why I took his money. Please, I'm freezing. Can I have a blanket?"

"No," Kathryn said.

Bell woke up in time to hear Newsom's last words. "You bitch, you stole my money! I hope you rot in hell!" Then he realized he was stark naked. He bellowed like a wild bull in heat.

"Give me my clothes! How dare you do this to me! How dare you!"

"Will you please just shut up?" Nikki said.

"Don't you dare tell me to shut up. Who do you think you're talking to?"

"Who do we think we're talking to? For goodness' sake, isn't it obvious we're talking to a naked guy with an itty-bitty little dick," the ever-blunt Kathryn said. "Hey, it rhymes." She giggled.

"It's getting light out," Alexis said. "It's almost seven o'clock."

Myra dropped to her knees. "Mr. Bell, my name is Myra Rutledge. I am going to ask you this once and only once. Nod if you understand."

"Kiss my ice-cold ass," Bell said.

"That was *really* rude, Mr. Bell. We do not tolerate rudeness. So, we're going to suit up and work you over," Kathryn said.

Alexis dived into her Red Bag and pulled out latex gloves and clear plastic raincoats, the kind Disney World issues to their customers when an unexpected rain shower crops up.

Annie reached for a screwdriver as Nikki spread clear plastic tarps all over the floor.

"Since I own this building, I don't think we have to worry too much if we make a mess, but tar is the dickens to get off, I'm told," Maggie said.

"Tar?" Bell bellowed.

"Oh, my God, what are you going to do with tar?" Newsom wailed pitifully.

"We're going to paint your entire bodies with

this black tar, and then we're going to . . . Myra, dear, since he talked so rudely to you, do you want to tell him what step two is?" Annie asked.

"Thank you for allowing me to speak, Countess. We're going to use this hair dryer to blow these feathers all over the wet tar," Myra said, motioning to a pile of feather pillows under the dining-room table. "Nikki, dear, do you want to tell Mr. Bell what step three is?"

"I'd love to tell him, Myra. Thank you for giving me the chance to speak," Nikki said. "Step three, Mr. Bell, is we're going to hang you up on the specially reinforced shower rod we installed earlier until you dry. Oooh, this tar really smells."

"Jesus Christ, you can kill us doing something like that! You're insane!" Bell shouted.

"Of course we're insane. We wouldn't be here otherwise," Annie said cheerfully. "You do know it is almost impossible to remove tar, don't you? Tar with feathers attached is *impossible* to remove. Why else do you think they put tar on roads?"

Adel Newsom squealed, then fainted dead away.

The women put on ski goggles, snapped their plastic raincoats into place, then pulled on their latex gloves.

"Last chance, Mr. Bell," Kathryn said as she removed the lid from a twenty-five-gallon can of coal black tar. She poured some of the tar into a bucket and picked up a paintbrush. "Where are the records? We want the account numbers for all your bank accounts. Give us what we want, and you're free to go."

After being revived so that she could appreciate what was about to happen, Adel Newsom was doing her best to crawl into herself. She fidgeted and squirmed until her back end made contact with the clothing the Sisters had removed from Bell. She saw his keys, his wallet, and his money clip lying on the floor, by his socks. She tore her gaze away from her lover's belongings long enough to cry out, "For God's sake, Baron, tell them what they want to know." Then she started to sob, her thin, scrawny shoulders shaking.

"Maybe he needs some incentives," Kathryn said.

"And that would be what, dear?" Annie asked curiously.

"Well, if we . . . uh . . . paint over his rectum and his . . . you know, that little thing, how long before things . . . you know, back up?" asked Kathryn.

The Sisters conferred. The final consensus was, not long at all. Newsom squealed again and fainted for the second time in a few minutes. The two surrogates sat huddled together, holding hands, as they tried to grapple with the craziness surrounding them.

Maggie was still texting, but she kept one eye on what was going on. She was grinning from ear to ear.

"We don't have a whole lot of time here, girls. We need that information, and we need it now,"

Nikki said. "It's obvious he was born stupid and never corrected the situation. Start with his thighs, Kathryn, and work upward. Alexis and Annie are going to start on Newsom. Wonder how those fake boobs are going to hold up under all that tar."

"Well, dear, this is just a guess on my part, but I assume they'll go *flat*. They use this stuff on roads for a reason. Cars go over it, and it packs down and becomes flat," Annie said with all the authority she could muster.

"That makes sense, Annie," Yoko observed, pointing to her own magnified breasts, which had come with a code number.

Resigned to the inevitable, Adel Newsom lay quietly, staring at her lover's things next to her. She sniffed. Everything smelled like the after-shave and cologne he drenched himself in, believing more was better. Even now the scent was almost overpowering. "Why don't you call his wife and ask her if Baron has a safe at home? I never believed she was the dimwit he made her out to be."

"Shut up, Adel, and leave my wife out of this. I do not have a safe at home."

"Like we're really going to believe you!" Kathryn said as she slapped a hefty amount of tar onto Bell's right thigh. "This goes on soooo easy. Shucks, we'll be done in no time. You enjoying this, Mr. Bell?" Bell flinched when she slapped another glob onto his left thigh. "We're getting there, sweetie. Next glob hits *the mark.*"

"Maggie, dear, do you have your camera ready?" Myra asked.

"Right here," Maggie said, holding up her left hand. "Just tell me when he's covered and hanging from the shower rod. I'm putting him on the front page!"

"Will you stop this crap already? You're just trying to scare me! Well, guess what? Baron Bell doesn't scare!"

"Guess what, Mr. Bell? This vigilante never says anything she doesn't mean." A load of tar hit the mark just as Kathryn finished speaking.

Myra noticed movement out of the corner of her eye. She turned to see Charles standing in the doorway. His face was whiter than the snow outside. "Not now, Charles. We're rather busy at the moment."

Charles turned and fled back to the bedroom.

"Flip him over, girls!" Kathryn said, dipping her brush into the bucket of tar.

Chapter 17

Bert Navarro, director of the Federal Bureau of Investigation, looked out at the sea of white that greeted him as he prepared to exit the Hoover Building, where he'd been a virtual prisoner, along with all the other agents in the building, since the snow started falling twenty-four hours ago.

He adjusted his aviator glasses against the blinding whiteness that surrounded him. He hated being out and about with a day's worth of beard, his clothes rumpled, his white shirt less than pristine. Considering the circumstances, he decided not to give his appearance a second thought.

Normally, he had nerves of steel, was great under pressure, and demonstrated clear thinking whatever the situation. This storm, though, with the power outages and resultant loss of communication with the outside world, had thrown him for a loop. He was worried about the vigilantes, especially Kathryn, and he was more than a little concerned about Jack and the others. He consoled himself with the fact that Jack was good at improvising, and he had Killer Harry on his team. Robinson and Espinosa always came through in the clench, so he shelved his concern for his friends. He had done what he could and hoped the others were doing the same thing.

Until the storm, Bert hadn't realized how much he depended on his cell phone to communicate with the outside world. He'd always taken power and convenience for granted, something he would never do again. Candles, flashlights that depended on batteries simply didn't do the job in his line of work.

Bert actually grinned when he heard his cell chirp inside his pocket. Hoping it was Kathryn, or possibly Charles or Jack, kept the grin on his face until he realized one of his least favorite people was on the other end of the line. He growled a greeting of sorts and waited for Mark Paterno, the head of the Secret Service detail at 1600 Pennsylvania Avenue, to state his case. For all the good it was going to do him. Bert pressed a button on his special cell that would allow him to record the conversation. It was a given that Paterno was doing the same thing.

Bert decided to wait out the agent. Finally he said, "You called me, remember. So what is it you want, Paterno?"

"It's not what I want, Mr. Director. It's what the president wants."

"Then have the president call me." Bert clicked

off the cell and counted, one-two-three. He clicked it on and waited again. "Don't ever hang up on me again, you asshole." Bert snapped the phone shut and put it on vibrating mode.

Bert Navarro carried three cell phones: his work phone, the special phone from Charles Martin, and his own personal phone. The Charles Martin phone took that moment to ring. The Bureau phone kept vibrating in his pocket. He ignored it as he concentrated on what Charles Martin was saying. "Got it. I'm waiting for my transportation." He listened again. "I'm outside in the pavilion. Nothing is moving. The city can't keep up with this storm. I heard a report as I was leaving that this is being billed as the storm of the century, and yet the White House is going ahead with the children's Christmas party. Have you heard how things are going over there?" Bert listened again, and asked, "What about the babies? The boys have it covered! I'd pay for that visual," he said, laughing. Bert went on to explain about hanging up on the head of the Secret Service. This time it was Charles who laughed.

"Do you care to tell me what the next step is?" Bert asked as he strained to look up and down the street to see if there was any sign of transportation coming his way. All he could see was a teenager carrying an inner tube, a man carrying a little dog, and two cars that were stuck in a snowbank. Most of the traffic lights appeared to be out. He brought his attention back to Charles and what he was saying. "Now *that's* a plan, Charles!" He listened again, then laughed so hard he doubled over. When he slipped the cell back into his other pocket, he was still laughing.

Bert stomped his feet to keep warm, the cell in his pocket vibrating continuously as he waited for the transportation that would take him to 1600 Pennsylvania Avenue.

Back at the *Post* apartment, Baron Bell was screaming his head off, while Adel Newsom stared off into space, resigned at what was to come. The two surrogates, their eyes red from crying, were still huddled together, praying.

"A little late with the prayers, aren't you?" Isabelle snapped. "What makes you think God is going to be in a forgiving mood at what you did to your own babies, selling them to the highest bidder? Right now you need to worry about what we're going to do to you. He's not doing so good," she said, jerking her head in Baron Bell's direction. "It is so not manly to squeal like that."

The surrogates cried harder.

Isabelle looked away in disgust in time to see Kathryn dip her brush into a second bucket.

"Make sure you get all those *nooks and crannies.*" Nikki giggled.

"I hear you!" Kathryn giggled in return. She wiggled the brush she'd just dipped into the second, restaurant-sized bucket, which was full of chocolate pudding with a licorice base. "Make sure you understand, Mr. Bell, once I seal up your rectum with this tar and that other stuff you have going on . . . in the front, you will probably *implode* in about ten hours. Come on, girls. Spread those flabby cheeks so I don't miss any of the nooks and crannies."

"Yuck," Yoko said.

"Oooh, he's so hairy back here!" Nikki grimaced.

"*STOP!* Okay, you bitch. I'll tell you what you want to know," Bell grunted.

"Too late," Annie said. "You snooze, you lose! Slap it on there, Kathryn! Seal him up tight!"

"Jesus, God, stop. Please," Bell begged, tears rolling down his cheeks.

"Listen to him," Adel Newsom pleaded. "You'll see he was the brains of this . . . this enterprise."

Kathryn stood up from her half crouch, the dark pudding dripping on the plastic tarp. The real tar she'd spread earlier was starting to harden up. She smiled. "Start talking, Mr. Bell."

"It's all there on my money clip. It looks like a money clip, but it's actually a Memory Stick. All my files and bank information are on it."

"Well, lookie here, girls," Nikki said, holding up a sheaf of bills attached to the Memory Stick. She ripped off her latex gloves, ran to the dining-room table, and inserted the Memory Stick into the laptop sitting there. "Wallah! It's all here. At least it looks like it is. Ooooh, this is *good.* The man is *rich!*

"Maggie, I'm going to upload these files. You'll have them in a minute. Wait! Where and how much money do you want me to transfer for all those adoptive parents?"

"We have an escrow account at the paper. Just a second. I'll send you the number of the account. Pick a number you're comfortable with, and it's a done deal. Remember, it is Christmas, so be generous. Babies are expensive. That means, be generous.

"And be certain to include funds to reimburse the parents they sold the babies to. We have to follow through on the promises we made when we explained that they had been the victims of a swindle. That the children they thought they were going to be able to adopt legally could not be adopted, because even though the surrogate mothers had signed off on the adoptions, the biological fathers had not and would not. That the babies were going to be returned to the families that had arranged for their conceptions and births, but if the 'buyers' would just not raise a fuss, not only would their money be returned but, more important, private adoptions through reputable parties would be arranged within the next year."

"Gotcha," Nikki said as she tapped at the keys on her laptop.

"What the hell are you doing?" Baron Bell snarled. "Stop that! I told you what you wanted to know. I said, stop it, goddamn it! Liars! You can't trust a woman no matter what."

"That is so true, especially with people like you," Kathryn said. She dipped her brush into the bucket of real tar and proceeded to paint the lawyer from the neck down. Myra and Annie were painting Adel Newsom, who just cried and sniveled. The two surrogates stared with unbelieving eyes at what was going on as they wondered if they would really be turned loose or strung up on the shower rod with the two lawyers.

"You are all going to be overnight sensations once we put you on YouTube," Yoko said. "I bet you'll get so many hits, the site will have to shut down."

"Just die already, all of you," Bell shouted as Kathryn continued to paint his body with tar and Nikki transferred his money to where it would do the most good.

"Yoo-hoo, Mr. Bell. I'm leaving fifty thousand dollars in your household account to see your wife through the year," Nikki commented. "I'm right now, right this second, processing a transfer of title to that palatial estate you once lived in. Mrs. Bell will have to sell it, and she'll be set for life."

"Piss on you!" Bell shouted.

"That does it!" Kathryn shouted as she demanded the lawyer be flipped again. She dipped her brush in the bucket of pudding and slapped it on his penis. "Now, let's see who is going to be pissing on whom. One more word out of you, and I'm stuffing your ears and nose with this stuff. That means shut up! Anything else, Nikki?" she called over her shoulder.

"Should we write Mrs. Bell a letter? You know, so she has something to look at from time to time when she thinks about that scumbag she was married to. What's your feeling on sending her some pictures?"

"That's a very good idea, dear," replied Myra. "I know I'd feel terrible if someone sent me pictures of Charles in . . . that condition. However, I really don't think it's going to be much of a shock to Mrs. Bell. Women always know in their hearts when their husbands cheat on them. She chose to ignore his philandering, from what we've been told, rather than confront him. So, no, I don't feel too sorry for her. Make it a kind letter."

"Okay, Myra, you're the boss," Nikki said cheerfully as she tapped away at the speed of light.

"Done!" Kathryn cried dramatically. "How's he look, girls?"

"Spectacular!" Yoko said.

The others agreed.

"Then let's hook him up!" Kathryn urged.

Charles poked his head into the doorway.

"Not now, dear!" Myra said when she spotted him.

Charles was gone in a flash.

"Boy, this stuff is sticky," Alexis said as she pulled the feather pillows out from under the dining-room table. "The tar, I mean, not the pillows."

"We knew what you meant, dear," Myra said as she fit the plug to the hair dryer into the electrical outlet.

Holding two feather pillows by the corners,

Annie, a devilish grin on her face, said, "One has to take one's fun wherever one can find it. Do you agree, girls?"

The Sisters nodded solemnly.

"Okay, Myra, on the count of three, let's rumble. Turn that baby on, and let's watch the feathers fly!"

Suddenly the room was a sea of white as feathers flew in all directions, most of them landing on the two tar-covered forms of Baron Bell and Adel Newsom. The Sisters swatted at the flying feathers as they settled in their hair and on every inch of their bodies.

"Spectacular!" Yoko chortled.

"You need to come up with a better word, dear," Annie shouted to be heard over the high-speed drone of the super-duper deluxe hair dryer, which, according to the box, promised to dry a full head of hair in forty-five seconds.

"We should have kept our raincoats on. We'll be picking feathers out of our ears for days," Kathryn grumbled.

"Oh, who cares? This is *fun!*" Alexis giggled. "Even the dogs are having fun!"

The Sisters turned to look at the two canines, who were jumping in all directions to catch the elusive feathers. They turned to view their handiwork the moment Myra turned off the high-speed hair dryer.

"They look like mummies! Very artful, if you like this kind of art." Myra turned to the door, knowing that Charles was there even without seeing him. "Not yet, dear, but soon."

Nikki and Isabelle helped the others drag Baron Bell into the bathroom. "How long before *it all* hardens up?" Nikki asked curiously. "Do you think the feathers will speed up the process?"

"Oh, yeah. It's hardening up as we speak." Kathryn cackled. "I sure hope that rod holds their weight. How about this? Since he's the heavier of the two, let's dangle Bell from the showerhead we rigged up to carry the weight of the two surrogates. Then Newsom can go on the rod all by herself. What'ya say?" She spit out a feather and laughed uproariously.

"That sounds awesome," Isabelle said. "Yoko is right. They do look spectacular."

"That means we have to loop a belt under his arms so we have something to hook onto the showerhead," Kathryn said.

"One belt coming up," Alexis said, running out to the dining room to return with Baron Bell's own belt. "Hoisted by his own petard. I love it, girls! Just love, love, love it!"

"Wow, it works! Look! If you touch him, you can make him swing around. This is way beyond clever. Next!" Kathryn shouted.

Myra and Annie, with Nikki's help, dragged Adel Newsom into the bathroom.

"If she gets bored," Nikki said, "she can swing her legs and slide back and forth on the rod. I had to borrow Charles's belt. He seems . . . *out of it,* poor thing. I finished the letter, and it will get sent sometime this afternoon. I checked three o'clock to be on the safe side. We should be far away by then, and Snowden and his people will be here to . . . take care of business."

"What are we going to do about the two surrogates?" Isabelle asked.

"I say we lock them up in the other bathroom and let Snowden turn them loose, with some very dire warnings of what will happen to them if they so much as breathe a word of what went on here. Before I came in here to help out, I had them sign all the legal forms. Those babies now belong to the Evanses and Dawsons forevermore," Nikki said.

"We need to make tracks, ladies," Annie said. "Time is marching on, and we don't want to be late for our gig at Sixteen Hundred Pennsylvania Avenue, now do we?"

"God forbid we should be late for something so momentous, Annie!" Myra said, tongue in cheek.

The Sisters scurried as they gathered up their belongings amid the sea of feathers. It was Annie who later said she didn't know why, but she stopped to listen to the conversation of the two surrogates. Her eyes popped wide at what she heard.

"Talk about Lady Luck smiling on us," Donna Davis said. "I thought it was all over when they found out about that BMW I bought. I can't believe you didn't spend the money they paid you, Joan!"

"Look, I did it for all the right reasons. I needed the money for my tuition. My parents are not wealthy like yours," Joan Olsen replied.

"I never wanted to take the baby back. I believed those evil people when they said they would put us on YouTube. That would kill my parents, and I'd never get a job. I've worked too hard to let those evil people ruin my life. I never had any intention of spending that money. In fact, I was trying to come up with a way to give it to the Evans family and the baby as well, then get out of town to study for the bar exam back home as soon as I graduated. I don't ever want to practice law in DC."

"You're stupid!" Donna Davis said.

"I'd rather be stupid than be someone like you, Donna."

Quicker than lightning, Annie had the door open and was dragging a protesting Donna Davis into the dining room. "One more. Give her the works, and don't spare the tar! I'll explain later."

The Sisters went to work as Maggie snapped picture after picture. Each time she moved, a flurry of feathers sailed upward and sent the two dogs into a frenzy of barking and jumping.

"Where do you want this one to go?" Kathryn asked as she pointed to Donna Davis, who was screaming at the top of her lungs.

"After what I heard, the bathroom is too private for her. How about we suspend her from the dining-room chandelier? We'll just hook her up, and her feet can rest on the table. If she moves, the chandelier will come out of the ceiling and she could get fried. Yep, I think that will work. Let's do it," Annie said.

"Kitchen, ladies," Myra said. "We have something important to decide."

With the Sisters, Maggie, and Charles assembled, Myra said, "Now that we have Bell's records, which go back for years, a lot of kids' lives could be ruined if they become public. The same is true for the records Maggie sent copies of to Nikki's old law firm. So I propose we get rid of all the records other than those we have already acted on. I do not want to be responsible for making hundreds of children miserable as they are torn from the only homes they have ever known. I know that it's unfair to the parents who lost them, but why make the kids suffer? What do you say?"

Every hand in the room rose in agreement.

"Myra," Charles said as the others started to make ready for their departure, "now I know just why I love you as much as I do."

Chapter 18

"This is a *horse,* Agent Thomas," Bert Navarro said, pointing to the animal waiting patiently for her new rider.

"Boss, you said transportation. You did not say what kind of transportation you required. Delilah—that's this horse's name—was the only game in town, and I had to steal her from some local cop. You might . . . uh . . . be hearing about that later today or tomorrow. Look around, boss. There's nothing on wheels moving."

Bert eyed the snorting steed, then his agent. He finally shrugged when he realized that Delilah was the only way he was going to get to Georgetown. "Okay, Thomas. You look dead on your feet. Go on up to the office, grab some z's, and get something to eat."

"Okay, boss. Listen, boss, stick to the middle of the road. Delilah goes where she wants to go, and she doesn't like to be crowded. Just give her reins a little tug if you want her to go right or left. Otherwise, she just goes straight. She's not good at backing up either."

"Shut the hell up, Thomas," Bert said as he struggled to get into the saddle. "You tell this to anyone, and your ass is grass. You hear me?"

"My lip is zipped, boss." The weary agent turned to head across the pavilion that would lead him inside the Hoover Building. He couldn't resist a parting comment. "Happy trails, boss."

Bert offered up a single-digit salute as he tried to adjust to his precarious seat. Delilah waited a moment, then moved off. "C'mon, old girl, you can do better than two miles an hour, can't you? You keep this up, we won't get there till the spring thaw." Delilah ignored him as she headed for the center of the road. "Shit!"

Bert yanked off his leather gloves and pulled out all three of his cell phones. The FBI phone was still vibrating like crazy. He ignored it as he punched in Kathryn's number and waited. A short kitchy-koo conversation followed, with Kathryn ending the conversation with, "We're ready and waiting!" Bert did his best to hunker into his heavy down jacket as the biting winds whipped at him. Delilah snorted happily, plumes of mist sailing upward from her nostrils.

The next call was to Jack Emery. He listened to Jack's tirade and had only one comment. "You guys have been changing shitty diapers? Is that what you're telling me? Damn, sorry I missed all that fun. What? Messy poo poo! That means a shitty diaper, right?" Bert grinned as he listened to Jack's continuing report. He interrupted when he couldn't take any more baby news. "I'll get there whenever this damn horse decides to get me there. She has only one speed, and there's no way to crank her into second gear.

"By the way, I just spoke to Kathryn. She said everything has been taken care of, and they're ready and waiting for us to pick them up for the trip to the White House for that goddamn party no one had the good sense to cancel. I had a run-in a little while ago with Paterno, the head of the White House Secret Service detail, and I hung up on him. The guy is a real prick, so be warned."

Bert listened again and replied, "I thought you knew Charles made it here. He even has the dogs with him. Old Home Week, Jack! Who's there? Who are you talking to?"

"A truckful of people. I mean a truck," replied Jack. "I think they're the real adoptive parents and some nurses that couldn't get here earlier. I gotta go, Bert. I'll see you when you get here."

Bert settled himself deeper in the saddle and let Delilah take her time. Sometimes it simply didn't pay to spin your wheels. "Attagirl, Delilah. As long as you get me there before midnight, I'll be a happy camper." Delilah snorted, and it seemed to Bert she was moving a tad faster. What had he said to create this change? "Ah, attagirl, Delilah. Boy, you can really strut your stuff here on this open road. Attagirl!" Damn, the old girl was actually working herself up to a trot. "Wheeee!" Bert shouted.

* * *

While Bert and Delilah made their way to Georgetown, Jack Emery was ushering in a gaggle of people, who immediately stampeded their way to the rows of babies, all of whom were sleeping peacefully.

Harry whistled, and the gaggle came to a dead stop. "Back up, ladies and gentlemen. Now, will the nurses step forward so we can do this trade-off in a nice, orderly manner? There are things you all need to know about these babies, even though they . . . have been out of your arms and homes for only a little while. Everyone is going to get their baby, so just be patient." He jerked his head in Espinosa's direction to indicate he should start his photography session, but Espinosa was already doing it.

"That sounded real good, Harry," Jack remarked. "All those parents listened to you like you were a doctor explaining a medical condition. I was impressed, and so were they."

Harry looked at his buddy suspiciously to see if Jack was making fun of him. He decided Jack was sincere, so he accepted the flattery he was heaping on him with good grace.

"What time is it?" Ted asked, a worried look on his face. "Maggie said she would personally kill us if we're late to the White House. Are you listening to me, Jack?"

"I am, but I have to pay attention to what's going on here, too. All we need is one baby going someplace it isn't supposed to go, and we might as well head to Siberia. We have to square this away. In case you forgot, these kids are what this is all about. That Christmas party at the White House is just the frosting on the cake."

"So what's the game plan, then, Jack?" asked Ted.

Jack was mesmerized by how Ted could talk, watch what was going on, and still text a message. "The minute each set of parents has its baby and Espinosa takes his picture, then a group shot, we're outta here. Those nurses remind me of my old grade-school teachers, who walked around with a ruler to smack the crap out of you if you moved a muscle. That means they are more than capable."

"Navarro is here, Jack," Harry hissed. "He's on a horse! Look! His feet almost touch the ground. How silly is that?"

"That's how you're going to look when you get on the horse that is assigned to you, Harry."

"Come on, Espinosa. How many shots you got left?" Ted bellowed.

"Just the group shot," Espinosa bellowed back, loud enough that the babies all started howling in unison.

Harry shook his head in disgust as he made his way to the one he called the bad burper. "Listen, ma'am, you have to put the baby like this, on your shoulder." He gave a quick demonstration, and even though the baby hadn't eaten, it burped. Harry looked so pleased, Jack patted him on the back.

"We're good to go. No one is going to leave with the babies until Snowden's men get here to *explain* things to these nice people. Everyone understands the rules, so that means we're free to head off into the sunset, but since there is no sunset, we're heading off to the horse barn to attach those four-legged creatures to the sleigh, which in turn will take us to the *Post* apartment, where we will be picking up . . . a few others in our quest to make the children of this great metropolis happy and contented."

"I really hate you, Jack," Harry said, slamming his way out the front door. The phalanx of horseflesh that greeted him made him falter.

"Stifle those feelings, Harry. Your trusty steed awaits. You want a boost?"

Jack picked himself up out of the snow to see Harry sitting tall in the saddle. "Eat me, Jack!"

Jack dusted himself off and climbed on his horse, whose name was Scarlet, according to Bert, whose apparent sincerity was matched only by his total ignorance about horses he had just seen for the first time in his life. "Well, Scarlet, it's just you and me in this white wilderness."

"What's my horse's name?" Harry asked with a catch in his voice.

"Cleopatra," Bert said with a straight face. "Ted, your horse's name is Aphrodite, and, Espinosa, your horse is named Delicious. I don't know the names of the other three that Snowden's men are riding. I have to go first because Delilah will travel only in the middle of the road. She's not too good about making lefts and rights, but we managed to get here."

In spite of himself, Jack laughed as he managed to get his horse behind Bert and his steed. "You getting all of this for our memory sampler?" he yelled to Espinosa.

"In living color!" was the response.

Fifteen minutes into their journey even Harry was perturbed. "Can't we go any faster? We're going to be late arriving at the White House if we don't pick up some speed."

Bert huffed and puffed. "You hear that, Delilah. They want speed. Let's give them some speed. Attagirl, attagirl, attagirl!" Delilah galloped down the road, Bert hanging on for dear life.

Jack almost swallowed his tongue as his horse kicked up her feet to follow suit. He took one quick glance at Harry, whose eyes were so glazed, he thought he was going to pass out. "Smile for Yoko, Harry!"

Harry came back to the land of the living with a squawk that could be heard a mile away.

"Hey, Harry," Jack said, peering at Harry's horse, "I think your horse is peeing. And guess what? If that horse's name is Cleopatra, then next year I'm going to volunteer to be a surrogate mother. And Bert's going to be Mother of the Year."

At that moment, Bert, unaware that his cover had been blown, bellowed, "Everybody slow down. We're going to be making a left turn." All the horses but Bert's turned left. "She can't back up. We have to turn around."

"And that expert on horse names and gender runs the FBI!" Harry said as he sailed down the street like he was headed to the O.K. Corral, with his six-guns at the ready.

And then they were at the horse barn, the horses snorting in rhythm as the huge doors leading into the barn were rolled open. Snowden's men burst out through the opening like they were shot from cannons. With scarcely any hesitation, they had the horses tethered and hooked to the sleigh. Sleigh bells jingled joyously.

"Which one is the lead horse?" Bert asked anxiously. "It can't be Delilah. She just goes straight. I don't know how she'll do in a group setting."

"And you would be?" one of Snowden's men asked.

"Him! He's the director of the fucking FBI, and the world's leading expert on horses," Harry said, pride ringing in his voice. The stupid look on the man's face was all the reward Harry needed or wanted.

"I'm going to make sure you get audited, you crazy Asian," Bert snarled.

"Take your best shot, Mr. Director. Lizzie made sure I'm clean as a whistle. Get your ass in this sleigh. We're running late."

"You getting all this, Espinosa?"

"Like I said, in living color."

It was 11:20 when the sleigh, driven by Bert Navarro, slid to a stop in front of the *Post* apartment building. Sleigh bells jangled merrily as the occupants of the sleigh climbed out and unhooked the first four horses, allowing the remaining four to pull the sleigh with Santa, his elves, and Ted Robinson.

Everyone stood pop-eyed as Charles Martin, aka Santa Claus, climbed into the sleigh. He looked more like Santa than Santa himself. Next to him was Myra Rutledge, aka Mrs. Santa Claus. Six elves dressed in red and green costumes climbed in alongside the two most important guests. As the sleigh bells jangled, the women and Santa kept up a running conversation that consisted of Bert was in charge, they were cleared to enter the White House grounds nearest the West Wing, where the sleigh would drive across the lawn as the children clustered around for a few merry ho-ho-ho's before the party departed the sleigh for the party room, where treats and presents would be handed out.

"That's the plan," Nikki said. "The White House and the Secret Service think Baron Bell is the Santa and Mrs. Santa is his office secretary. That was the last thing we had Bell do before we left the apartment. Annie held a gun to his head, and he did it without a peep. We should be good to go. Everyone cross their fingers that we pull this off. How'd it go with the babies?" she yelled to Ted.

"Just fine," Ted yelled back. "How long ago did Maggie leave?"

"About ten minutes before we did. Espinosa is uploading the pictures as we speak, and Maggie is going to do her best to get out a special edition for early morning tomorrow."

"What about Bell and his friends?" Ted

shouted as the horses galloped down the middle of the road.

"Snowden's people were waiting in the lobby when we left. They'll use the city sanitation truck Bert had his people leave at the curb. They're history. Don't give them another thought," Yoko said, her eyes on her beloved, who she thought belonged on a horse.

She had such a dreamy look on her face, Isabelle gave her a swat.

"He looks like John Wayne," Yoko gushed.

Isabelle rolled her eyes, then burst out laughing. "Don't ever lose your imagination, honey."

Up ahead, Espinosa looked over at Bert. "Shouldn't you get there before us? We're supposed to be crowd control. What are you supposed to be?"

"The guy who shoves his foot up Paterno's ass when we get there. He's the guy in charge of the Secret Service at the White House, and we hate each other's guts. He's going to want to do an inspection of the sleigh, card everyone, so to speak, then talk into his sleeve for an hour before he pronounces us fit to enter the sacred grounds of the White House."

"We're doomed then," Espinosa said.

"Nah, we got the good guys on our side. I called Lizzie, who called the president, and Connor will be waiting for us. Once in a while I get it right, Espinosa."

Espinosa nodded sagely. "Hey, you want me to take a picture of that horse, the one that can't do rights and lefts?"

"Yeah. Frame it and give it to me for Christmas." Bert guffawed.

"The White House is coming up!" Jack shouted. "Right turn, Ted! Whoa. I said right turn. Oh, shit, Delilah is leading. Right turn, Ted!"

"I'm trying!" Ted yelled. "Okay, got it. Attagirl, Delilah!"

Delilah, hearing her favorite words, picked up her feet and galloped down the driveway, past the cordon of Secret Service agents, her partners joining in the jaunt and the sleigh careening to the right, then the left, the sleigh bells jangling at full throttle.

The agents, guns drawn, assumed a firing position until Bert bellowed, "Stand down, gentlemen! I *SAID*, stand down!" In the stillness the only sound to be heard was that of the hammers being drawn back.

"Do what the director is telling you, Agent Paterno. *STAND* down! If you don't, I'll shoot you myself. Do you understand?" Martine Connor said loud enough to be heard a block away.

"Go away, Agent Paterno, get out of my sight. And take your men with you. I don't want to see your face the rest of the afternoon. If I do, you'll be patrolling the Tidal Basin.

"Welcome to the White House, gentlemen. Thank you so much for all your help today. I want to personally apologize to all of you. We simply could not cancel the party and disappoint the children. Follow me, please, so we can get the festivities under way."

Bert Navarro hung back, the last in line. He looked over at Paterno and gave him his middle finger. "Hey, Mister Secret Service Man, never be impressed with yourself, because there's always someone out there ready to cut you down to size. Today it's me. Lucky you!"

Whatever Paterno was about to say, he changed his mind, a murderous look on his face.

"Espinosa, tell me you got a picture of that!" Bert shouted.

"In living color, like all the others," Espinosa assured him.

Bert laughed.

Ninety minutes later, the party nearing its end, the president walked around the huge room, admiring the mountain of torn gift wrap and the happy smiles on the faces of the children, their presents under their arms as their parents herded them together for a group shot, which would make the evening news around the world.

Connor knew there was something off-kilter about the whole afternoon, but she couldn't quite put her finger on exactly what it was. She discounted the confrontational meeting earlier between the head of her Secret Service detail and the director of the FBI. No, it was something else. She moved off to the side to stand next to her secretary, who was beaming happily.

"It was a wonderful party, wasn't it, Madam President? There's nothing like Santa Claus and his helpers to make a child's eyes go wide. I remember so well how it was when I was a little girl."

"Hmm." *Santa Claus and his helpers.* Connor let her gaze travel across the room to where Santa and his wife were getting up from their thrones. She watched as Santa threw his empty sack over his shoulder and belted out a few ho-ho-ho's to the children's delight. Mrs. Claus, while meaty, wasn't exactly round where it counted. The last time she'd seen Baron Bell, he didn't appear to be more than five-nine, maybe five-ten at the most. This Santa looked to be six foot two or so. *Hmm. And those elves. Wigs, a little latex, some greasepaint, a costume, and you have . . .*

The president's cell vibrated in her pocket. She turned away when she clicked it on and spoke. "You cheated, Lizzie. You had me give them clearance."

Lizzie laughed, that tinkling sound Martine loved to hear even when it meant Lizzie won the round. "They would have gotten in with or without your help, Marti. We both know that."

"I do know that. The big question now is, do I let them know I know, or should I play stupid?"

Lizzie laughed again before the connection was broken.

The White House photographer appeared at the president's elbow. "I'd like to take a group shot of you, Santa, and the others outside if you're up to it, Madam President."

Martine Connor smiled. "Absolutely, but only if the sleigh is facing out to the road and Santa and his helpers are in the sleigh, ready to drive off." The photographer frowned but nodded as he watched the president don a scarlet cape trimmed in faux ermine. The last thing she did was plop a bright red Santa hat on her head. "I'm ready," she trilled.

Outside, Bert Navarro was astride Delilah and had her pointing straight out. "This is not good, boys. Here comes the president and the photographer. We should have been out of here twenty minutes ago. Make damn sure those gates go down, and, Espinosa, you ready to turn the power off?"

"Yep," said Espinosa.

The horses pawed the ground as they snorted and bellowed. The sleigh bells jangled, the sound crystal clear as Martine walked up to the sleigh, her hand extended in greeting or thanks. No one was quite sure. Behind her, the Secret Service agents were lined up, watching what was happening.

"Merry Christmas, ladies. You, too, Mr. Martin," she said. "Shhh, no one knows but me. Now, let's all smile pretty for the cameras. By the way, I could have taken you, just so you know."

"Sorry, Madam President, not on your best day," Annie said.

The president smiled. "You're probably right. I do have my pride. Merry Christmas!"

Annie leaned over the side of the sleigh. She was close enough to whisper, "We'll be back if you don't keep your promise."

"I know, Annie. I'm working on it. The papers are actually on my desk."

"Attagirl, Madam President. We don't have a lot of patience."

The magic words galvanized Delilah, who took off at a full gallop. Annie fell back into the sleigh as the horses rumbled down the road to the gate that somehow magically closed the minute the sleigh went through.

Martine stood in the snow and laughed until the tears rolled down her cheeks.

"You get all that, Espinosa?" Jack bellowed.

"In living color, Jack!"

Back at the gate Mark Paterno was bellowing for someone to call a goddamn electrician.

"Why?" the president asked. "They made their getaway. And to think you head up my Secret Service detail." She shook her head in disgust.

"What are you talking about, Madam President?" said Paterno.

"The vigilantes! They just left in the sleigh. Right under your nose, Agent Paterno! Merry Christmas! I'll see you after the New Year. By then all your bad publicity should be just a memory. No, you are not going to Camp David with me."

Martine took a deep breath as she walked back to her lonely digs in the White House. She offered up a salute of sorts to the defiant women known as the vigilantes and wished with all her heart that she was one of them.

"Merry Christmas, ladies!"

Epilogue

New Year's Eve!

With the clock ticking down, the guests on Big Pine Mountain threw on wraps and ran to the center of the compound, where Charles and Myra were standing, their hands full of the sleigh bells from Baron Bell's sleigh that they had brought back to the mountain.

The solid wall of evergreens and tall pines whispered and trembled, their scent intoxicating, while the blanket of stars overhead winked at and twinkled down on the happy guests.

In unison, the guests started to count down.

"Six!"

"Five!"

"Four!"

"Three!"

"Two!"

"One!"

"Happy New Year!"

The happy, joyous sounds rang over the

mountain as the guests slapped one another on the back, kissed each other, and wiped at their eyes.

A new year had just been ushered in.

In just eleven hours and fifty-five minutes, another momentous fete would take place: Myra and Charles's wedding.

Laughing and singing, the guests made their way back to the main building for their third and last champagne toast of the evening. They gathered around the twelve-foot-tall Norwegian spruce tree, which glowed with brightly colored lights, the angel on top of the tree smiling down on them. The guests held their glasses high as they toasted in the New Year and whatever it would hold for all of them.

Eyes misty, they sang, mostly off-key, "Auld Lang Syne."

And then it was time to call it a night.

One by one the guests made their way to their separate rooms, until the only people left in the room were Myra, Annie, and Isabelle.

"How about some coffee, girls? I'm so wired, I know I will never be able to fall asleep. I'll make it," Myra said.

"It's just us again, Annie," Isabelle said. "This isn't working for me. I guess you know that, huh?"

"I do, dear. I can't believe you missed Stu Franklin by three minutes. He was waiting right there on the curb, just like he said he would. Then those damn mounties made him move, making it impossible for us to pick him up.

There will be another time, dear. Trust me on that."

Isabelle smiled. "I know. I'm just feeling blue, that's all. I'm sorry Fish's flight was canceled. The storm, the weather, it just fouled everything up. But, like you said, tomorrow is another day."

Both women stared at the beautiful tree, each busy with her own thoughts, until Myra came back with a tray filled with coffee cups, cream, and sugar.

"I am so proud of all of us. This whole week we never talked business, not once. We just enjoyed each other's company and all that wonderful food Charles prepared for us. I do wonder, though, how Mr. Bell and his friends are doing."

"I kept up on the aftermath by reading the papers online. I think it's safe to say Washington had its knickers in a knot when Maggie's headlines ripped around the world. I think it's wonderful that none of the adoptive parents would talk to the press. All they want to do is put this mess behind them and raise their families. We did good, Myra."

Myra smiled. "We did, didn't we? So many memories. I'm sorry about Fish and your young man, Isabelle."

Isabelle shrugged, as did Annie. The shrugs meant life would go on no matter what.

"We really should try to get some sleep, ladies," Annie said. "How will it look if we have dark circles under our eyes as Myra takes her vows?"

"They have makeup for that," Myra said. "You two go on to bed. I think I need some alone time. I want to . . . I just . . ."

"We understand, Myra. Come along, Isabelle."

At the door, both women turned and waved at Myra, but she was staring at the beautiful tree, her memories taking her back in time. Tears rolled down her cheeks, and she made no move to stop them.

"Mummie, Mummie, please don't cry. This should be the happiest day of your life."

"Oh, darling girl, you came. I was so hoping you would. I am happy. I just wish you were here with me."

"I am, Mummie, in spirit."

"It's not the same thing. I want to wrap my arms around you, to feel the beat of your heart, to kiss you on the cheek, to hold your hand, to hear you laugh. I want to *see* you. I need to see you, darling girl."

"Look up, Mummie!"

Myra raised her eyes to look at the angel sitting on top of the tree. It was made of gossamer, with gold wings and a halo. She blinked when she saw the wings on the angel flutter. Then she blinked again when the angel left its perch and sailed around the room before it made its way back to perch on top of the tree. "Oh, dear God!" Myra whispered.

"I hope you don't want an encore, Mummie. That took all my energy. Go to sleep, Mummie. I'll see you

at the wedding in just a few hours. I'm going to be your invisible flower girl."

Myra woke with a start. She looked around, a dazed look on her face when she remembered her dream. Was it a dream? She craned her neck to look up at the angel on top of the tree. It wasn't nestled in the top branch, the way it had been earlier. In fact it looked like someone had just stuck it there without securing it to the branch. One of the wings looked bent. Myra smiled; then she laughed as she struggled to her feet to make her way to bed to try and get a little sleep. She was gathering up her coat and boots when the angel toppled from the tree. Myra ran to the tree and caught the gossamer decoration before it hit the floor. She clutched it to her chest and somehow managed to throw on her coat without letting loose of it.

When Myra woke three hours later, the angel was back on top of the tree.

Later, after the wedding, when she told Charles about her dream, she said, "It was the most wonderful dream I have ever had in my life."

Annie was smiling from ear to ear. "It's amazing that Barbara's dress fits you, and Alexis did not need to do a thing to it. You look beautiful, Myra."

Sensing movement to her right, Myra turned to see a line of snowbirds perched outside the window. "Listen, Annie! I think they're saying I'm pretty. Over and over they keep chirping. Isn't this just too wonderful for words?"

"Sounds to me like they're saying Pritzie, Pritzie, Pritzie. Or maybe they're saying Prizzi, Prizzi, Prizzi. Isn't there some kind of cockamamie law firm in the District named Prizzi, Prizzi, Prizzi, and Prizzi?"

"I don't know and I don't care. I'm going with they're here to tell me I look pretty. Do not rain—er, snow—on my parade today, Annie. Now, tell me the truth. Do you think I'm being . . . I don't even know what term to use about me being married in my daughter's wedding dress. Silly maybe? Maudlin?"

"Good Lord, no! I think it's wonderful. Beyond wonderful. I know wherever Barbara is, she's happy seeing you in her wedding dress. I hear the music, so it's time to walk down the hall and out to the big room, where your husband-to-be awaits. I have to go first, so wait thirty seconds before you follow me. I have to be in place."

"Go already," Myra said, "so we can . . . God, I am so nervous. The worst part is I'm not even going to get a *real* ring until next month."

"Oh, poo, like that matters. I'm going, I'm going. Remember, small steps."

Myra heard a few oohs and ahs as she made her way to where Charles was waiting for her. Nellie, her book open in front of her, smiled. Myra tried to smile, but her lips wouldn't move. When Nellie got to the part about the ring—and later she said she couldn't remember the words—Myra felt her spirit daughter nudge her.

"I'm here, Mummie. Open your hand."

Myra looked down at her clenched hand and slowly opened it. Her knees buckled, and she would have fallen except for Annie, who reached out to take her arm. Nestled in the palm of her hand was a plain gold wedding band. She knew without reading the inscription inside the ring that it was her daughter's wedding ring.

"My wedding gift to you, Mummie."

Myra's heart soared as Charles reached for the ring and slipped it on her finger.

Nellie beamed. "You may now kiss the bride!"

Don't miss Fern Michaels's
brand new and already wildly popular
new series,
The Godmothers!

Here is a special excerpt from the first book,

THE SCOOP,

a Kensington trade paperback on sale now.

Chapter 1

Charleston, South Carolina

It was an event, there was no doubt about it. Not that funerals were, as a rule, events, but when someone of Leland St. John's stature bit the dust, it became one. The seven-piece string band playing in the downpour, per one of Leland's last wishes, had turned it into an event regardless of what else was going on in the world.

Then there was the tail end of Hurricane Blanche, which was unleashing torrents of rain upon the mourners huddled under the dark blue tent and only added to the circuslike atmosphere.

"Will you just get on with it," Toots Loudenberry mumbled under her breath. She continued to mutter and mumble as the minister droned on and on. "No one is as good as you're making Leland sound. All you know is what I told you, and I sure as hell didn't tell you all that crap you're spouting. He was a selfish, rich, old man. End of story."

Toots's daughter leaned closer to her mother

and tried to whisper through the thick veil covering her mother's head and ears. "Can't you hurry it along? It's not like this is the first time you've done this. Isn't this the seventh or eighth husband you've buried? I'm damn glad that preacher said his name, or I wouldn't even know who it is that's being planted. I gotta say, Mom, you outdid yourself with all these flowers."

Toots rose to the occasion and stepped forward, cutting the minister off in midsentence. "Thank you, Reverend." She wanted to say his check was in the mail, but she bit her tongue as she took a step forward and laid her wilted rose on top of the bronze coffin. She stepped aside so the other mourners could follow her out from under the temporary tent, which was open on all four sides. She stepped in water up to her ankles, cursed ripely, and sloshed her way to the waiting limousine, which would take her back home. "That's just like you, Leland. Why couldn't you have waited one more week, and the rainy season would have been over? Now my shoes are ruined. So is my hat, as well as my suit. Too bad you don't know how much this outfit cost. If you did, you would have waited another week to die. You always were selfish. See what all that selfishness got you. You're dead."

"What are you mumbling about, Mom?"

Toots slid into the limousine and kicked off her sodden shoes. Her black mourning hat followed. She looked over at her daughter, Abby, who looked like a drowned rat, and said, "Of all my husbands, I liked Leland the least. I resent having to attend his funeral under these conditions. He was my only mistake. But one out of eight, I suppose, isn't too bad."

Abby reached for a wad of paper napkins next to the champagne bottle that seemed to come with all limousines. "Why didn't you just crisp him up?"

Toots sighed. "I wanted to, but Leland said in his will that he wanted to be buried with that damn string band playing music. One has to honor a person's last wishes. What kind of person would I be if I didn't honor his, even if he was a jerk?"

"Don't you mean if you didn't honor those last wishes, what's-his-name's money would have gone to the polar bears in the Arctic?"

"That, too." Toots sighed.

The woman born Teresa Amelia Loudenberry, Toots to her friends, stared at her daughter. "How long are you staying, dear?"

"I have a four o'clock flight. I left Chester with a sitter, and Chester does not like sitters. There's just enough time for me to grab something to eat at your post feast, change into dry clothes, and get outta here. Can't you hear California calling my name? Don't look at me like that, Mom. I didn't even know that guy you married. I met him at your wedding, and that's the sum total of our relationship. If I remember correctly, you said he was a charmer. I expected a charmer. I did not get a charmer. I'm just saying."

"Maybe I should have said snake charmer,"

Toots said vaguely. "Leland was like this gorgeously wrapped present that when opened was quite . . . tacky. I was stunned, but I did marry the man, so I had to make the best of it. He's gone now, so perhaps we shouldn't speak ill of him. I'll mourn for ten days for the sake of appearance, then get on with my life. I'm going to find a hobby to keep myself busy. I'm sick and tired of doing good deeds. Anyone can do good deeds. Anyone can garden and grow one-of-a-kind roses. I need to do something that will make a difference, something challenging. Something I can really sink my teeth into. That's another thing. Leland wore dentures. He kept them in a cup in the bathroom at night. I could never get used to that. He wasn't very good in bed, either."

"That's probably more than I need to know, Mom."

"I'm just saying, Abby. I don't want you to think your old mom is callous. You have to admit I did have seven happy marriages. I should have hung up my garter belt when Dolph died. Did I do that? No, I did not. I let Leland sweep me off my feet, dentures and all. Sometimes life is so unfair.

"That's enough of a pity party for me. Tell me how it's going out there in sunny California. How's the job going? What's the latest hot gossip, and who is doing what to whom in Hollywood?"

Abby Simpson, Toots's daughter by her first husband, John Simpson, the absolute love of

Toots's life, was a reporter for a second-rate tabloid, *The Informer*, based in Los Angeles. She was a second-string runner, which meant she had to hit the pavement and find her own stories, then elaborate on them for the public's insatiable appetite for Hollywood gossip.

"Rodwell Archibald Godfrey, otherwise known as Rag to us underlings, called me into his office and told me he wants more product. I can't make it happen if it isn't out there. All the A-list papers seem to get the stories first. I think this is just another way of saying he is not happy with my work. I applied to the other tabloids, but they're full up and not taking on anyone new. I'm doing my best. I just manage to make my mortgage payment every month and have enough left over to buy dog food. No, you cannot help me, Mom. I'm going to make it on my own, so let's not go down that road. My break is coming, I can feel it. By the way, I brought a stack of future issues for you to read. I have stuff in all of them."

"I can't get used to the idea that you people make all that stuff up, then it happens. And you print weeks in advance of what's happening," Toots said.

Abby laughed. "It's not quite that way, but you're close. Well, we're home, and you have guests. You really know how to throw a funeral, Mom."

"Event, dear. *Funeral* is such a dreary word. It conjures up all kinds of dismal thinking."

Abby laughed as she climbed out of the limo

and marched up the steps to the wide veranda of her mother's house.

Both women raced upstairs to change into dry clothing before they had to meet with the guests who would be coming by to pay their last respects.

Toots looked at herself in the long mirror in her room. Yes, she did look bedraggled, but wasn't a widow supposed to look a little bedraggled? "Black is not my best color," she muttered to herself as she tossed her mourning outfit into a heap on the floor in the bathroom. She donned another black dress, added a string of pearls, brushed out her hair, sprayed on some perfume, and felt refreshed enough to go downstairs and socialize for an hour or so.

Burying the dead was so time-consuming. Even the aftermath took an eternity. All she wanted to do was retire to her sitting room to read the pile of tabloids Abby had brought with her. Not for the world would Toots ever admit that she was addicted to tabloid gossip. But for now, she had a duty to perform, and perform it she would. She had all evening to read her treasured tabloids and guzzle a little wine while doing so. She'd drink to Leland, and that would be the end of this chapter in her life.

Time to move on. Something she was very good at.

Chapter 2

The minute the last guest walked out the door with a go-bag of food, the bereaved Toots galloped up the stairs and headed for her three-hundred-square-foot bathroom, where she ran a bath. She made two trips to the huge Jacuzzi with the pile of tabloids, four scented candles, a fresh bottle of wine, and her favorite Baccarat wineglass. She paused a minute to decide which bath salts she wanted to use, finally settling on Confederate jasmine since the scent was more or less true to the flower. She was, when you got right down to it, a transplanted Southern belle.

Toots stripped down, and the clothes she was wearing went on top of the sodden outfit she'd discarded earlier. She'd never wear them again. Then again, since she was a stickler for protocol, maybe she'd tell her housekeeper, Bernice, to leave them until her ten days of mourning were up. That way she wouldn't be cheating. And to think she had to wear black, which really made her look washed out, for another ten days. Nine more if you counted today. Well, she was definitely counting today.

Toots sniffed at the delicious aroma emanating from the Jacuzzi. Wonderful! She lowered herself into the silky water and sighed happily. Toots leaned back and savored the first few moments of the exquisite bath before leaning forward to pour herself a glass of the bubbly that Leland had bought by the truckload for his wine cellar.

"To you, Leland," Toots said as she held her wineglass aloft. She turned up the glass and swallowed the contents in one long gulp. Now she could move on. She'd done her duty.

Toots refilled her glass, leaned back, and fired up a cigarette. Smoking was a truly horrible habit, but she didn't care. She was way too old to worry about what was good or bad for her. She was all about living and didn't give a thought to the fact that cigarettes would interfere with that. Besides, she had every vice there was. She loved vices because they made for such good conversations. She liked to drink, smoke, was a sugar addict and a closet tabloid reader. She'd long ago convinced herself that being a vegan made up for all her bad habits. That shit, Leland, was forever giving her grief for her, as he put it, unsavory habits. "Screw you, Leland!"

Toots was on her third glass of wine and on page four of the issue she was reading before she realized she couldn't remember what she'd just read. What was wrong with her? Nothing ever interfered with reading her beloved tabloids. Until now. She closed her eyes and tried to figure out what it was that was interfering with her universe.

Something was lurking somewhere inside her. She'd already scratched Leland. Abby was okay, at least for the moment. Did she feel rudderless? Did she need a man in residence? Hell no, she didn't. Then what was bothering her? The nine days of mourning she allowed herself? She snorted. Any woman worth her salt could get through nine days of mourning by going out to breakfast, lunch, and dinner every day. Fit in a little shopping, and she'd be good to go.

By the fourth glass of wine, Toots decided she needed . . . no, she didn't need, she *wanted* to stir up some trouble. She needed some excitement in her life. Her thoughts carried her back in time to when she was young and full of piss and vinegar with her friends. Friends she hadn't seen near enough throughout the past twenty years. They e-mailed, called, and sent Christmas cards, but life got in the way sometimes. Maybe it was time to call all of them and invite them for a visit. They were, after all, Abby's godmothers. Everyone thought it strange that her daughter had three godmothers. Especially that shithead, Leland. She didn't find it strange at all. Neither did her friends.

Toots peered into the wine bottle. Empty! She climbed out of the tub, dried off with a towel the size of a tent, powdered herself, slipped into a black nightgown—because she was in mourning—and tottered out to the minioffice in her bedroom. It wasn't really an office, just a little table where she sat to write notes to people she didn't give two shits about, pay a few bills that she didn't want her business manager to know about, and use her laptop to check out TMZ and Page Six several times a day.

Toots fired up her laptop and proceeded to type an e-mail to her friend Mavis, who lived in Maine in a little clapboard house near the ocean.

"I want you to come for a visit, Mavis. You were always the one with the ideas. How soon can you get here? By the way, I just buried Leland today, and I'm in a funk."

Five minutes later, the laptop pinged receipt of a return e-mail.

"Sorry, Toots, I can't afford a trip like that. I can't leave Coco, my dog. She's really my only friend these days. I'm sorry your dog Leland died. I didn't even know you had a dog. It's terrible when your beloved pet dies. Sorry, Toots, I'd love to see you, but my pension just won't cover a trip at this time."

Toots blinked. How weird that Mavis thought Leland was a dog. She wondered why she thought that, then it dawned on her what her old friend meant.

She hit the REPLY button.

"I'll send a first-class ticket for you and Coco. Leland was my husband."

The next response from Mavis was: *"LOL, I forgot you married again. Too bad, too sad. You'll get over it, Toots, you always do. I'll be happy to accept your tickets and look forward to seeing you. It's been way too long. Are the others coming, too?"*

Toots fired back, *"I'm working on it now. More tomorrow."*

Toots's next e-mail was to Sophie, who'd married a philanderer, now with one foot in the grave and the other on a banana peel, according to Sophie's latest e-mail. It was a known fact among the foursome that Sophie hated her husband and was only sort of/more or less taking care of him because of the five-million-dollar insurance policy she'd taken out on him some years ago. "I'm sticking around long enough to collect, then I'm outta here," she'd said.

"Sophie, I'm e-mailing you to invite you for a visit. I'm willing to send you a ticket if you can clear your calendar. It's been way too long since we've seen each other. I have something in mind that I think you and the others will find interesting. It will be like old times."

Sophie's response came through so quickly that Toots was surprised. *"I can't leave him here alone. This old bird is taking way too long to die. I didn't pay that mountain of premiums all these years to get aced out of the payoff. Besides, I want him to sweat every day and wonder if I'm going to give him his meds and feed him. Which, of course, I do. What kind of person would I be not to do that?"*

Well, Toots decided, she could certainly relate to that. *"Not to worry, Sophie. I'll get you a nurse 24/7 for your husband. So you'll come, then? By the way, I buried Leland today."*

Sophie shot back. *"Okay, I'll clear my schedule that's not really a schedule. Just let me know when my departure date is. Who is Leland?"*

Toots responded to her e-mail. *"I'll get back to you on the date. Leland was my husband. I have to do that ten-day mourning thing. Nine days if you count today. I am definitely counting today. You can watch me and know what it's like, so you'll know how to behave when that dud you married bites the dust. Mourning is tricky. You have to do it just right, or people will talk about you."*

"What number is Leland?" Sophie queried. *"I think you've been married more times than Elizabeth Taylor."*

Toots quickly replied, *"Leland was number 8, and I am* never *getting married again. More tomorrow. I have to e-mail Ida now. She's going to be tough. Remember how we hated each other and pretended we didn't? I think she's still ticked off that I married the guy she wanted. She'd be a widow now if I hadn't. I tried to tell her he was a big nothing, but he did have all that money."*

Toots didn't bother waiting for a response before she e-mailed Ida. She got right to the point. *"Ida, it's Toots. I'm e-mailing you to invite you for a visit. Mavis and Sophie have agreed to come, and it will be like old times. I have this plan, Ida, and I want to involve all of us in it. I hope you aren't still holding a grudge against me. It's time for us to forget about all that old silly stuff. Believe it or not, I did you a favor by stealing whatever his name was. Even his money didn't make up for how boring he was. But he was gentle and considerate. So, what do you think? By the way, I buried Leland today. I'm in mourning, have nine days to go."*

Ida's response was short and curt. *"Count me in. Tell me when you want me to arrive. Oh, boo hoo about Leland."*

Toots rubbed her hands together and closed her laptop. She was on a roll, she could feel it. Though what this big plan was, she hadn't a clue just yet. She'd think of something. She always did.

Chapter 3

Toots had wakened at five A.M. every day of the week for as long as she could remember, but today, on her tenth and final day of mourning, she woke up at three, more excited than she'd been in ages. Sophie, Mavis, and Ida would be arriving first thing in the morning. Today was her "get my ass in gear" day.

Out of habit she quickly made her bed. She'd let Bernice, her friend and housekeeper, worry about dusting and vacuuming later. This day was to be a new beginning for her. She wanted to live like a woman half her age, not like some old fuddy-duddy who buried husbands like ancient treasures, then spent the rest of her life memorializing them. No, no, no, that was not for her.

Thrilled she could finally toss her black mourning clothes, Toots chose a bright hot-pink blouse to wear with a cherry red skirt. Just a bit over five-seven, and thankfully she hadn't acquired a hump on her back like many women her age, her reddish-brown hair still glistened.

Of course she colored her hair, but that was her own secret. She tied her hair in a loose topknot. *Not bad for sixty-five,* she thought as she gazed in the full-length mirror. Three of her husbands had told her she looked like Katharine Hepburn, though for the life of her she couldn't recall which ones. It didn't matter anyway. She smiled at her reflection. The colors were loud, but after ten days of black, she planned to dress like a rainbow from here on. No more husbands, so there would be no need for black. With that thought in mind, Toots yanked everything black out of her closet, tossing all of it into a laundry basket. She'd donate the clothes to charity. That accomplished, Toots headed downstairs to the kitchen, her favorite room in her house.

The old pine floors shone like molten gold. With the sunrise, Toots knew the freshly washed windows would sparkle like diamonds. She and Bernice had spent yesterday scrubbing and shining them with white vinegar and newspapers. Red and emerald green throw rugs were scattered around the floor like Christmas gumdrops. Custom-made red cabinets, which Leland had called gaudy and tacky, lined three walls. On the fourth wall was a fireplace made from large rocks she had gathered herself in the mountains of North Carolina. Leland had thought that was cheap. She'd reminded him this was *her* house, and he was free to live in the guesthouse anytime he chose. He chose to stay put, the old shit. But he'd kept his mouth shut after that. Well, Leland was dead and gone. She could paint the walls purple if she wanted to.

Obliterating all thoughts of her deceased spouse, Toots prepared a pot of coffee, found her cigarettes in the kitchen drawer where she hid her secret supply of PayDay candy bars. When the coffee finished brewing, she filled her favorite Maxine cup with the hot brew. Cigarettes and coffee in hand, she went outside to sit on the back veranda.

She loved this time of day. The birds were starting to awaken, the potpourri of their chirping music to her ears. The flowers and shrubbery were still glazed with early-morning dew. Freshly plowed dirt from her neighbor's garden seasoned the morning air, reminding her that summer was just around the corner. The bouquet of night-blooming jasmine she'd gathered last night sat in a vase on a wicker side table, filling her senses with its pungent odor. God, she loved this place. She couldn't imagine living anywhere else in the whole world.

Taking a big swallow of coffee, Toots went over her mental "get my ass in gear" list. She and Bernice had worked like troopers yesterday cleaning most of the house inside and out. Pete, her longtime friend and gardener, weeded the flower beds, spruced up the shrubs, cut the grass, then trimmed the dead leaves from her two angel oaks. The hummingbird feeders were replenished, dried corn sprinkled around for the squirrels in hopes they would stay away from her bird feeders, but that was a lost cause. She did this every year and saw no reason to stop anytime soon. She had a routine, liked sticking to it most days, but there was a yearning in her now, something she hadn't been able to silence since Leland's death. The best she could come up with was that a sort of restlessness was flowing through her veins. Was this what getting old felt like? Lost, with no sense of purpose? No! No! No! She would not allow herself a pity party by believing in that crap.

Her best friends in the whole world were on their way for a visit. A dark mood was not on her agenda. She liked to count her blessings and reminded herself of all she had to be thankful for. At sixty-five she was healthy as a horse, according to her physical three months ago. She had a beautiful daughter who seemed to be thriving in Los Angeles. Her dearest friends were still alive. She had more money than JPMorgan Chase, at least today she did, and she didn't see that changing anytime in the near future. Life was lookin' good.

She took a slurp of the now-cold coffee, lit another cigarette, and inhaled the toxins before releasing the acrid smoke into the fresh air. Ida would be on her ass like white on rice when she found out that Toots still smoked. Ida thought everything in life that felt good was actually bad for you. Breathing was bad for you, according to her. Mavis said Ida had something the professionals called OCD, obsessive compulsive disorder, whatever the hell that was. Didn't anyone just get constipated anymore? Why did every disease have to be reduced to initials?

New beginnings, Toots thought as she went inside to refill her cup. *Brand-spanking-new beginnings.* No husbands to fret over, not that she ever had, but for the first time in a very, very long time, Toots was on her own. She wasn't sure if she liked the idea or not. She'd always had some distant family close by or, God help her, a husband to contend with. With Abby on the West Coast and her friends scattered across the country, Toots realized that the feelings she'd been experiencing were feelings of loss, of not being needed. Shit. Someone always needed something. She would simply find a new need, fill it, and live heartily.

Never one to wallow in self-pity, Toots drank two more cups of coffee and smoked three more cigarettes before fixing herself a bowl of Froot Loops cereal doused liberally with extra sugar and whole milk. She laughed loudly at what she thought of as her wicked ways.

"What on earth are you doing up at this hour laughing like a loon in *my* kitchen?" Bernice asked from the front door, where she'd been watching her crazy employer, whom she loved more than she had ever loved her own deceased husband.

Toots almost jumped out of her skin. "Damn, Bernice, you scared the snot out of me! I didn't hear the front door open. I might ask you the same thing. Why are you here so early?"

"We have a long list of things to do today. You said so yourself last night. All those hoity-toity friends of yours will be here soon. I wouldn't want them to think you lived like anything but a queen. I'm here at your command. Remember how you taught me to say that after your third husband died?"

Toots grimaced. She couldn't remember any such thing, but she nodded anyway.

Bernice was more friend than employee. When Toots had told her about her friends' upcoming visit, Bernice wasn't the least bit thrilled. Not wanting her to feel left out of the swing of things, she'd asked her to help with a few extra chores, hoping it would make her feel included, part of the gang, but instead Bernice acted like she'd been stung by a nasty bunch of bees, then mumbled something about being the hired help.

"Oh, stop it already! You're acting like a baby. You don't have to stick around while the girls are here. I'm sure you have plenty of other activities to occupy your time." Toots and Bernice both knew this was bullshit. Bernice's family consisted of a son she hadn't seen or heard from in four years and was supposedly traveling the world in search of his roots.

"If you weren't my employer, I'd tell you to just kiss my wrinkled old ass," Bernice said with a trace of her old humor.

"Yeah? And if you weren't my favorite employee, I'd tell you you're fired. So there," Toots shot right back.

"Did you drink the entire pot of coffee?" Bernice asked.

"Yep, what's it to ya?" Toots singsonged. "You the coffee police this morning?"

"You know I like at least three cups before I start working. Make another pot while I fix myself some toast."

"Yes, sir—ma'am!" Toots said, smiling. This was their normal morning routine. Bernice was a bit on the possessive side, though in a good way, when it came to her friendship with Toots. The truth was, Toots knew she'd just lie down and die if Bernice deserted her. She consoled herself that once Bernice got to know the girls on this visit, since they would all be here at once, she'd come around. They'd have plenty of time for gabbing and getting to know each other all over again. Bernice included.

The phone rang, alarming Toots. She'd learned through eight marriages that early-morning and late-night phone calls never brought good news. She hesitated before answering, then remembered there weren't any more husbands to bury.

"Hello?" she said in a brisk voice.

"Mom, are you really awake at this god-awful hour or just pretending to be?" Abby asked.

"I could ask you the same question. Knowing you're on the West Coast probably means you are winding down your night's work. So what gives? Why are you calling me at this ungodly hour? You're okay, aren't you?" Toots asked anxiously.

"It depends on what you mean by okay. Am I healthy? Yes. Is my mortgage paid? Yes. Is Chester okay? Yes to that, too." Abby sighed. Chester was the German shepherd that Abby had adopted three years ago on Christmas Day. Abby called her

Sweet Baby Love for short. Chester never responded to that endearment.

Toots knew her daughter, and she knew that she wouldn't call her at this time of day, or early morning as was the case, unless there was truly something bothering her. "So what's the problem? Is it a man? If you've met another jerk, and he needs to be taken care of, I'll be on the next flight out."

Abby ignored the gibe. "Mom, I just heard some disturbing news. It seems dear old Rag is in trouble. The entire staff knew he had a gambling problem. We just didn't know to what extent. We had a staff meeting yesterday afternoon. He told us he was putting *The Informer* up for sale. Said he was tired of working, but we all know it's to pay off his gambling debts. He spends most weekends in Vegas. I don't know what I'm going to do for a job. In one of his usual small spiteful moods, he told us one of the conditions to selling the paper would probably be that all former employees have to go. I'm just venting here, Mom."

"Oh, honey, that's terrible. From everything you've told me about him, he might just do himself in. You also said he threatens to sell from time to time and never does. Hold tight until you have something a little more definite to go on. Just out of curiosity, do you have any idea how much he's asking for the paper?" Toots asked, as an idea hit her like a lightning bolt.

"I don't know, Mom. I'm sure *The Globe* or *The Enquirer* will pick it up for a song if it really does go up for sale. If they do, they've got plenty of people to staff or pick up the slack. It just pisses me off that someone else's bad habit is putting me and a handful of others out of a job. I just hate the thought of possibly having to collect unemployment."

"You could come home, Abby. *The Post and Courier* would hire you in a heartbeat. You know that." Amanda Lawford, the owner and publisher of *The Post and Courier,* had worked with Toots on at least a dozen mutual committees and had told her time and again if Abby ever decided to move back to Charleston, she'd give her a job on the crime beat. Abby hadn't been interested. Maybe this time things would be different.

"Thanks, Mom, but no, thanks. I'm twenty-eight years old. The last thing I want to do is come crawling home with my tail between my legs. Besides, Amanda Lawford just wants me around to date that nerd son of hers."

Toots laughed. "You're right about that. He always asks about you when I see him."

"Tell him I said hello next time you see him. He's not a bad guy, just not my type. Besides, I could never date a guy named Herman. Reminds me of that show I used to watch as a kid."

"The Munsters!" Toots laughed as she recalled how Abby sat glued to reruns of the old television show and, to her knowledge, never missed an episode.

"Yep, that was it. So when do all my godmothers arrive? I can't believe you actually orchestrated a visit for them at the same time. It's been like forever since I've seen them."

"Come home, and you can see them, Abby. They'd love to see you," Toots encouraged. "I'll buy you a ticket."

"The timing is off. With the dark stuff about to hit the fan at the paper, I don't think it would be in my best interest to take a vacation. Besides, I was just there."

"Your room is waiting if you change your mind. Bernice takes great pleasure in freshening your room every day in case you decide to make a spur-of-the-moment visit."

"Thanks, Mom. You're the best, but right now I just needed to cry on your shoulder. I'll figure something out. I can always work for the *Los Angeles Times*. I get e-mails from my former editor at least once a month trying to lure me back."

"You wouldn't be happy writing about stuffy politicians and government," Toots said.

Toots could hear Abby's deep sigh over the phone. "If it comes down to that, I'll consider it. I have bills to pay, and no, I'm not going to allow you to cover my ass, so let's not even go there, okay?"

Toots smiled in spite of herself. Abby was just like her father. Fiercely independent. "Whatever you say, dear. Just know that help is out there if things get too rough."

"How did I ever get so lucky to wind up with a mother like you?" Abby asked.

"The luck of the draw, kiddo," Toots said. She hoped Abby would remember those words in six months.

Chapter 4

Toots raced around the kitchen, opening and closing drawers. "Where is my address book? I know it's in here somewhere."

"It's on your desk in your room. Remember, you always leave it there," Bernice said between bites of toast.

"Of course! You're right. What was I thinking?" Toots snapped.

"You weren't," Bernice quipped.

"Would you stop it already?" Toots tossed over her shoulder as she raced upstairs. She heard Bernice mutter something just as she found her address book on her desk. Toots laughed and shook her head. Bernice had been with her since Abby was a baby. At the time, she'd been recently widowed herself, with a young son, when she'd answered an ad for a housekeeper Toots had placed in the paper back in New Jersey all those years ago. When John Simpson, her one true love and Abby's father, died in a car accident, they'd left New Jersey behind with no regrets.

Bernice hadn't hesitated for a skinny minute when Toots asked her to come to Charleston. Abby had been five at the time. Where had all the years gone?

Bernice knew her better than had all eight of her husbands put together. She'd been with her through the good times and the bad. While a dear friend, Bernice was forever mindful of her position as an employee. Toots trusted her to the ends of the earth.

Toots flipped through the pages until she found the number for her stepson, Christopher Clay. She looked at the clock and realized it was probably too early to call. Shit! If Christopher was anything like his father, he got up with the chickens. Toots dialed the number despite the three-hour time difference. This was important. Screw propriety. As she waited for the call to go through, she tried to remember where Garland, Christopher's father, ranked on the husband scale. Maybe the fourth. Christopher had been in boarding school when they married.

Toots remembered fearing Chris would view her as his evil stepmother, but that hadn't been the case at all. Garland's first wife, Chris's mother, had died when Chris was a baby. He'd been thrilled at the prospect of having a "real mom," and they'd hit it off from the beginning. To this day, Toots still thought of him as her son. When Garland died and left her everything, she'd immediately turned the millions over to Chris, who'd just started law school. She'd kept the home they'd shared simply because Chris hadn't been ready for the responsibility of home ownership at the time. When the time was right, she'd give him the house as well. Toots had fond memories of their life together. She hoped Chris's memories were just as pleasant.

"This better be good," a throaty voice came over the wire.

"Christopher, good morning! It's Toots, how goes it, baby?" she said cheerfully. Everyone in Hollywood called each other baby.

The voice on the other end of the line chuckled. "I should have known it was you. Typhoon Toots, you're the only one crazy enough to call me this time of night . . . morning." Typhoon Toots was a name Chris had bestowed on her the week he'd graduated from college and she'd arranged the party of all parties for two hundred of his friends in a matter of just a few hours.

Toots smiled. She'd always admired and respected her stepson and was glad they'd remained close through the years. She knew she could count on him no matter what. When Abby had decided to move to Los Angeles, knowing Chris was there in the wings to watch over her was a tremendous weight off Toots's shoulders. He was as responsible as his father had been.

"Look, I'm sorry for this early-morning call, but it's important; otherwise, I wouldn't be calling. I need some legal advice, Chris, and you were the first person who came to mind. Plus you're in Los Angeles, which stacked the deck."

"Thanks for the vote of confidence, Toots. What's going down in LA?"

"It's Abby," she said. "She's in trouble."

"Damn! Why didn't you say something?"

"I'm saying it now. And, Christopher, it's not life-threatening. At least not at this point." Toots did have thoughts of choking Rodwell Archibald Godfrey, but she kept them to herself. "Clearly, Abby is alive and well, or I wouldn't be talking to you. She's having trouble at work."

"She still writing for that rag?"

Abby replied in a firm yet kind tone. "Yes, Christopher, she is still writing for that rag. She loves her work regardless of who approves or disapproves."

"No need to defend her, Toots. I'm an entertainment attorney. We don't rate so high in the legal world, either. So what kind of trouble has Abby gotten herself into?"

That was more like it. It reminded her of why she'd married Garland. He'd had a quick wit and all of his own teeth. Like father like son.

"The paper's owner needs to pay off his gambling debts. He told the staff he's selling the paper."

Christopher laughed. "What does this have to do with Abby? Doesn't she want to work for someone else? She's good, Toots. She could have her pick of beats at any of the large newspapers."

"As her mother, I already know that! Abby absolutely loves working for a tabloid," Toots said, her voice crisp and clipped. "Sorry, Chris, I'm just so ticked off right now. I didn't mean to go all snarly on you. Apparently one of the conditions in selling the paper is that the current employees, including Abby, have to go their own way. Abby says it's the owner's way of being petty and spiteful, and I tend to agree, but then again, I know nothing about how newspapers work."

"Toots, I know where this is heading, and as an attorney, I am going to advise you to stay out of it. Financially, *The Informer* is a flop. It's low on the tabloid totem pole. Very low, as I'm sure Abby's told you. I haven't a clue what the circulation is, but—"

"Find out as soon as possible. Offer them double their asking price. No questions, Chris. It is what it is."

"It's not a good investment, Toots. I strongly caution you against going down this road. You just said you don't know anything about newspapers. If your mind is made up, I won't stop you, but I am going on record that it is a poor move. I'm not keen on acting as your broker, either. Have you really thought this through, Toots? What does Abby think about this?"

Damn, how did she know he would ask her about Abby? "I have thought it through, Chris." Toots took a deep breath and let it out in a loud swoosh. "Currently, Abby is unaware of my intentions."

"I assume you don't plan to share them with her, either," Chris said sourly. He was not liking this conversation one little bit.

Was she that obvious? Hell yes. She was a mother. She had to do what she had to do for her daughter. Any woman/mother in her right mind would do whatever she could to help her daughter's career. So what if it was just the type of unscrupulous excitement she'd been looking for anyway? She couldn't wait to tell Sophie, Mavis, and Ida.

"Your assumption would be correct, darling boy."

"Okay, Toots. Give me a day or so to get the ball rolling."

"You're a good man, Chris, just like your father. I knew I could count on you."

Ten minutes later, Toots was downstairs pouring her umpteenth cup of coffee. There was a twinkle in her eye that hadn't been there since . . . forever.

"Bernice, I have a good bottle of scotch hidden around here somewhere. I say let's find it and make a toast." Toots ran around the kitchen, rifling through the cupboards, searching for the bottle. She found it next to the Comet cleanser beneath the sink. Bernice held out her empty mug. "Mind telling me what we're toasting?"

Suddenly, Toots was afraid she'd jinx the possible deal if she spoke about it before it was a fait accompli. She'd always been superstitious. "Yes. No. I'm not exactly sure. Never mind." Toots held her Maxine cup high. "Here's to new beginnings and happy endings."

The women clinked their mugs together, spilling coffee and liquor on the newly polished floor. Bernice dropped a kitchen towel onto the floor and used her foot to mop up the spill.

"I do like the way you clean, Bernice dear, but the Ladies' Society would frown on that particular method. Personally, I don't care; I'm just saying. I'm thinking they would call us both tacky," Toots said, before pouring each of them another bounteous spot of scotch.

"You didn't think that way yesterday while you were working me like a mule."

"Oh, for crying out loud, Bernice, stop whining. I did not work you like a mule yesterday. You have the cushiest job in Charleston," Toots said, before tipping her mug back.

"Don't get carried away, Toots."

They both laughed at the absurdity of their state of affairs. Each had it made, and they both knew life couldn't be better. They just liked to devil one another to, as Bernice put it, get the other's goat.

"So now that we're half snockered, do you want to tell me why we're drinking scotch at five o'clock in the morning?" Bernice asked.

"Nope, but let's just say this. I might be taking a trip to the West Coast. Soon. As in day-after-tomorrow soon."

"What about your friends? You can't just leave me here to entertain them! I don't even know them." Bernice started to flutter around like a lost hen.

"They'll come with me, of course. You can

come with us, too, if you want, you know that, Bernice. I'm not leaving you out."

"Not me! No, ma'am, I will *not* get on an airplane. That's not in my job description. I'll stay here and make sure Pete keeps the bird feeders full, thank you very much."

"Oh, Bernice, you need to live a little. Life's too short to allow fear to bog you down."

"Toots, I'm seventy years old. If God wanted me to fly, he would have given me wings. I've made it this far in life without flying, and I plan on keeping it that way. I've never been on an airplane in my life. I don't think it's going to matter one way or another at this point in time if I'm fearful of flying or not. I just can't see how it would improve my life," Bernice said, in defense of her lifelong fear of flying.

Toots thought about what her housekeeper had just said. She supposed it made sense from Bernice's point of view. "You're probably right, but still, you could give it some thought."

"Still nothing. It's unnatural. If people were meant to fly, we would've been born with wings." Bernice made her usual argument when the topic of air travel came up, and she never cared how repetitive she was.

"I suppose you're right about that, too, but you don't know what you're missing. There are still so many places I want to visit. Actually, I plan to become bicoastal. It's the new 'in thing' with seniors, at least healthy, well-to-do seniors." If she succeeded in purchasing *The Informer,* she would *have* to live bicoastal.

"You're certainly well qualified for that lifestyle," Bernice said tartly.

"Yes, I am, I won't disagree. Now let's get my 'ass in gear' list and zip through what's left. I still have some shopping to do. I think I'll have Pete drive me since I've . . . imbibed a little."

"Well, I, for one, need to rest a minute. That booze doesn't sit well in my stomach this early. We should have eaten some cornflakes first. Go on to the store. I'll put the fresh sheets on the guest beds while you're gone."

"Good idea. Thank heavens Walmart never closes. If you think of anything we didn't put on the list, call my cell," Toots called over her shoulder. Grabbing her purse and the keys to her Town Car, she walked out the back door without another word as she went in search of her gardener.

Two hours later, the early-morning sun flashed through the kitchen window as Toots dumped fourteen bags on the countertop. She skimmed through her list, checking off each item as she removed it from a bag. "Damn, something *is* up with Ida," she said out loud.

Bernice skirted through the kitchen like a summer breeze. "You back already?"

"Yes. Six in the morning is the perfect time to shop. There are no lines. Look at all this stuff." Toots indicated three bags of disinfectant and germ-killing products.

Bernice foraged through the bags. "What's

all this for? We've got plenty of cleaning supplies."

A bit bewildered, Toots shook her head. "Ida said she'd need a few things for her visit. This must be what Mavis was telling me about. Something about Ida's fear of germs. She called it OCD, obsessive compulsive disorder."

Bernice removed a box with a picture on the front label that resembled a cell phone. "What kind of dumb-bunny gadget is this?"

"It's called a germ-zapping light. Apparently you wave it around a germy area, and it's supposed to kill off any germs in ten seconds. E. coli, staphylococcus, salmonella, cold and flu germs, stuff like that. Mavis said Ida wouldn't come if I didn't buy one."

"Think she'll wave it over the toilet seat? Lord, I'll have to douse it with Clorox every two minutes."

Toots laughed. "Probably, but I don't think you need to concern yourself with Ida's germ disorder. I've bought everything under the sun and then some. Besides, this house is as clean as it's going to get. So what if there's a little germ here and there? Ida will just have to get over it."

"I suppose," Bernice said as she began transferring the canned goods and staples Toots had purchased to the pantry shelves. "I don't see why the need for all this food. You said yourself you gals were going to the West Coast. Who's going to eat all this?" she asked, waving her arm around to indicate the already overstocked shelves.

"Actually, Bernice, I'm stockpiling just in case I'm in California longer than planned, you know, more than, say, ten days. I don't have a clue at this juncture just how long I'll be staying, so I want to go with a free mind, knowing you and Pete will be covered until I get back. The freezer is chock-full." Toots wondered if she was putting the cart before the horse. Yes, she probably was, but she had a feeling this "project" might turn into something more than a simple bicoastal quickie business venture.

Maybe what she should do was cover all her bases and have Christopher check into purchasing a jet and hiring a full-time pilot so she wouldn't have to give up her Charleston digs. She beamed at the thought. *Yes*, she thought, it was all doable.

"Did you get any of those raspberry jelly rolls I like?"

"Don't I always? I don't see how you eat the silly things and not gain an ounce."

"The same way you do, Typhoon Toots. I smoke, drink, and thrive on the adrenaline rush I get when I see the stock market climbing. It keeps my metabolism high. Don't tell anyone I said that, because they won't believe you, but it's the honest-to-God truth." Bernice cackled.

"I'm sure it is." W*hen pigs fly.*

Do you enjoy the Sisterhood novels,
but missed the very first book in the series?

Here's a special look back at where it all began!

WEEKEND WARRIORS,

a Zebra paperback on sale now.

Prologue

Washington, D.C.

The traffic was horrendous on Massachusetts Avenue, but then it was always horrendous at this time of day. Rush hour. God, how she hated those words. Especially today. She slapped the palm of her hand on the horn and muttered under her breath, "C'mon you jerk, move!"

"Take it easy, Nik," Barbara Rutledge said, her eyes on the slow moving traffic. "One more block and we're there. Mom won't mind if we're a few minutes late. She hates it that she turned sixty today so the longer she has to wait for the celebration, the better she'll feel. I don't think she looks sixty, do you, Nik?"

"Are you kidding! She looks better than we do and we're only thirty-six." She leaned on the horn again even though it was an exercise in futility. "Just tell me one thing, why did your mother pick the Jockey Club for dinner?"

"The first crab cakes of the season, that's why.

President Reagan made this restaurant famous and all her political friends come here. If you want my opinion, thirty bucks for two crab cakes is obscene. I can eat lunch all week on thirty bucks if I'm careful. Mom pitched a fit last week when I took her to Taco Bell for lunch. We both ate for five bucks. She was a good sport about it but she can't understand why I don't tap into the trust fund. I keep telling her I want to make it on my own. Some days she understands, some days she doesn't. I know she's proud of me, you, too, Nik. She tells everyone about her two crime fighting girls who are lawyers."

"I love her as much as you do, Barb. I can't imagine growing up without a mother. I would have if she hadn't stepped in and taken over when my parents died. Okay, we're here and we're only thirty minutes late. This isn't the best parking spot in the world but it will have to do and we're under a streetlight. In this city it doesn't get any better than that."

"We really should hit the powder room before we head for the table. Mom does like spit and polish, not to mention perfume and lipstick," Barbara said, trying to smooth the wrinkles out of her suit. Nik did the same thing.

"I spent the day in court and so did you. We're supposed to look wrinkled, messy, and harried. Myra will understand. Ooops, almost forgot my present," Nik said, reaching into the backseat for a small silver-wrapped package. She handed Barbara a long cylinder tied with a bright red ribbon. "Your brain must be as tired as mine. You almost forgot yours, too. What about this pile of books, Barb?"

"They're for Mom. I picked them up today at lunchtime. You know how she loves reading about murder and mayhem. I'll give them to her when we leave."

Myra Rutledge was waiting, a beautiful woman whose smile and open arms welcomed them. "My girls are here. We're ready to be seated now, Franklin," Myra said.

"Certainly, madam. Your usual table, or would you prefer the smoking section with a window view?"

"The window, Franklin," Barbara said. "I think tonight in honor of my mother's birthday you two can have a cigarette. Just one cigarette after dinner for both of you. I will of course abstain. Yes, yes, yes, I know we all quit but this is Mom's birthday and I say why not."

Myra smiled as she reached for her daughter's hand. "Why not indeed."

"This is so wonderful," Myra said, sitting down and leaning across the table. "My two favorite girls. I couldn't ask for a better finale to my birthday."

"Finale, Mom! Does that mean when you go home, you and Charles won't celebrate?"

"Well . . . I . . . perhaps a glass of sherry. I did ask Charles to come but he said this was a mother daughter dinner and he would feel out of place. No comments, girls."

"Mom, when are you going to marry the guy?

You've been together for twenty years. Nik and I know all about the birds and the bees so stop blushing," Barbara teased.

"Yes, and it was Charles who told you two about the birds and the bees." Myra smiled.

Charles Emery was Myra's companion slash houseman. When his cover was blown as an MI 6 agent his government had relocated him to the United States where he'd signed on as head of security for Myra's Fortune 500 candy business. His sole goal in life was to take care of Myra, a job he took seriously and did well. Both girls were grateful to his attention to Myra, lessening her loneliness when they went off on their own.

Myra's eyes sparkled. "Now, tell me everything. Your latest cases, who you're dating at the moment, how our softball team is doing. Don't leave anything out. Will I be planning a wedding any time soon?"

It was what Nikki loved about Myra the most, her genuine interest in their lives. She'd never invaded their privacy, always content to stand on the sidelines, offer motherly support and aid when needed but she never interfered, or gave advice unless asked. Nikki knew Myra enjoyed the times the three of them spent together, loved the twice-monthly dinners in town and the occasional lunches with her daughter or perhaps a short stroll along the Tidal Basin.

Yes, Myra had a life, a busy life, a life of her own beyond her girls. She sat on various charitable boards, worked tirelessly for both political parties, did numerous good deeds every day, was active in the Historical Society and still managed to have time for Charles, Barbara, and herself.

"You staying in town tonight, Mom?"

A rosy hue marched across Myra's face. "No, Barbara, I'm going home. No, I didn't drive myself. I took a car service so don't fret about the trip to McLean. Charles is waiting for me. I told you, we'll have a glass of sherry together."

"No birthday cake!" Nik said.

The rosy hue crept down Myra's neck. "We had the cake at lunchtime. Charles needed a blowtorch to light all the candles. All sixty of them. It was very . . . festive."

"How does it feel to be sixty, Mom?" Barbara asked, reaching for her mother's hand across the table. "You told me you were dreading the day."

"It's just a number, just a day. I don't feel any different than I did yesterday. People always talk about 'the moments' in their lives. The special times they never forget. I guess this day is one of those moments. The day I married your father was a special moment. The day you were born was an extra special moment, the day Nikki came to us was another special moment, and then of course when the candy company went 500. Don't laugh at me now when I tell you the other special moment was when Charles said he would take care of me for the rest of my life. All wonderful moments. I hope I have years and years of special moments. If you would get married and give me a grandchild I would run up the flag, Barbara. I don't want to be so old I dodder when you give birth."

Nikki poked Barbara's arm, a huge smile on her face. "Go on, tell her. Make your mother happy on her sixtieth birthday."

"I'm pregnant, Mom. You can start planning the wedding, but you better make it quick or I'll be showing before you know it."

Myra looked first at Nikki to see if they were teasing her or not. Nikki's head bobbed up and down. "I'm going to be the maid of honor and the godmother! She's not teasing, Myra."

"Oh, honey. Are you happy? Of course you are. All I have to do is look at you. Oh, there is so much to do. You want the reception at home in the garden, right?"

"Absolutely, Mom. I want to be married in the living room. I want to slide down the bannister in my wedding gown. I'm going to do that, Mom. Nik will be right behind me. If I can't do that, the wedding is off."

"Anything you want, honey. Anything. You have made me the happiest woman in the whole world. Promise that you will allow Charles and me to babysit."

"She promised me first." Nikki grinned.

"This is definitely 'a moment.' Do either of you have a camera?"

"Mom, a camera is not something I carry around in my purse. However, all is not lost. Nik has one in her car. I'll scoot over there and get it."

Nikki fished in her pocket and tossed her the keys.

"I'm going to be a mother. Me! Do you believe it? You'll be Auntie Nik," Barbara said, bending over to tweak Nikki's cheek. "I'll ask Franklin to take our picture when I get back. See ya," she said, flashing them both an ear-to-ear grin.

"I hope you had a good day, today, Myra. Birthdays are always special," Nikki said, her gaze on the window opposite her chair. "Knowing you're going to be a grandmother has to be the most wonderful thing in the world. I'm pretty excited myself." She could see Barbara running across the street, her jacket flapping in the spring breeze. "Do you remember the time Barbara and I made you a birthday cake out of cornflakes, crackers, and pancake syrup?"

"I'll never forget it. I don't think the cook ever forgot it either. I did eat it, though."

Nikki laughed. "Yes, you did." She was glad now she had parked under the streetlight. She could see several couples walking down the street, saw Barbara open the back door of the car, saw her reach for the camera, saw her sling it over her shoulder, saw her lock the door. She turned her attention to Myra, who was also staring out the window. Nikki's gaze swiveled back to the window to see Barbara look both ways for oncoming traffic, ready to sprint across the street at the first break. The three couples were almost upon her when she stepped off the curb.

Nikki was aware of the dark car that came out of nowhere, the sound of horns blowing and the sudden screech of brakes. Myra was moving off her seat almost in slow motion, her face a mask of disbelief as they both ran out of the restaurant. The scream when it came was so tortured, so animal-like, Nikki stopped in her tracks to reach for Myra's arm.

The awkward position of her friend's body was a picture that would stay with Nikki forever. She bent down, afraid to touch her friend, the friend she called sister. "Did anyone call an ambulance?" she shouted. She heard a loud, jittery response. "Yes."

"No! No! No!" Myra screamed over and over as she dropped to the ground to cradle her daughter's body in her arms. From somewhere off in the distance, a siren could be heard. Nikki's trembling fingers fumbled for a pulse. Her whole body started to shake when she couldn't find even a faint beat. Maybe she wasn't doing it right. She pressed harder with her third and fourth fingers the way she'd seen nurses do. A wave of dizziness riveted through her just as the ambulance crew hit the ground running. Tears burned her eyes as she watched the paramedics check Barbara's vital signs.

Time lost all meaning as the medical crew did what they were trained to do. A young woman with long curly hair raised her head to look straight at Nikki. Her eyes were sad when she shook her head.

It couldn't be. She wanted to shout, to scream, to stamp her feet. Instead, she knuckled her eyes and stifled her sobs.

"She'll be all right, won't she, Nikki? Broken bones heal. She was just knocked unconscious. Tell me she'll be all right. Please, tell me that. Please, Nikki."

The lump in Nikki's throat was so large she thought she would choke. She tried not to look at the still body, tried not to see them straighten out Barbara's arms and legs. When they lifted her onto the stretcher, she closed her eyes. She thought she would lose it when the young woman with the long curly hair pulled a sheet up over her best friend's face. Not Barbara. Not her best friend in the whole world. Not the girl she played with in a sandbox, gone to kindergarten with. Not the girl she'd gone through high school, college, and law school with. She was going to be her maid of honor, babysit her baby. How could she be dead? "I saw her look both ways before she stepped onto the curb. She had a clear path to cross the street," she mumbled.

"Nikki, should we ride in the ambulance with Barbara? Will they let us?" Myra asked tearfully.

She doesn't know. She doesn't know what the sheet means. How was she going to tell Myra her daughter was dead?

The ambulance doors closed. It drove off. The siren silent.

"It's too late. They left. You'll have to drive, Nikki. They'll need all sorts of information when they admit her to the hospital. I want to be there. Barbara needs to know I'm there. She needs to know her mother is there. Can we go now, Nikki?" Myra pleaded.

"Ma'am?"

"Yes, officer," Nikki said. She loosened her hold on Myra's shoulders.

His voice was not unkind. He was too young to be this kind. She could see the compassion on his face.

"I need to take a statement. You are . . ."

"Nicole Quinn. This is Myra Rutledge. She's the mother . . ." She almost said, "of the deceased," but bit her tongue in time.

"Officer, can we do this later?" Myra interjected. "I have to get to the hospital. There will be so much paperwork to take care of. Do you know which hospital they took my daughter to? Was it George Washington or Georgetown Hospital?" Myra begged. Tears rolled down her wrinkled cheeks.

Nikki looked away. She knew she was being cowardly, but there was just no way she could get the words past her lips to tell Myra her only daughter was dead. She watched as police officers dispersed the crowd of onlookers until only the three couples remained. Where was the car that hit Barbara? Did they take it away already? Where was the driver? She wanted to voice the questions aloud but remained silent because of Myra.

Nikki watched as the young officer steeled himself for what he had to do. He worked his thin neck around the starched collar of his shirt, cleared his throat once, and then again. "Ma'am, your daughter was taken to the morgue at George Washington Hospital. There's no hurry on the paperwork. I can have one of the officers take you to the hospital if you like. I'm . . . I'm sorry for your loss, ma'am."

Myra's scream was primal as she slipped to the ground. The young cop dropped to his knees. "I thought she knew. I didn't . . . Jesus . . ."

"We need to get her to a doctor right away. Will you stay with her for a minute, officer? I need to get my cell phone out of the car to make some calls." Her first call was to Myra's doctor and then she called Charles. Both promised to meet her at the emergency entrance to GW Hospital.

When she returned, Myra was sitting up, supported by the young officer. She looked dazed and her speech was incoherent. "She doesn't weigh much. I can easily carry her to the cruiser," the officer said. Nikki nodded gratefully.

"Can you tell me what happened, officer? Did you get the car that hit Barbara? Those couples standing over there must have seen everything. We even saw it from the restaurant window. Did they get the license plate number? I saw a dark car, but it came out of nowhere. She had a clear path to cross the street. He must have peeled away from the curb at ninety miles an hour."

"I ran the license plate one of the couples gave us, but it isn't going to do any good."

"Why is that?" Nikki rubbed at her temples as a hammer pounded away inside her head.

"Because it was a diplomat's car. That means the driver has diplomatic immunity, ma'am."

Nikki's knees buckled. The young cop reached out to steady her.

"That means he can't be prosecuted," Nikki said in a choked voice.

"Yes, ma'am, that's exactly what it means."

Chapter 1

Sixteen months later

It was dusk when Nikki Quinn stopped her cobalt-blue BMW in front of the massive iron gates of Myra Rutledge's McLean estate. She pressed the remote control attached to the visor and waited for the lumbering gates to slide open. She knew Charles was watching her on the closed-circuit television screen. The security here at the estate was sophisticated, high-tech, impregnable. The only thing missing was concertina wire along the top of the electrified fence.

Nikki sailed up the half mile of cobblestones to the driveway that led around to the back of the McLean mansion. When she was younger, she and Barbara referred to the house as Myra's Fortress. She'd loved growing up here, loved riding across the fields on Barbara's horse Starlite, loved playing with Barbara in the tunnels underneath the old house that had once been used to aid runaway slaves.

The engine idling, Nikki made no move to get out of the car. She hated coming here these days, hated seeing the empty shell her beloved Myra had turned into. All the life, all the spark had gone out of her. According to Charles, Myra sat in the living room, drinking tea, staring at old photo albums, the television tuned to CNN twenty-four hours a day. She hadn't left the house once since Barbara's funeral.

She finally turned off the engine, gathered her briefcase, weekend bag, and purse. Should she put the top up or leave it down? The sky was clear. She shrugged. If it looked like rain, Charles would put the top up.

"Any change?" she asked, walking into the kitchen.

Charles shook his head before he hugged her. "She's gone downhill even more these last two weeks. I hate saying this, but I don't think she even noticed you weren't here, Nikki."

Nikki flinched. "I couldn't get here, Charles. I had to wait for a court verdict. I must have called a hundred times," Nikki said, tossing her gear on the countertop. Her eyes pleaded with Myra's houseman for understanding.

Charles Martin was a tall man with clear crystal blue eyes and a shock of white hair that was thick and full. Once he'd been heavier but this past year had taken a toll on him, too. She noticed the tremor in his hand when he handed her a cup of coffee.

"Is she at least talking, Charles?"

"She responds if I ask her a direct question. Earlier in the week she fired me. She said she didn't need me anymore."

"My God!" Nikki sat down at the old oak table with the claw feet. Myra said the table was over three hundred years old and hand-hewn. As a child, she'd loved eating in the kitchen. Loved sitting at the table drinking cold milk and eating fat sugar cookies. She looked around. There didn't seem to be much life in the kitchen these days. The plants didn't seem as green, the summer dishes were still in the pantry, the winter placemats were still on the table. Even the braided winter rugs were still on the old pine floors. In the spring, Myra always changed them. She blinked. "This kitchen looks like an institution kitchen, Charles. The house is too quiet. Doesn't Myra play her music anymore?"

"No. She doesn't do anything anymore. I tried to get her to go for a walk today. She told me to get out of her face. I have to fight with her to take a shower. I'm at my wit's end. I don't know what to do anymore. This is no way to live, Nikki."

"Maybe it's time for some tough love. Let me see if she responds to me this evening. By the way, what's for dinner?"

"Rack of lamb. Those little red potatoes you like, and fresh garden peas. I made a blackberry cobbler just for you. But when you're not here, I end up throwing it all away. Myra nibbled on a piece of toast today." Charles threw his hands in the air and stomped over to the stove to open the oven door.

Nikki sighed. She straightened her shoulders before she marched into the living room where Myra was sitting on the sofa. She bent down to kiss the wrinkled cheek. "Did you miss me, Myra?"

"Nikki! It's nice to see you. Of course, I missed you. Sit down, dear. Tell me how you are. Is the law firm doing nicely? How's our softball team doing? Are you still seeing that assistant district attorney?" Her voice trailed off to nothing as she stared at the television set whose sound was on mute.

Nikki sat down and reached for the remote control. "I hope you don't mind if I switch to the local station. I want to see the news." She turned the volume up slightly.

"Let's see. Yes, I'm still seeing Jack, and the firm is doing wonderfully. We have more cases than we can handle. The team is in fourth place. I'm fine but I worry about you, Myra. Charles is worried about you, too."

"I fired Charles."

"I know, but he's still here. He has nowhere to go, Myra. You have to snap out of this depression. I can arrange some grief counseling sessions for you. You need a medical checkup. You have to let it go, Myra. You can't bring Barbara back. I can't stand seeing you like this. Barbara wouldn't approve of the way you're grieving. She always said life is for the living."

"I never heard her say any such thing. I can't let it go. She's with me every minute of every day. There's nothing to live for. The bastard who killed my daughter robbed my life as well. He's out there somewhere living a good life. If I could just get my hands on him for five minutes, I would . . ."

"Myra, he's back in his own country. Shhh, listen. That man," Nikki said, pointing to the screen, "was set free today because of a technicality. He killed a young girl and he's walking away a free man. Jack prosecuted the case and lost."

"He must not be a very good district attorney if he lost the case," Myra snapped. Nikki's eyebrows shot upward. Was that a spark of interest? Childishly, she crossed her fingers.

"He's an excellent district attorney, Myra, but the law is the law. The judge let things go because they weren't legal. Oh, look, there's the mother of the girl. God, I feel so sorry for her. She was in court every single day. The papers said she never took her eyes off the accused, not even for a minute. The reporters marveled at the woman's steadfast intensity. Every day they did an article about her. Jack said she fainted when the verdict came in."

"I know just how she feels," Myra said, leaning forward to see the screen better. "What's she doing, Nikki? Look, there's Jack! He's very photogenic."

Nikki watched as the scene played out in front of her. She saw Jack's lips move, knew he was saying something but she couldn't hear over the voices of the excited news reporters. She saw his arm reach out but he was too late. Marie

Lewellen fired the gun in her hand point-blank at the man who killed her daughter.

The television screen turned black and then came to life again.

Barnes looked directly into the camera, his eyes wide with shocked disbelief. Blood bubbled from his mouth. "I . . . should have . . . killed . . . you, too . . . you bitch!"

"You killed my little girl. You don't deserve to live. I'm glad I killed you. Glad!" Marie Lewellen screamed.

Barnes fell face forward onto the concrete steps of the courthouse.

Chaos erupted but the camera stayed positioned, capturing the ensuing panic.

"Oh, my God!" was all Nikki could say.

Myra reared back against the cushions. "Did you see that! That's what I should have done! I hope she killed the son of a bitch! Is he moving? I can't see. Is he dead, Nikki? Charles, come see this. Why didn't I have the guts to do what that woman just did?" Myra shouted, her skinny arms flailing up and down. "If she killed him, I want you to defend her, Nikki. I'll pay for everything. Use your whole firm. Every expert, every specialist in the world. She killed him. She got in his face and killed him. Tell me he's dead. I want to know if he's dead!"

Nikki looked at Charles, who was busy staring at the ceiling. "He's dead, Myra."

"Look, look! They're handcuffing her. They're going to take her to jail. I want you to leave right now. Post her bail, do something. Don't let them keep her in jail. Say you'll take her home with you. Tell them she won't be a menace to society. Charles, get my checkbook."

"Myra, for God's sake, simmer down. It's not that easy."

"The hell it isn't. She was crazed. Temporary insanity. Are you going to do it or not, Nikki?"

"Yes, but . . ."

"Don't give me buts. You're still sitting here. I never asked you to do a thing for me, Nikki. Never once. I'm asking you now."

"I didn't say I wouldn't do it, Myra. I need to think. I need to talk to Jack. I can have my paralegal go down to the station. Tomorrow morning will be time enough. There is no way in hell she's getting out of jail tonight. She has to be arraigned. Can you wait for morning, Myra?"

"Yes, I can wait for morning." Myra swung around. "Charles, did you see what that woman just did? I would cheerfully rot in prison if I had the guts to do that. First thing in the morning, Nikki. I want you to call me with a full report."

"You don't answer the phone, Myra," Nikki said sourly.

"I'll answer it tomorrow. Isn't it time for dinner? Let's eat off trays this evening. I want to see what happens to that poor woman. They'll be reporting on this for hours. Does she have other children? A husband? Isn't anyone going to answer me?"

Nikki's jaw dropped. Charles spun around on his heel, a smirk on his face.

"I can tell you what Jack told me. She has two

other children, and yes, she has a husband. She's a homemaker. She works at a Hallmark shop on weekends for extra money that goes for all the little extras young kids need. Her husband is a lineman for AT&T. Her two boys are nine and eleven. Jenny, the daughter that was killed, worked after school till closing at the same Hallmark shop. She had a flat tire the night she was killed. She was fixing it herself when that creep offered to help and then he snatched her and dumped her body out near Manassas. Jack said they're a very nice family. Marie went to PTA meetings and they went to church as a family on Sunday."

"They'll need someone to take care of the boys, to cook and do all the things a mother does in case they don't let her out right away. Charles, find someone for the family. Use that employment agency we use when we do our spring cleaning. I hope they give her a medal. Someone should."

"Myra, for God's sake, she killed a man in cold blood. She took the law into her own hands. Civilized people don't do things like that. That's why we have laws."

"Where was the law when that bastard killed my daughter? Did Barbara get justice? No, she did not! My daughter is dead and no one paid for that crime. My unborn grandchild is dead and no one paid for that crime either. I'll go to my grave never having seen my grandchild. Don't talk to me about justice. Don't talk to me about the law because I don't want to hear it. Those laws, the justice that freed that man . . . *suck.*"

Nikki looked up to see Charles standing in the doorway. She watched as both his clenched fists shot upward. In spite of herself, she grinned. Myra was alive and belching fire. All she had to do was get her to calm down and maybe, just maybe, she would return to the land of the living.

It was midnight when Jack Emery finally returned Nikki's call. She crawled into bed, her head buzzing with the evening's events.

"Did you see it, Nikki?"

"Of course I saw it. Myra and Charles saw it, too. I'll say one thing, it snapped Myra out of her fugue. At least for now. She wants me to defend Marie Lewellen. I said I would."

"You can't defend her. It's open and shut. Insanity isn't going to hold up. She admitted to buying the gun at lunchtime from some punk on the street. That goes to premeditation. They've charged her with first degree murder. I'll be prosecuting, Nikki."

"Pass on it, Jack. You did enough to that woman."

"What the hell is that supposed to mean, Nikki?"

"It means that asshole got off. That's exactly what it means, Jack. Myra was right when she said it sucked. You didn't fight hard enough. He was guilty as sin and you damn well know it."

"The judge threw out . . . why am I defending myself? I did the best job I could under the circumstances. I tried to stop her at the courthouse. I was seconds too late. Don't go sour on me now. Turn it over to someone else in your firm, Nikki."

"I can't do that, Jack. I promised Myra. She's never, ever, asked anything of me. I have to do what she wants. I'm going to give you the fight of your life, too."

"If you take this case on that means we aren't going to be able to see one another until it's over, at which point we'll probably hate each other's guts. Is that what you want?"

Nikki's mind raced. No, it wasn't what she wanted but she knew where her loyalties lay. She loved Jack Emery. "Beg off, Jack. Let some other A.D.A. take the case."

"I guess I'll see you in court, Counselor," Jack said coldly.

It was his tone, not his words, that sparked her reply. "You bet your sweet ass you'll see me in court." Nikki snapped her cell phone shut and threw it across the room.

Nikki punched at the thick downy pillows. She knew she wasn't going to be able to sleep now. She felt like crying. A second later she bounded out of the twin bed and ripped down the covers from the bed that once belonged to Barbara. If she wanted to, she could stick her hand under the pillow and pull out Barb's old beat-up teddy bear and hug it to her chest the way Barb had done every night she slept in the bed.

It almost seemed sacrilegious to touch it. Instead she picked up the pillow and looked down at the tattered bear named Willie. She almost stuck her finger in the hole under Willie's chin but changed her mind. She lowered the pillow and went back to her own bed. Tears rolled down her cheeks. "God, I miss you, Barb. I think about you every day. I just had a fight with Jack. At least I think it was a fight. I wish you were here so I could call you up and tell you all about it." She punched at the down pillows again. Maybe she needed to read herself to sleep. Her gaze traveled to the built-in bookshelves across the room. The three top shelves were hers because she was taller than Barbara. The three bottom shelves belonged to Barbara and were loaded with everything *but* books. No, she was too wired-up to read.

The first month she'd come here to live, Myra had knocked out two walls and turned this room into a two-girl bedroom. They'd spent so many hours in here, huddled in their beds, giggling, telling secrets, talking about boys and sharing all their hopes and dreams. Even the bathroom had twin vanities and twin showers. Myra didn't stint and she didn't favor one over the other. She simply had enough love for both of them. She looked now at the twin desks, the colorful swivel chairs, the bright red rocking chairs. It seemed so long ago, almost like a lifetime. She stared at the colorful rockers and at the cushions they'd made at camp one year. Barbara's was perfect, her stitches small and neat. Her own was sloppy, the seams loose. But it wasn't the cushions that held her gaze. The chair was rocking, moving slowly back and forth. She looked up to see if the fan was on. A chill washed down her spine. She shuddered as she reached for her robe. Maybe Charles had left some coffee in the pot. If not, she could make some more.

Nikki walked down the long hallway to the back staircase that led to the kitchen. She blinked when she saw Myra and Charles sitting at the table, highball glasses in their hands. She blinked again. "I couldn't sleep," she mumbled.

"We couldn't either," Myra said.

"After what we saw on television this evening, I can understand why. I'm going to make some coffee."

"Nikki, Charles and I want to talk to you about something."

Nikki reached for the coffee canister. There was an edge to Myra's voice. A combative edge. Something she'd never heard before. "About what, Myra? I said I would take Marie Lewellen's case."

"I know. That's just a small part of it. Do you remember a while back when you told Charles and myself about two young women who came to see you? Kathryn Lucas and Alexis Thorne, only that wasn't Alexis Thorne's real name at the time?"

"I remember," Nikki said, measuring coffee into the stainless steel basket.

"You helped Alexis by going outside the law.

You couldn't help Kathryn because the statute of limitations had run out but if there was a way to help her, would you do it?"

Nikki felt herself freeze. "Are you talking about inside the law or outside the law, Myra?"

"Don't answer my question with a question. Would you help her?"

"I can't, Myra. There's nothing I can do for her. I looked at everything. Time ran out. Yes, I feel sorry for her. I understand how it all went down. She waited too long, that's the bottom line."

"You looked the other way for Alexis. You knew someone who was on the other side of the law and you got her a new identity, you helped her start a small home business as a personal shopper and you made it happen for her. You believed in her when she told you her story. She was a victim, she didn't deserve to go to prison for a whole year. She can never get that year of her life back. The men and women who turned her into a scapegoat walked free and are living the good life and her life is ruined. Kathryn is a victim and no one is helping her. Marie Lewellen could spend the rest of her life in jail unless you can get her off. Legally."

Nikki sat down across from Myra and Charles. "I think this would be a real good time for you to tell me *exactly* what you two are talking about."

"The system you work under doesn't always work," Charles said.

"Sometimes that's true," Nikki said carefully. "For the most part, it works."

Myra looked at Nikki over the rim of her glass. "What if we take the part that doesn't work and make it work? What if I told you I was willing to use my entire fortune, and you know, Nikki, that it is sizable, and use it to . . . make that system work. For us. For all the Maries, the Kathryns, and the Alexis Thornes who got lost in the system."

"Are you talking about going outside the law to . . . to . . . avenge these women? Are you talking about taking the law into your own hands and . . . and . . ."

Myra's head bobbed up and down. "Charles can help. He dealt with criminals and terrorists during his stint at MI 6. You're an attorney, a law professor. With your brains, Charles's expertise, and my money, we could right quite a few wrongs. It would have to be secret, of course."

"And you just now came up with all this?" Nikki said in awe. "No!"

"Yes," Myra and Charles said in unison.

Nikki looked at her watch. "Just eight hours ago, give or take a few minutes, you were practically comatose, Myra. You didn't want to live. You were so deep in your misery and your depression I wanted to cry for you. Now you're all set to take on the judicial system and dispense your own brand of justice. You'll get caught, Myra. You're too old to go to jail. They aren't kind to old people in jail. NO!"

Myra took a long pull from the highball glass. "If I can't satisfy my own vengeance, maybe I can do something for others where the system failed." She spoke in a low, even monotone. "Kathryn Lucas, age thirty-eight. Married to Alan Lucas, the love of her life. Alan had multiple sclerosis as well as Parkinson's disease and lived in a wheelchair. They owned an eighteen-wheeler, Alan's dream. In order to keep his dream alive for him, Kathryn drove the rig and Alan rode alongside her. One night when they stopped for food and gas, Kathryn was raped at a truck stop by three bikers. Alan was forced to watch and could not help his wife. Rather than report the rape and destroy what was left of her husband's manhood, she remained silent. She did nothing. She carried it with her day and night for the next seven years until Alan died. Needless to say, whatever was left of the marriage after the rape, died right then and there. The day after she buried her husband she went to you, gave you all the information she had on the case and you turned her away because the stupid statute of limitations had run out. You told me she had a partial license plate, her husband took pictures, and she said one of the bikers was riding an old Indian motorcycle. You said she told you they belonged to the Weekend Warriors club, probably white-collar professionals out for a fling. Charles said there aren't many Indians in existence and they're on every biker's wish list. It shouldn't be hard to track it down. You just sit there, Nikki, and think about three men raping you while Jack is forced to watch. You think about that."

"Myra, I don't have to think about it. I feel

terrible for Kathryn Lucas. Yes, she deserves to have something done but she waited too long. The law is the law. I'm a goddamn lawyer. I can't break the law I swore to uphold."

"The circumstances have to be brought into consideration. I need you to help us, Nikki."

"What is it you want me to do?"

"We could form this little club. You certainly know plenty of women who have slipped through the cracks. Like Alexis, Kathryn, and many others. We'll invite them to join and then we'll do whatever has to be done."

Nikki stood up and threw her hands in the air. "You want us to be *vigilantes!*"

"Yes, dear. Thank you. I couldn't think of the right word. Don't you remember those movies with Charles Bronson?"

"He got caught, Myra."

"But they let him go in the end."

"It was a damn movie, Myra. Make-believe. You want us to do the same thing for real. Just out of curiosity, supposing we were able to find the men that raped Kathryn Lucas, what would we do to them?"

Myra smiled. "That would be up to Kathryn now, wouldn't it?"

"I don't believe I'm sitting here listening to you two hatch this . . . this . . . what the hell is it, Myra?"

"A secret society of women who do what has to be done to make things right," Myra said solemnly.

"It could work, Nikki, as long as we hold to

the secrecy part," Charles said quietly. "There is that room in the tunnels where you and Barbara used to play. You could hold your meetings there. No one would ever know. I know exactly how to set it all up."

Nikki struggled for a comeback that would make sense. In the end, she said, "Jack Emery will be prosecuting Marie Lewellen. We'll be adversaries."

"I see," Myra said. She slapped her palms on the old, scarred tabletop. "Then you have to get her out on bail and we'll find a way to whisk her and her family away to safety. I have the money to do that. It will be like the Witness Protection Program. Charles can handle all that."

Nikki sat down with a thump. "If I don't agree to . . . go along with this, what will you do?"

Myra borrowed a line from her favorite comedian. "Then we'll have to kill you," she said cheerfully. "So, are you in?"

"God help me, I'm in."

If you love the Sisterhood series,
but are wanting a non-Sisterhood "fix" from
Fern Michaels,
you are in luck!

Her next stand-alone novel will be
coming from Kensington in May 2010.

Turn the page for a special preview of

RETURN TO SENDER,

the wonderful new bestseller by Fern Michaels.

Prologue

January 13, 1989
Dalton, Georgia

Rosalind Townsend, whom everyone called Lin, held her newborn son tightly in her arms as the orderly wheeled her to the hospital's administration office. A nurse tried to take him from her so she could tend to the business of her release, but she refused to give him up.

After eighteen hours of agonizing labor without any medication, she'd delivered a healthy six-pound eight-ounce baby boy. She wasn't about to let him out of her sight.

She'd named him William Michael Townsend. A good, solid name. She would call him Will.

Like his father's, Will's hair was a deep black, so dark it appeared to be blue. Lin wasn't sure about his eyes at this point. She'd read in her baby book that a newborn's eye color wasn't true at birth. Nothing about him resembled her, as she was fair-haired with unusual silver-colored eyes and milk white skin.

She gazed down at the securely wrapped bundle in her arms and ran her thumb across his delicate cheek. Soft as silk. He yawned, revealing tender, pink gums. Lin smiled down at her son. No matter what her circumstances, she made a vow to herself: she would devote her life to caring for this precious little child.

Lin had spent the past seven months preparing for this day. During the day she worked at J & G Carpet Mills as a secretary. Five evenings a week and weekend mornings, she waited tables at Jack's Diner. Other than what it cost for rent, food, and utilities, Lin saved every cent she made. She had to be conservative, because it was just her and Will. She'd allowed herself a week off from both jobs so she could bond with her son, adjust to her new life as a mother. While she would've loved spending more time with her son, being the sole caregiver and provider made that impossible. She'd lucked out when Sally, a coworker at Jack's and a single mother to boot, had asked her if she would sit for her two-year-old daughter, Lizzie. In return, Sally would look after the baby on the days that she wasn't working. Lin had agreed because she had to. There were still the days to cover, but Sally gave her a list of reliable sitters she'd used in the past. Dear Sally. Only five years older than Lin but so much wiser to the ways of the world. They were fast becoming good friends. Sally was the complete opposite of Lin—tall, olive-skinned, with beautiful brown eyes that had a slight upward slant, giving her an Asian look. Lin had called three of the sitters: two high-school girls and one elderly woman. She would meet with them later in the week. Lin was sure that if Sally approved, she would as well.

Sadly, there would be no help from Will's father or her parents. Lin recalled her father's cruel words when he learned she was pregnant.

"May you burn in hell, you little harlot! You've disgraced my good name. Get out of my house. I don't ever want to lay eyes on you again or your bastard child!"

Lin had appealed to her mother in the hope she would intervene, but, as usual, her mother had cowered behind her father, accepting his word as law. Lin would never allow a man to intimidate her the way her father did her mother.

Never.

"Miss?"

Lin directed her attention back to the woman behind the administration desk. "Yes?"

"If you'll sign here and initial here." The woman slid a single sheet of paper across the desk.

Lin signed the paper, releasing the hospital from any liability. Since she had no health insurance and refused public assistance, she could only afford to stay in the hospital for twenty-four hours. She'd spend the next two years paying a hundred dollars a month until her debt was paid in full.

The woman behind the desk reached into a drawer and pulled out a thick envelope. "Here, take these. You might find them useful."

Lin took the envelope, peered inside. Coupons for diapers, formula, baby lotion, and anything else one might need. She gave the woman a wan smile. "Thank you."

"You're welcome."

Throughout her pregnancy, she had visited the local dollar store once a month. She'd purchased generic brands of baby items that were on the list of layette necessities she'd read about in the baby book given to her by her obstetrician. Lin didn't have extra money to spend on a homecoming outfit for the baby, so she'd gone to Goodwill and found a secondhand pale blue sweater set. She'd carefully hand washed it in Dreft detergent. Subsequently it had looked good as new. Someday, she swore to herself, her son wouldn't have to wear secondhand clothes.

The orderly wheeled her back to her room, where she dressed in the maternity clothes she'd worn when admitted to the hospital the day before. She ran her hand across her flat stomach. Now she would be able to wear the uniform Jack required, thus saving wear and tear on her few meager outfits. She gazed around the room to make sure she wasn't leaving anything behind. Had it only been twenty-four hours since the taxi had dropped her off at the emergency room? It seemed like a week.

Lin carefully removed the sweater set she'd placed in her overnight bag. With ease, she dressed her son, smiling at the results. Will looked like a little prince in his blue outfit from Goodwill. Briefly, she thought of his father and their weeklong affair. What would his reaction be when he saw his son for the first time? After months of indecision, she'd finally written him another letter two months ago, the first one since she had been on her own, and mailed it to his parents' address in New York, the only way she knew to contact him. She'd begged Nancy Johnson, a girl Will's father had introduced her to, for his phone number as well, but the woman had been adamant about not revealing more of her friend's personal life. She'd told Lin that if Nicholas wanted her to have his phone number, he would have given it to her. The harsh words had stung, but there was more at stake than her raw feelings. She had a child to consider. She'd written a lengthy letter, revealing her pregnancy, telling Nicholas he would be a father shortly after the new year. Weeks passed without a response. Then just last week she'd trudged to the mailbox only to find the letter she'd sent unopened and marked RETURN TO SENDER.

What's one more rejection? she'd asked herself.

Her father hadn't accepted her, either. Her mother had once told her that he'd always dreamed of having a son. At the time, Lin had been terribly hurt, but as the years passed, she learned to set those feelings aside. She'd been the best daughter she knew how to be in hopes of gaining some kind of approval, and maybe even a bit of love and affection from both parents, but that was not to be. When she told her parents about the decision to keep her baby, they were mortified and humiliated. She'd been tossed out of the only home she'd ever known with nothing more than the clothes on her back.

A soft, mewling sound jerked her out of the past. "It's okay, little one. I'm right here."

With the quilt that Irma, Jack's wife, had made for him, Lin gently wrapped Will in a snug bundle. It was below freezing outside. Lin had halfheartedly listened to the local weather report as it blared from the television mounted above her bed. An ice storm was predicted. Meteorologists said it could be the worst in north Georgia history. With only two small electric space heaters, her garage apartment would be freezing. How she wished she could take Will to her childhood home. While it wasn't filled with love, at least it would be warm.

But Lin recalled the torturous evenings of her childhood. She would rather die than subject her son to such a strict and oftentimes cruel upbringing. Every evening, as far back as she could remember, she'd had to pray while kneeling on the hardwood floor in the living room as her father read from the Bible.

A die-hard Southern Baptist who considered himself a man of God, her father had constructed a pulpit for himself in the center of the living room from which he would gaze down at her with disdain, as though she weren't good enough. Then, as if that weren't bad enough, he'd make her recite the names of all the books of the Bible in order. If she missed one, he would make her start from the beginning until she named them correctly. Once, when she was about seven or eight, she remembered spending an entire night on her knees praying. She'd prayed hard, her father watching her the entire time. Little did he know she'd been praying for his immediate death. Many times she'd wet herself while on her knees in prayer. Her father wouldn't allow her to change her clothes or bathe afterward.

"The devil lives inside you, girly! Taking a shower ain't gonna cleanse your dirty soul!"

She'd winced the first time she'd heard those words. After a while, she became immune to his cruel words. She'd even gotten used to smelling like urine. The kids at school were relentless, calling her Miss Stinkypants. And she would do what she always did when she was hurting.

She prayed.

Every night that she knelt on that cold, hard floor, she prayed for her father's death. Not once in the seventeen years that she had lived in her father's house had he ever relented on this evening ritual. She had thick, ugly calluses on her knees to prove it.

When she left home, or rather when she was thrown out, she made a promise to herself: she would *never, ever* kneel again.

Freezing definitely held more appeal.

She checked the room one last time. One of the nurses waited to wheel her downstairs, where the hospital's courtesy van would take her and Will home.

In the lobby, the automatic doors opened,

and a gush of icy air greeted her, smacking her in the face. She held Will close to her with one arm and carried her small suitcase with the other. The driver, an older black man, opened the door and reached for her bag. "You best hop inside, miss. This here cold ain't good for the young'un." He nodded at the bundle in her arms.

Shivering, Lin stepped carefully up into the van. Thankful for the warm air blowing from the heater's vents, she sat on the hard vinyl seat and realized she was still very sore from the delivery. Her breasts felt as though they would explode. She couldn't wait to get home to nurse Will. She'd only be able to do so for the week she was home. Then she'd have to resort to formula. She'd calculated the expense, and while it was very costly, she would manage. Unfortunately, she had no choice.

"Thank you," she said to the driver as she placed Will in the car seat beside her. When Lin had discovered she was pregnant, she'd been frightened, fearful of having inherited her parents' harsh and unloving manner. However, when Will was placed in her arms, the love she felt for him was the most natural thing in the world. Her worries had been for naught.

When mother and son were secure in their seats, the driver made his way through the parking lot. Waiting at the traffic light, he perused a stack of papers attached to a clipboard. "Tunnel Hill, ma'am?"

"Yes, just make a left on Lafayette, then take

the second right." Lin hated having to take Will home to a one-room garage apartment. Someday they would have a home with a big yard with flowers, a white picket fence, and lots of trees for him to climb. Will would have a swing set, and she'd watch him play. Yes, she would see to it that Will had a good home, and, whatever it took, she would make sure he had an education.

Lin remembered her father telling her years before that it was foolish for women to go to college, a waste of money. He'd assured her then that he would not contribute to her education, so after she'd preenrolled at Dalton Junior College during her senior year of high school, she'd saved enough money for the first year.

Having spent three terrifying nights alone in a cheap motel after her father threw her out, she'd made her first adult decision. Instead of using the money for college, she'd paid three months' rent on an apartment. In retrospect, her father's attitude had worked out well since it forced her to save for her education. If not, there wouldn't even be a place for her to bring Will.

The driver parked in her landlady's driveway. She hurriedly removed Will from the car seat and took her bag from the driver. "Thank you. I appreciate the ride."

"Jus' doin' my job, miss. Now scoot on outta here. That ice storm's gonna hit real soon."

"Yes, I know. Thanks again for the ride."

Lin felt rather than saw the driver watching

her as he slowly reversed down the long driveway. She didn't feel creepy at all, because she knew he was good and decent and just wanted to make sure she made it inside safely. A stranger cared more about her well-being than her own flesh and blood. Sad. But she smiled at her thoughts. She had the greatest gift ever, right here in her very own arms.

Holding Will tightly against her chest, she plodded down the long drive that led to the garage apartment. She felt for the key in her pocket, then stopped when she heard a whining noise. Putting her bag on the ground, she checked Will, but he was sound asleep. She heard the sound again.

"What the heck?" she said out loud.

On the side of the garage, at the bottom of the steep wooden steps that led to her apartment, Lin spotted a small dog and walked behind the steps where he hovered. Holding Will tightly, she held out her hand. Its brownish red fur matted with clumps of dirt, the ribs clearly visible, the poor dog looked scruffy and cold. He or she—she wasn't sure of the animal's gender—whined before standing on all fours, limping over to Lin, and licking her outstretched hand.

She laughed. "You sure know the way to a girl's heart."

"Woof, woof."

With the ice storm ready to hit, there was no way Lin could leave the poor dog outside. She fluffed the matted fur between its ears and decided that the dog was going inside with her.

"Scruffy, that's what I'm going to call you for now. Come on, puppy. Follow me." The dog obeyed, staying a foot behind Lin as she made her way up the rickety steps while holding Will against her chest.

Unlocking the door, Lin stepped inside and dropped her bag on the floor. Timidly, Scruffy waited to be invited in. "Come on, Scruffy. You're staying here tonight. Something tells me we're going to get along just fine."

Two unwanted strays, Lin thought.

Scruffy scurried inside and sat patiently on the kitchen floor. With Will still clutched to her chest, Lin grabbed a plastic bowl from her single cupboard, filled it with water, and placed it on the cracked olive green linoleum. She took two hot dogs out of her minirefrigerator, broke them into small pieces, and placed them on a saucer next to the bowl of water. "This should tide you over for a bit. I've got to feed the little guy now."

Scruffy looked at her with big, round eyes. Lin swore she saw thankfulness in the dog's brown-eyed gaze.

With her son still clutched in her arms, Lin managed to remove her jacket before loosening the blanket surrounding him. Making the necessary adjustments to her clothing, Lin began to nurse her son. Reclining on the floral-patterned sofa, she relaxed for the first time in a long time.

Her son was fed and content. She'd inherited an adorable dog, however temporarily, and she was warm.

For a while, that would do. Someday their lives would be different.

Lin stared at the sleeping infant in her arms. "I promise you, little guy, you'll have the best life ever." Then, as an afterthought, she added, "No matter what I have to do."

Chapter 1

Friday, August 31, 2007
New York University

Will's deep brown eyes sparkled with excitement, his enthusiasm contagious, as he and Lin left University Hall, a crowded dormitory for freshmen located at Union Square. If all went as planned, Will would reside in New York City for the next four years before moving on to graduate school to study at North Carolina State University College of Veterinary Medicine, one of the most prestigious veterinary institutions in the country.

"I just hate that you're so far away from home. And in New York City, no less," Lin said for the umpteenth time. "With all the remodeling and holiday parties going on at the restaurant, I doubt I'll be able to make the trip north for Thanksgiving. I don't want you to spend your holiday alone."

"Mom, I said I'd come home if I could. And I will. I promise," Will said. "Besides, I'm a big boy now. I just might like spending some time alone in this big city full of hot chicks."

Laughing, Lin replied, "I'm sure you would." She watched her son as they rode the elevator downstairs. Over six feet tall, with thick, raven black hair, Will was the spitting image of his father, or at least her memory of him.

Lin recalled all those years ago when she'd first met his father. She'd fallen head over heels in love while he'd been visiting a friend in Georgia. Briefly, Lin wondered if Will would follow in her footsteps or his father's. She prayed it wasn't the latter, though she had to admit she really didn't know how he'd turned out. But she didn't want her son to take after a man who denied his son's existence. Lin knew he was very wealthy, but that didn't mean he was a good man. Good men took care of their children, acknowledged them.

Three weeks after she'd brought Will home from the hospital, she'd sent his father a copy of their son's birth announcement along with a copy of the birth certificate. She'd shamelessly added a picture of herself just in case he'd forgotten their brief affair. Throughout the years, she had continued to send items marking Will's accomplishments, the milestones reached as he grew up. Photos of the first day of school; first lost tooth; then, as he aged, driver's license; first date; anything she thought a father would have been proud of. Again, all had come back, unopened and marked RETURN TO SENDER. After so many years of this, she should have learned, should have known that Will's father had no desire to acknowledge him. To this very day, she'd never told Will for fear it would affect him in a way that she wouldn't be able to handle. Recalling the hurt, then the anger each time she and her son were rejected, Lin tucked away the memories of the man she'd given herself to so many years ago, the man she'd loved, the man who had so callously discarded all traces of their romance and in so doing failed to acknowledge their son's existence. When Will had turned twelve, she'd told him his father had died in an accident. It had seemed enough at the time.

But as Jack, her former employer and substitute father, always said, "The past is prologue, kiddo." And he was right. She'd put that part of her life behind her and moved forward.

The elevator doors swished open. The main floor was empty but for a few couples gathered in the corner speaking in hushed tones. Most of the parents were either visiting other dorms or preparing for the evening banquet. Will hadn't wanted to attend, but Lin insisted, telling him several of the college's alumni would be speaking. She'd teased him, saying he might be among them one day. He'd reluctantly agreed, but Lin knew that if he truly hadn't wanted to attend, he would have been more persistent.

She glanced at the exquisite diamond watch on her slender wrist, a gift from Jack and Irma the day she'd made her last payment on the diner she'd purchased from them eight years ago. "I'll meet you in the banquet hall at seven.

Are you sure you don't want to come back to the hotel?"

Will cupped her elbow, guiding her toward the exit. "No. Actually, I think I might take a nap. Aaron doesn't arrive until tomorrow. It might be the last chance I have for some time alone. I want to take advantage of it."

Will and his dorm mate, Aaron Levy, had met through the Internet during the summer. Though they hadn't met in person, Will assured her they'd get along just fine. They were studying to become veterinarians and both shared an avid love of baseball.

"Better set your alarm," Lin suggested. Will slept like the dead.

"Good idea." He gave her a hug, then stepped back, his gaze suddenly full of concern. "You'll be okay on your own for a while?"

Lin patted her son's arm. "Of course I will. This is my first trip to the city. There are dozens of things to do. I doubt I'll have a minute to spare. Though I don't think I'll do any sightseeing today, since I made an appointment to have my hair and nails done at the hotel spa."

Will laughed. "That's a first. You never do that kind of stuff. What gives?"

"It's not every day a mother sends her son off to college." She gently pushed him away. "Now go on with you, or there'll be no time to relax. I'll see you at seven."

Will waved. "Seven, then."

Lin gave him a thumbs-up sign, her signal to

him that all was a go. She pushed the glass door open and stepped outside. The late-afternoon sun shone brightly through the oak trees, casting all sorts of irregular shapes and shadows on the sidewalk. The autumn air was cool and crisp. Lin walked down the sidewalk and breathed deeply, suddenly deliriously happy with the life she'd made for herself. She stopped for a moment, remembering all the struggles, the ups and downs, and how hard she'd worked to get to where she was. Abundant, fulfilled, completely comfortable with her life, she picked up her pace, feeling somewhat foolish and silly for her thoughts. She laughed, the sound seemingly odd since she was walking alone, no one to hear her. That was okay, too. Life was good. She was happy, Will's future appeared bright and exciting. The only dark spot in her life was her father. Her mother had died shortly after Lin had moved into Mrs. Turner's garage apartment. She'd had to read about it in the obituaries. Lin had called her father, asking how her mother had died. He told her she'd fallen down the basement steps. She suspected otherwise but knew it would be useless, possibly even dangerous to her and her unborn child, if she were to pry into the circumstances surrounding her mother's death. She'd tried to establish a relationship with her father on more than one occasion through the years, and each time he'd rebuffed her, telling her she was the devil's spawn. Her father now resided in Atlanta, in a very upscale nursing home, at her expense. Lin was sure his pure meanness had launched him into early onset Alzheimer's.

Lin thought it was time for her to proceed at her own leisurely pace, kick back, and totally relax for the first time in a very, very long time.

Lin continued to ponder her life as she walked down the sidewalk toward a line of waiting taxis. After ten years of working at Jack's Diner, when she'd learned that Jack and Irma were considering closing the place, she'd come up with a plan. Though she'd skimped and saved most of her life, for once she was about to splurge and do something so out of character that Jack had thought she'd taken temporary leave of her senses. She'd offered him a fifty-thousand-dollar down payment, a cut of the profits, and a promissory note on the balance if they would sell her the diner. It took all of two minutes for Jack and Irma to accept her offer. Since they'd never had children and didn't think they'd have a chance in hell of selling the diner given the local economy, closing the doors had seemed their only option.

Lin laughed.

She'd worked her tail off day and night and most weekends to attract a new clientele, a younger crowd with money to burn. She'd applied for a liquor license and changed the menu to healthier fare while still remaining true to some of the comfort foods Jack's was known for, such as his famous meat loaf and mashed potatoes. Within a year, Jack's was booked every night of the week, and weekends months in advance. From there, she started catering private parties. With so much success, she'd decided it was time to add on to the diner. In addition to two large private banquet rooms that would accommodate five hundred guests when combined, she added three moderately sized private rooms for smaller groups. The remodeling was in its final stages when she'd left for New York the day before. She'd left Sally, her dearest friend and manager, in charge of last-minute details.

Lin quickened her pace as she saw that the line of taxis at the end of the block had dwindled down to three. She waved her hand in the air to alert the cabbie. Yanking the yellow-orange door open, she slid inside, where the smell of stale smoke and fried onions filled her nostrils. She wrinkled her nose in disgust. "The Helmsley Park Lane." She'd always wanted to say that to a New York cab driver. Though it wasn't the most elite or expensive hotel in the city, it was one that had captured her imagination over the years. Its infamous owner, known far and wide by the well-deserved epithet the Queen of Mean, had been quite visible in the news media when Lin was younger, especially when she'd been tried and convicted for tax evasion, extortion, and mail fraud, and had died just over a week before.

Through blasts of horns, shouts from sidewalk vendors hawking their wares, and the occasional bicyclist weaving in and out of traffic, Lin enjoyed the scenery during the quick cab ride back to the hotel. New York was unlike any city in the world. Of course, she hadn't traveled outside the state of Georgia, so where this sudden knowledge came from, she hadn't a clue, but still she knew there was no other place like New York. It had its own unique *everything*, right down to the smell of the city.

The taxi stopped in front of the Helmsley. Lin handed the driver a twenty, telling him to keep the change. Hurrying, Lin practically floated through the turnstile doors as though she were on air. She felt like Cinderella, and the banquet would be her very own ball, with Will acting as her handsome prince. He would croak if he knew her thoughts. Nonetheless, she was excited about the evening ahead.

She dashed to the elevator doors with only seconds to spare. She'd lost track of time, and her salon appointment was in five minutes. They'd asked her to wear a blouse that buttoned in the front so she wouldn't mess up her new do before the banquet. She punched the button to the forty-sixth floor, from which she had an unbelievable view of the city and Central Park. Lin cringed when she thought of the cost but remembered this was just a onetime treat, and she was doing it in style.

She slid the keycard into the slot on the door and pushed the door inward. Overcome by the sheer luxuriousness, she simply stared at her surroundings, taking them in. Lavender walls with white wainscoting, cream-colored antique tables at either end of the lavender floral sofa.

The bedroom color scheme matched, though the coverlet on her bed was a deep, royal purple. She raced over to the large walk-in closet, grabbed a white button-up blouse, and headed to the bathroom. This, too, was beyond opulent. All marble, a deep Jacuzzi tub, a shower that could hold at least eight people, thick, soft, lavender bath towels and bars of lilac soaps and bath beads placed in crystal containers gave Lin such a feeling of luxury, and it was such a novel feeling, she considered staying in the room her entire trip. She laughed, then spoke out loud. "Sally would really think I've lost my marbles." She'd discussed her New York trip with her, and they'd made a list of all the must-see places. If she returned empty-handed, Sally would wring her neck. She'd bring her back something special.

They'd practically raised the kids together, and Sally felt like the older sister she'd never had. And she'd bring Elizabeth, Sally's daughter, something smart and sexy. She'd opted to attend Emory University in Atlanta instead of leaving the state as Will had. Sally told her she was glad. Not only did she not have to pay out-of-state tuition, but Lizzie was able to come home on the weekends. She would graduate next year. Where had the time gone?

She hurried downstairs to the spa for her afternoon of pampering.

Three hours later, Lin returned to her room to dress for the banquet. The hairstylist had talked her into a pedicure and a facial. After an afternoon of being catered to, she felt like royalty. Of course, it all came at a price, one so high she didn't dare give it another thought, or she'd have such a case of the guilts that she'd ruin the evening for herself and Will. No, she reminded herself again, this was a once-in-a-lifetime trip. As she had explained to Will, it wasn't every day that he went away to college. Besides, she wanted to look her best at the banquet, knowing there would be many well-to-do parents attending with their children. No way did she want to cause Will any embarrassment just because she was a small-town hick who ran a diner. Her accomplishments might mean something in Dalton, but here in New York City she would just be seen as a country bumpkin trying to keep up with the big-city folk, even though her net worth these days could probably match that of many of New York's movers and shakers.

Discarding her self-doubts, Lin took her dress out of its garment bag. She'd ordered it from a Macy's catalog four months ago. She slid the black, long-sleeved silk dress over her head, allowing it to swathe her slender body. Lin looked at her reflection in the full-length mirror. With all the skipped meals and extra work at the diner, she'd lost weight since purchasing the dress. The curve-hugging dress emphasized her tiny waist. She twirled around in front of the mirror. *Not bad for an old woman,* she thought.

"Shoot, I'm not *that* old." She cast another look in the mirror and slipped her feet into her ruby red slingbacks she'd been dying to wear since she'd purchased them two years ago. Lin remembered buying them on a trip to Atlanta as a prize to celebrate her first million. On paper, of course, but still it was monumental to her, since she'd clawed her way to the top. It hadn't been all rainbows and lollipops, either.

Clipping on the garnet earrings Sally and Irma had given her for her thirtieth birthday, she returned to the mirror for one last look before heading downstairs.

Five-foot-three, maybe a hundred pounds soaking wet, Lin scrutinized her image. The stylist had flat-ironed her long blond hair, assuring her that it was the current style, and, no, she was not too old to wear her hair down. Her face had a rosy glow courtesy of Lancôme and a facial. The manicurist had given her a French manicure, telling her it, too, was "in vogue." After leaving the spa, she returned to her room with a few makeup tricks under her belt. Plus, her hairstylist had sashayed back and forth, showing her the fashionable way to strut her stuff so that she'd be noticed when making an entrance. While that was the last thing on her mind, she'd had a blast with the women, more than she cared to admit. Lin had confessed that she hadn't had time for such things as a girl, but she hadn't explained why.

She glanced at her watch. Six-fifteen. It was time for Cinderella to hail her carriage.

"Get off it!" If she continued thinking along those lines, she would have to commit herself.

Lin visualized her mental checklist. Purse, lipstick, wallet, cell phone, and keycard. All of a sudden her hands began to shake, and her stomach twisted in knots. It wasn't like she would be the only parent there. Unsure why she was so jittery, she shrugged her feelings aside, telling herself she simply wanted to make a good impression on Will's professors and classmates. Plus, she wasn't on her own turf, and that in and of itself had the power to turn her insides to mush.

Instead of exiting through the turnstile doors, Lin allowed the doorman to open the door for her. Discreetly, she placed a twenty in his hand and hoped it was enough. Sally told her you had to tip everyone for everything in the city. Lin calculated she'd be broke in less than a year if she remained in New York.

"Thank you, ma'am," the elderly man said as he escorted her to a waiting taxi.

Okay, that was worth the twenty bucks. She would've hated to chase down a cab in the red heels.

The inside of the taxi was warm. Lin offered up a silent prayer of thanks that there were no strange odors permeating the closed-in space. She would hate to arrive at the banquet smelling like cigarettes and onions.

More blaring horns, shouts, and tires squealing could be heard. Lin enjoyed watching the throngs of people on the streets as the driver managed to weave through the traffic. Lord, she loved the hubbub, but she didn't think she could tolerate it on a daily basis.

Poor Will. She smiled. *Not* poor Will. After

the slow pace of Dalton, he would welcome this. It was one of the many reasons he chose to attend NYU in the first place. He'd wanted a taste of the big city. Lin thought he was about to get his wish and then some.

Twenty minutes later, the cab stopped in front of the building where the banquet was being held. She offered up two twenties, telling the driver to keep the change.

"Do you want me to pick you up later?" the driver asked as he jumped out to open her door. Lin thought the tip must have been a tad too generous.

"Uh, I'm not sure. Do you have a card?" she asked.

He laughed. "No card, lady, but if you want a return ride, you gotta ask for it."

"Of course. Midnight. Be here at midnight." Now she was starting to *sound* like Cinderella.

"Will do."

Her transportation taken care of, Lin stepped out into the cool night air.

A SPECIAL INTERVIEW WITH FERN MICHAELS

QUESTION: With so many novels of yours published—many of which are *New York Times* bestsellers—did you ever imagine you would have such a prolific and successful career as a writer? How did you first get started? What put you on the path to becoming an author?

FERN MICHAELS: Never in a million years did I imagine I would be where I am today. I think I knew someway, somehow, that I was going to write *something* someday in the fourth grade when I wrote a story about a tadpole and the teacher gave me a big red A. What put me on the path to writing years and years later was when my youngest son went off to kindergarten and my husband told me I had to get a job. Being a wife and mother did not qualify me to go into the outside workforce. Plus, and most important, I didn't have a car to get to and from work. So I thought I would try my hand at writing a book. It was that simple. What was even more amazing was that the storytelling came easy to me. Please note, I did not say the *writing* came easy—it was the storytelling part that worked for me.

QUESTION: *Razor Sharp* marks the fourteenth book in the Sisterhood series. When you started the series with the first seven books, did you ever think it would become so successful, and you'd still be writing about the Ladies of Pinewood so many years later?

FERN MICHAELS: I've kept the series going because so many fans wrote and asked me to continue. But even I had withdrawal from the Sisterhood when I finished what I thought was the last one with number seven [*Free Fall*] and had a long break before finally starting to write *Hide and Seek.* I lived with those characters during the first seven books for so long they were part of me. The bottom line was, those wonderful characters were not ready to ride off into the sunset, and I made the decision to continue because there were so many more stories in my head that needed to play out.

QUESTION: What is it about the characters in your Sisterhood novels that allows for you to connect so deeply with readers, and how did you first conceive of these women on your pages? Is there any thread of you in any of these characters?

FERN MICHAELS: I have a lot of friends and meet a lot of people, and as women do, we moan and groan about injustices we see and experience along the way. One would say, boy, if I could just get even in some small way, or, somehow that guy/gal shouldn't be able to get away with this or that! Then I would sit down and plot all these different revenge theories that maybe would work or maybe wouldn't, but since it is all fiction, these gals could do whatever, and I could control the outcome. The "Sisters" all kept reminding me I was a storyteller. In the end, I was convinced that the woman hadn't been born yet who didn't want some sort of revenge in her life. I just ran with it. The seven women of the Sisterhood and the new characters that I developed along the way are composites of those same friends, family, and to some extent some of my neighbors. Even the guys. Is there any thread of me in those characters? Oh yeah! In every single one.

QUESTION: To the disappointment of many fans, *Final Justice* was going to be the "second end" to the Sisterhood series. But to everyone's delight, the stories keep coming. When will you decide to end this successful series, and what have the reactions of your fans been?

FERN MICHAELS: To end the series after *Final Justice* was my original intention because twelve books is a lot in a series. But . . . remember now, I am a storyteller and I still have more stories swirling around in my head. When I sent off *Final Justice* to my publisher, I stood at the FedEx place holding the box and felt physically sick. I thought I was going to cry. It was like saying good-bye to a group of my best friends that I was never going to see again. I went home in such a funk I made a pot of coffee and drank it all . . . black. Then I was so wired up I didn't know what to do. When I don't know what to do, I write. I posted a letter to my readers on my website and let it run for ten days. I asked my readers if they wanted me to end the series. I got over three thousand replies. All but twenty-two wanted me to continue it. Of the twenty-two, eleven of them said no only because they thought I wouldn't write other books. But I assured them that I am still writing non-Sisterhood books, including *Mr. and Miss Anonymous*, the upcoming *Return to Sender*, and of course the Christmas novellas I do for Zebra's anthologies every year. You know what they say: it isn't over till the big lady sings.

QUESTION: While many people know you through your writing, not many people are aware of your charitable work, which includes buying bulletproof vests for police dogs and creating day-care centers set up for the needs of single mothers. You also created the Fern Michaels Foundation, which grants scholarships to needy children. How did you get involved in these projects, and why is philanthropy such an important part of your life?

FERN MICHAELS: When I was a kid my old Polish grandmother said something to me that I didn't understand at the time but do understand now. She said when God is good to you, you must give back. I do my best. A day doesn't go by in my life that I don't thank God for all He has done for me. How could I do less? I have a new project right now, which is our local police department in the town where I live. With the passing of my daughter due to a heart condition way before her time several years ago, I wanted to do something in her memory. So I made sure every officer in the department had a defibrillator and was trained to use it, a thermal-imaging camera, plus every officer now has a taser, along with training and hiring a new police officer every year to help safeguard the people in my little town.

QUESTION: With the publication of several books a year, along with your ongoing charity work, how do you manage to balance writing, home, family, and book events with all this going on in your career and life?

FERN MICHAELS: I don't know how to answer that other than to say I take it one day at a time, look at what the day holds when I get up in the morning, and put things in the order of importance. Somehow or other I manage to do what has to be done, even if it takes me till bedtime. My kids tell me I have grease on my sneakers, otherwise I wouldn't be able to do what I do. I love it.

QUESTION: Where do you draw your inspiration from? Are there any specific people—friends, family members, etc.—that help provide the characters found in your novels?

FERN MICHAELS: Just everyday life. I think my brain is on overdrive from eight in the morning till around midnight. I hear, I see, I smell, I think, and I write it down. Sometimes it can be something really silly. Like the day I was babysitting my grandson and he was watching cartoons and it was Alvin and the Chipmunks and they were shouting, "Finders keepers! Finders keepers!" I had been struggling for a title on the book I was writing at the time. You guessed it—turned out to be *Finders Keepers*.

QUESTION: Throughout all of the years you've been writing and promoting your novels, what have been the most rewarding and memorable experiences for you?

FERN MICHAELS: Oh my gosh, there are so many! I'm going to give you two, but they are sad. A lady's daughter e-mailed me and said her mother was dying, literally dying, and had maybe a month to live if she was lucky. She had read the first two books in the Kentucky series and wanted to know how the third one ended because she wouldn't be here when it came out. The third book was done and in production, but there were months to go before it would be in stores. I called my publisher, Kensington Publishing, and somehow they found a way to get the advance galleys to me to send to the daughter. The daughter e-mailed me later and said every day she read to her mother and they finished the book *in time.* The second incident was almost identical, but this lady was a friend of someone who had brain cancer and was in a hospice. She wanted the fourth Sisterhood book [*The Jury*] so her friend could read it to her. I sent it along with a roomful of flowers. You just can't forget things like that, ever. And I never will. I like to think I make people's lives a little happier with my storytelling. Now, if you want to go in the other direction, I was inducted into the New Jersey Literary Hall of Fame along with such notables as Mary Higgins Clark, Peter Benchley, Belva Plain, and many others (I lived in New Jersey at the time), and you better believe that was a thrill!

QUESTION: Now that the Sisterhood is still going strong and topping the bestseller lists with every book, what is the next thing you can tell readers that you're excited about? What will 2010 and beyond bring?

FERN MICHAELS: I'm sure not ready as of this moment to put the Sisterhood series behind me, but I do have other things I'm excited about. Especially my brand-new series called the Godmothers. Again, some feisty ladies, led by eight-times-widowed Teresa "Toots" Amelia Loudenberry, getting their way in the world and having a lot of great times while they're at it. I think these books are even more fun than the Sisterhood books, and I hope my readers find them just as entertaining. The first book is *The Scoop,* in September 2009, and then I have another non-Sisterhood novel called *Return to Sender* coming in the spring of 2010. So I'm working on all kinds of things, but in my off-hours, my brain is swirling with Sisterhood stories. I can multitask.